COTTAGE COUNTRY KILLERS

A Crime and Mystery Collection

Edited by
Vicki Cameron and Linda Wiken

Published by

GENERAL STORE
PUBLISHING HOUSE

Box 28, 1694 Burnstown Rd., Burnstown, Ontario, Canada K0J 1G0
Telephone 1-800-465-6072 Fax (613) 432-7184

ISBN 1-896182-53-4
Printed and bound in Canada

Cover design by Hugh Malcolm

Copyright © 1997 The Authors
General Store Publishing House
Burnstown, Ontario, Canada

No part of this publication may be reproduced, stored in a retrieval system
or transmitted, in any form or by any means, without the prior written permission
of the publisher or, in case of photocopying or other reprographic copying, a licence
from CANCOPY (Canadian Copyright Licensing Agency), 6 Adelaide Street East,
Suite 900, Toronto, Ontario, M5C 1H6.

General Store Publishing House gratefully acknowledges assistance from the Ontario
Arts Council and Canada Council.

Canadian Cataloguing in Publication Data

Main entry under title:
    Cottage country killers: a crime and mystery collection

ISBN 1-896182-53-4

1. Detective amd mystery stories, Canadian (English)
2. Canadian fiction (English) – 20th century.
I. Cameron, Vicki. II. Wiken, Linda.

PS8323.D4C68 1997   C813'.087208054   C97-900178-1
PR9197.35.D48C68 1997

Second Printing, March 1999.

TABLE OF CONTENTS

Too Many Guys Named Bill	*Rose DeShaw*	1
Eb and Flo	*Joy Hewitt Mann*	15
The Inheritance	*Barbara Fradkin*	16
Widow's Weeds	*Sue Pike*	34
Hunting Lessons	*Joy Hewitt Mann*	42
Getting Rid of Cottage Pests	*Rosemary Aubert*	43
Up The Pole	*Liz Palmer*	48
Mea Culpa	*Jane Tun*	60
September Mourn	*Audrey Jessup*	73
It's in the Bag	*Joy Hewitt Mann*	83
Conspicuous Presumption	*Pat Wilson and Kris Wood*	84
Partner-in-Crime	*Joy Hewitt Mann*	94
August is the Lamb of Winter	*Michelle Marcotte*	95
Holding Down the Fort	*Therese Greenwood*	100
Murder by Moonlight	*Marguerite McDonald*	107
It's No Mystery To Me	*Joy Hewitt Mann*	123
Hear No Evil	*Linda Wiken*	124
Accidents Can Happen	*Joan Boswell*	136
It Must Have Been the Sherry	*Brenda Missen*	147
Unnaturally Inclined	*Joy Hewitt Mann*	159
The Language of Flowers	*Maureen Jennings*	160
Full Moon, Blue Lake	*Mary Jane Maffini*	169
Zebra Mussels	*Vicki Cameron*	186
An Accident Waiting to Happen	*Joy Hewitt Mann*	188

TOO MANY GUYS NAMED BILL

by Rose DeShaw

"Just old Bill, an ordinary guy. You meet him on the street and never notice him" – Showboat

She stood there in her nightdress screaming, barefoot in the snow. Her cold hands gripped mine and my sister's, the house in flames behind us.

My earliest memory of Mother.

I wasn't yet three and even then I was trying to calm her. Strong emotion, they say, that comes at such a time causes the event to cling longest to the walls of the mind. That must be why I can still smell the 3 AM burning of that small home, hear the crackling of toys, books and crib, hoses making a puddle of my baby quilt.

Every detail comes back, clear as yesterday. Sleepy neighbours rushing from a warm yellow kitchen to drag us inside, the wail of the firetruck and tall men in black rubber coats who would turn cozy warm bed, blankets and pillow into ice sculpture. The shortwave radio call bringing my father home.

It was our first fire.

"If you could get time off from the library, Wilda, I'd like to give your mother a little holiday," my father, Bill Lauren, said. He picked up his fishburger and took a bite.

As senior office manager for a firm of accountants, Dad could take all the time he wished while at my level I could barely manage half an hour off. I looked at the old windmill tilter, feeling the waves of energy that tensed his short frame; red hair hinting at the remarkable temper erupting whenever he ran up against one of life's little frustrations.

"Are you thinking of a cruise or something?" I was kidding.

Dad would never allow a body of water to come between him and his employment. This holiday would be something nearby where the office could call him if they needed to know what he'd done with the new pencils or where you smacked the 486 to make it stop beeping.

"The company lawyer, Bill Hoskit, has offered me the use of his cottage for a nominal fee. His house in town suddenly burned down so he's got to stay around and sort that out." Dad took another bite, not looking at me.

I stopped plastering tartar sauce on my kaiser like mortar on a brick and looked at him uneasily. "You discussed the . . . fire?" I said cryptically.

"I shared some of our fire experiences, yes," my father said. "Which led to his offer of the cottage."

"So you warned him about Mother?"

"I fail to take your meaning," he murmured and began to line up his french fries by length around the rim of his plate. Never in so many words have I heard my father admit we have a family arsonist. The blazes that consumed my childhood were a series of unfortunate accidents according to him. In the light of such an obvious omission it seemed odd that he was the one to set up the precautions we took around Mother.

So had he or had he not told the lawyer Bill about her? If he had, it didn't seem likely we'd be offered the cottage.

Dad was going on about Bill Hoskit. 'Generous' pretty well defined the man according to him. Bill our future landlord was on the board of directors for a local halfway house where he'd been active in finding jobs and accommodation for those rejoining society from various institutions. Much too good to be true. Maybe not a hawk in dove's clothing but something. For starters he was a lawyer. I'd sort out what was what when I met the man but first we had to decide about the cottage.

Living with an arsonist in the family takes a bit of getting used to. Fires have always been Mother's way of communicating when she's backed against a wall. Let the front hall fill with tennis rackets and golf clubs, the living room overflow with too many plants, magazines and books, dishes be left out in the kitchen and all of a sudden Mother stops complaining. It's her silences you learn to listen for.

First come small hints like a spring rain, then a deluge of complaints thunder forth. Then the lull before her firestorm.

So far it's only been a house or two, a garage that wasn't in great shape anyway and a storage barn full of family memorabilia. Since we picked up on her pattern we've been fire free for several years now. Still you always consult the arsonist in the family before you make any sudden moves like a cottage holiday. As it would probably be a flammable wooden building, she would have to really like the idea and we would have to keep it tidy.

I have always wished my parents communicated like normal people. Burning things down to get my preoccupied father's attention is over the top. There's his work, the clubs where he's usually on the executive and the night school courses that enhance his hobbies. Mere words would never make it through that barrier of distractions but smoke always seems to do the trick.

And after the smoke, the insurance. "I kept the premiums paid up," my father would say indignantly. So far none of the causes of our fires had been questioned, nor laid officially at Mother's feet. Accident. Faulty wiring. Combustible materials. I had to admit she was pretty good. Each time we'd moved to a more substantial house in another province. Brick and slate. No frame buildings, no gas. A nice library within walking distance, which probably influenced my choice of careers. And Mother's nose stuck back into a fantasy novel.

Since she's partial to firebreathing dragons it's a good thing she came of age at the time when science fiction had begun dissolving into quests and fairy tales. Mother would have found no peace in robots and machinery to conquer space. The only space she'd ever wanted to conquer was that which separated her from my father.

Guinevere Lauren, a small, compliant dreamy woman with wispy brown hair pulled back in an old-fashioned twist, little floral print dresses, always stockings and pumps with a heel. I've never seen her in anything you couldn't call, 'ladylike.'

"I'm counting on you to help make this a real holiday," my father said. He was eating his french fries in order, tallest first.

"Does that mean you'll only be out on weekends?" I asked warily.

"No, no. No clubs, no classes. We'll enjoy Bill's cottage in peace and let the office run itself this summer."

"How do you work it, both of you named Bill," I asked curiously. "Don't you mix up your messages sometimes?"

"He is most properly 'William' at the office," my father said stiffly. "And of course we have regular clients of the same name. There's no real difficulty. It's simply a matter of paying attention."

I choked back a comment. Won't you come home, Bill Bailey? There were never two less attentive people than my parents. The caretakers in our family had been my sister Janice and I, but now Janice had washed her hands of the pair of them and trotted off to a job in Halifax, urging me to follow suit.

"Let her smoke him like a piece of bacon if she must, Willy," she said before she left. "But we've got our lives to live." Tough love, parent-style.

I wanted a life of my own too, freedom, travelling, a husband and children some day. Still a small flammable summer cottage didn't seem quite the place to leave them to their own devices. Not that the time was ever right. I'd just pace my cage more often as they got older and odder till one day maybe our tender relationship would come to resemble that of Lizzie Borden and her parents. I felt trapped and depressed as I asked about holiday time at work.

The library was prepared to give me my two weeks in mid-July at short notice if I could be available for emergencies. "That will be a marvelous break," Mother said when we told her at dinner. "A little cottage in the woods."

A break from doing what? I studied her, wondering how it would be to withdraw as she did when a responsibility came up. Or did she know very well what she was doing? Most of the time she appeared to have dipped only a toe into the dimension inhabited by the rest of us. Gripping her dream world like a flotation device, now and again Mother would peer into our reality, find it not to her liking, torch it and retreat.

I'm not saying I didn't resent all this. "Mosquitos, blackflies and snakes," I said, trying to decide how far she had come this time. My father gave me a dark look and began to talk about taking a minimum of belongings.

"And while we're away would be a good time to get a new roof, send the living room furniture to be reupholstered, have the furnace cleaned and the painters in upstairs," he added.

"What? No driveway paving? No landscaping?" An office manager is always managing but I saw his point. We could buy a lot of fire safety from Mother with all that sparkling newness.

Bill our new landlord drove out with us Sunday to show us around. My cynicism melted like a popsicle on a stove as Bill and I talked. A burly man built like a tree, curly blonde hair like willow leaves in autumn, eyebrows like nests in the branches. A mature tree, stable and rooted and terribly unlawyerlike. "I was so sorry to hear about your fire," my mother said.

"Yes, well, these things happen," Bill said, giving her a searching look. He had been told mother's history, I decided, but due to something giving in his nature was prepared to let us have the cottage anyway. Maybe his recent fire had left him vulnerable.

I remember standing in the crowd during Mother's last arson, watching my bedroom roof fall in on the closet that contained my entire fall wardrobe including my new winter coat. Misery at such a time is a combination of guilt and helplessness. Wasn't there something I could have done to prevent this, I asked myself then? But there hadn't been anything. Bill seemed to share the feeling.

We turned onto a side road that wasn't more than a swoop of gravel and dirt. Half a mile in, a handful of cottages started to appear through the trees. The road wound around these like taffy on a stick. On a rise at the top was the cottage, somewhat isolated but with a tremendous view of the lake below.

"I'll give you the quick tour," Bill said jangling the keys. "Then we can run over to see where the general store and the gas station are. Not much else around here for supplies."

We got out and eyed the small structure under the cedars with varying enthusiasm. An arsonist's dream, I thought. All dry timber with shutters and gingerbread, set in a carpet of pine needles with the forest not ten feet from the door. Then we whipped through a kitchen and bathroom where I was glad to see indoor plumbing. There were three small but adequate bedrooms upstairs and a living room with a working fireplace if the flecks of ash on the poker were any indication. Cozy nights around the fire were for some other family.

"I think I'll stay here, dear, if you don't mind," Mother said, sinking down on the sofa. "I'd like to get to know it on my own. You go ahead with Bill."

"And Bill," I added. My father waggled his eyebrows at me and I signalled back that it looked okay. Mother was communicating. It was when she didn't talk we had to worry.

We left Bill's car pulled up by the cottage and headed down to the lake with Dad. When we got back, Mother was standing in the open doorway looking agitated.

"A man called by for you, dear," she told my father. "An insurance man. He said he'd tried the office and they sent him out here. He's coming back tonight."

Surely Dad's office wouldn't sic a salesman on us? Which meant they thought this was important. I felt my stomach lurch. "What company, Mother. Did he say?"

"He left a brochure." She handed me a folder. It had been several years but I still recognized the logo from the company that had paid out on our last fire.

I couldn't tell if Dad did or not. He was too busy complaining. "I told those fools at the office not to give out the address," he fumed. "Here we are trying to have a proper holiday and some idiot comes around to sell me insurance. Well, I'm not going to be home when he arrives, I can tell you that."

"Good enough, Bill," our landlord Bill said. "There's a chicken dinner tonight at that Methodist church we passed by the lake. The ladies put on quite a spread."

"That's where we'll be then," my father said with a satisfied grin. "Let him find nobody home. He'll have driven clear out here from the city for nothing." Bill said he had to get back to the city but to call if we needed anything. I went out to the porch and watched his tail lights vanish then reappear through the trees on the twisty road down the hill.

About six, Mother complained of a headache. "If I put out the lights and lie down, it'll be the same as if nobody's home," she said firmly. "I don't feel like a crowd tonight."

"And I don't feel like lying around in the dark," I objected.

She finally agreed not to answer either phone or door and we'd come back early with a plateful of chicken for her supper. It seemed perfectly reasonable. Mother had no reason to hate the house yet anyway. Once this pesky insurance man was off the premises we could relax and enjoy our holiday, my father said.

Since no one questioned why a man would come out here to sell insurance to holidayers who obviously wanted to leave the business world behind, I didn't mention my fear that perhaps he hadn't. With a last look back at the cottage we headed for the church.

Dinner was dished with a generous hand. I finished a piece of home-baked pumpkin pie swimming in whipped cream and looked idly out the tall windows in the church hall. Just as I realized they faced our hill, I saw the flames. It looked like a signal fire for low-flying planes. I pushed my pie away and pointed to the window. Dad stumbled to his feet and together we flew out the door to the car. The usual recriminations crowded into my head. Why had we left her alone? Because she seemed happy and our only other choices were hanging around to beat off the insurance man or carrying her kicking and screaming to the dinner.

The road back was clogged and impassable. Bored cottagers, eager for the entertainment of a fire, blocked the road. We abandoned the car at the first layby and ran the rest of the way on foot. At the top a ring of cars had been parked with headlights on to illuminate the scene. Dad and I split up to search. There was a hiss of water from the hose of the single fire truck and the usual smell of burning. Two volunteer firemen came out carrying an immobile, blanket-swathed figure on a stretcher. "Didja see that can of paraffin back there," I heard one man say as I approached. "This fire was set."

Maybe for the very last time, I told myself, fighting hysteria. What I'd stumbled into was a recurring nightmare. Sometimes in these dreams the blanket-wrapped shape has my sister's face, sometimes my father's. The worst news was, as the ash-laden wind touched my cheek, this time I was awake.

"I'm looking for my mother, Guinevere Lauren," I said as I came closer. My voice shook. "Do you know," I gulped, "if that's a woman?"

"Too badly burned to say," the first man answered. "Job for forensics."

The horror on my face seemed to be too much for his partner. He gestured at a group of trees beyond the lights. "Some woman was outside when we drove up."

I didn't dare hope. Probably only a neighbour or a fire-loving tourist. I ran past the sizzling timbers, through the beams of light where a small group of people stood and sat. On a lawn chair, wrapped in a quilt my mother was telling whoever would listen that she'd heard a noise, gone down, found the cottage in flames and managed to stumble outside but was afraid to go any further through the dark, unknown woods.

I saw Dad had slipped easily into his anger like a comfortable old coat to shield himself from more dangerous emotions like sorrow or pity. Between my parents I was beyond feeling, shocked into the kind of silence a soldier might feel, done with fighting. The volunteer fire chief, Sid Abel, looked at the uncommunicative three of us and offered a temporarily vacant cottage he was taking care of, owned by his brother-in-law away at a reunion in the States. Mr. Abel took us over, unlocked the place and put on coffee. I wish I didn't have experience sitting with the smell of smoke in the house of strangers. Still, the cottage crowd had been kind.

"You said nobody's missing, Mr. and Mrs. Lauren," the fire chief asked when we were sitting around with our mugs full. "But we took a body out of that cottage." He looked around at us then pulled out a car registration. "Truck was driven into the woods up there. Registered to a William Jenkins. Ring any bells?"

Nobody heard any. "Is this cottage available?" my father brushed the unknown Jenkins aside and concentrated as usual on his own needs.

The chief gave a discreet cough which I took to mean we'd burnt down one cottage already. But he said he'd see what he could do. Certainly we could stay the night and use the facilities. This way we'd be handy for further questions in the morning. Mother and I went to bed and Mother went to sleep.

Dad said he'd bunk in the other room. "I'll call Bill first and tell him what happened," he said.

"I wish you didn't work with him," Mother said suddenly. "I don't trust him."

I looked at her sharply. She seldom expressed such a strong dislike of anyone. But at least Bill was safe from any demonstration of her antipathy, now that his cottage had burned down like his house in town. I hoped he was fully insured.

Insurance! Maybe William Jenkins was the insurance man? But what would a salesman have been doing in the house? Unless he really was an investigator, poking around for something he thought might be evidence. And then what? Had he fallen asleep, waiting in the dark and Mother, thinking she was alone, had done it again, this time with no advance warning? I looked over at her sleeping so peacefully in the other twin bed. It was a logical conclusion given our history. I went to sleep with the smell of smoke in my nostrils. Maybe tomorrow, when Mother and Bill met again I would be able to figure out what had happened from their conversation.

Next day when I got downstairs, Mr. Abel, the fire chief, was in the kitchen eating pancakes. Dad stood at the stove flipping more while Mother absently stirred a cup of tea with a pencil and made notes on a pad of paper she'd gotten somewhere.

"Do you suppose Bill had something to do with the fire?" she asked Abel.

"He went back to town," Dad interrupted. "Your irrational dislike of the man shouldn't make you paranoid. She means the man who rented us the cottage," he told Abel who was looking at him curiously. "I remember where I saw the name William Jenkins," he continued, changing the subject. "You were asking about him last night."

"Guy who died in the fire," Abel nodded. "We sure could use some help."

Dad brought a plate of pancakes over to the table and sat down. "He sold policies to fenceposts," he continued. Nobody seemed to get it. "In the insurance industry, fenceposts mean customers that aren't there," Dad said patiently. "The salesman writes a policy using a fake name and address, then sends in the first premium which usually isn't more than a hundred dollars. But the company pay him for the sale upfront, some six hundred dollars. Then he lets the policy lapse and writes another one. They caught this Jenkins with enough posts for a whole field and he did some provincial prison time." He took a bite of pancake.

"Would any insurance company have hired him after that?" I asked.

"Probably," Dad said bitterly. "With all these mergers in the business, nobody knows who's who anymore. Besides even if they remembered him, the man has paid his debt to society. He certainly proved he knows how the field works."

"Insurance doesn't explain why he was in the cottage," Mother said quietly.

"Maybe he picked up a little sideline in prison. Like burglary or maybe arson," the fire chief chuckled and wiped syrup off his lips. "Anyway, between the county sheriff and the O.P.P. they'll sort it out. Great breakfast," he said, pushing his plate away as he got up and stretched. "I've got to get back, Bill," he told my father. "Don't worry about a thing. Someone'll probably be over to see you soon."

Arsonists didn't usually die in their fires, even though I feared Mother had last night. Dad was as prickly as a clump of burdock as I washed up and he wielded a tea towel. Mother kept working on what looked like a list. With anyone else it would be itemizing what we'd lost in the fire. Mother probably hadn't come that far into reality yet.

After a short silence Dad threw the towel in the general direction of the sink and said he was going to see if any of our personal effects had escaped the blaze. Escape. I suppose it runs in the family. Mother with her escapist fiction and Dad and I blocking out our fears with activity. After the door slammed behind Dad, Mother got up and twitched the curtains. She didn't seem to know what to do with her hands.

At first I was puzzled until I realized she was bookless. Whatever she'd brought up to read had burned last night. Mother wasn't used to wandering around in our dimension.

"Why don't I walk down to the store and see if they've got any fantasy novels? I noticed a rack by the window," I said. Maybe out of range of Mother my thoughts would cease to spiral in their present hopeless litany. Mother arrested and charged with our other fires, going to prison while Dad died of humiliation and a broken heart. In any event she'd need a book.

Mother cheered up immediately. "See if they've got Weis and Hickman's *Fire Sea,*" she said. "It's Volume 3 in the Death Gate cycle." As usual last night's fire seemed to have gone right out of her mind. I knew the arson was probably subconscious but I couldn't help resenting how little the fires seemed to touch her.

The paperback rack yielded second-hand copies of Bradbury's *Farenheit 451*, Moorcock's *An Alien Heat* and a reprint of Zebrowski's *Ashes and Stars.* The cover blurb said: *"Their planet was reduced to a burned-out cinder."* I knew how they felt. I settled for Farmer's *Traitor To The Living* as the most appropriate of the bunch. I wondered as I paid for the book if the person who stocked the reading rack was just cold or a candidate for a support group with Mother.

Sunlight dappled the forest floor through branches of pine and cypress as I trudged slowly back. Hawks sailed purposefully overhead and sailboats dotted the bits of lake I could see through the trees. I sat down on the beach feeling a chill of real hatred for my life the way it was now. I would love to be on my own with nothing on my mind except sunbathing. I must have fallen asleep after the late night. When I woke up the sun was lower than I thought it should be. I started quickly up the hill.

When I reached the cottage, Mother was gone. Had she panicked and run?

Our car was gone too. Maybe Dad had come back and taken her somewhere, I tried to calm myself. But there was no note for the one left behind to worry.

The only person I could think to call was my sister who would say I told you so and add that I'd better get out before I was toast. The coffee was cold. Mother had been gone awhile. I sat down and thought of decent women who went to prison. The ladylike headmistress who had killed the diet doctor and spent her time inside teaching the other female inmates. Or the otherwise nice wives who had done in abusive husbands in order to protect their families. Mother might survive. I had heard prisons have pretty good libraries. Maybe she would only be aware now and then of her surroundings.

There was a knock at the door. "YOUR MOTHER BURNED DOWN THE ONLY THING I HAD LEFT!" Bill the lawyer and ex-landlord stood on the doorstep pointing a demented finger at me. His autumn hair seemed to be deciduous. As he lowered his head I could see pink scalp where his fingers had raked it back. "That cottage was in my family for generations," he continued in a low, hissing voice. "I should have known better than to rent it to a recovered arsonist. Recovered, hah!"

I pretended I hadn't heard any of this, the way I do when schizophrenics at the library tell me they hear voices in the books that aren't on tape. "My parents are out just now," I said. "Would you like to wait?" I hoped he wouldn't but he stepped inside. I could see his grief over losing the cottage was heartfelt. Nevertheless he wasn't being very supportive given all the work he was supposed to have done with the halfway house. Or maybe he was okay with trouble as long as it wasn't his.

The door opened and Dad came in, brushing soot and ashes off the cuffs of his light-coloured slacks. "Where's your mother?" he asked abruptly, frowning at Bill.

"I thought she was with you," I said.

Bill glared back at Dad. I could feel accusations leaping across the craggy surface of his brain, no doubt images of My Mother The Torch igniting cottage after cottage, causing lawsuit after lawsuit against the one who had brought her here. Bill Hoskit had just opened his mouth when Mother trotted in, looking elegant and composed.

"YOU!" Bill the lawyer whirled around and planted his index finger against Mother's startled little nose. "YOU FIREBUG! Why don't they keep you locked up where you belong?"

"How dare you . . . " my father growled like a terrier addressing a Great Dane. Mother held up her hand and he stopped in confusion. She stepped back, smiling.

"I'm so glad you're here, Mr. Hoskit," she said politely. "If Willy could make us some coffee perhaps we can get to the bottom of this." She looked around at the seating arrangements. "We'll need a few of the kitchen chairs, I think, dear," she said to my father who was looking rabbit-punched. "I've brought some guests."

"What IS all this?" I heard my father demanding. I hurried into the kitchen so as not to miss a word. As the door swung shut I could hear the sound of several people tramping up the steps and into our cottage.

"Guinevere," my father was repeating in a tragic voice when I got back with a trayful of coffee mugs. "Where were you and who are all these men?" Using Mother's full name showed the depth of his distress. Guinevere tied to the stake, flames licking her feet while her Lancelot was unable to save her.

"You know Mr. Abel, the fire chief," my mother said, indicating the three men who now sat around the living room. "And this is Mr. Higgins, the county sheriff. Mr. Smith is from the fire inspector's office. None of them is named Bill." She crossed her dainty feet and folded her hands in her lap. "There are altogether too many men named Bill around," she added softly and contemplated her hands.

Dad cleared his throat as though he were about to speak. Mother continued hastily. "After last night's fire my family didn't seem very interested in digging up any more information so I decided it was probably up to me. I woke up wondering if the insurance man had really asked for my husband or if he wanted Bill the lawyer instead. After all, it was Mr. Hoskit's cottage. And if it was important enough for William Jenkins to interrupt Bill's holiday, we ought to know why. I asked Mr. Abel what address Jenkins' car was registered to. Then I went over this morning to pay my respects."

Mother paused and took a sip of her coffee. "It turned out that William Jenkins was living in the halfway house that Bill supervises. For some reason I started wondering if the fire marshall in town had heard of him. And I happened to catch the inspector at a good time." She gestured to the tall man to her right.

"We had just finished an investigation concerning Mr. Hoskit's other house in town, that told us it had been torched by an arsonist for hire known as Willy the Wick. William Jenkins," he added for clarification. "Then Mrs. Lauren appeared, asking to speak to anyone who wasn't named Bill."

The three officials chuckled but the rest of us were in no laughing mood.

"When this little lady told us the connection between Jenkins and Hoskit," the inspector continued, "and that Jenkins was found dead here last night at a fire in Hoskit's other house, why, we thought it was time to come around and ask what was up? Jenkins was strictly a citybug. How come he's suddenly up at the lake?"

"Coroner says he didn't burn to death," the sheriff added. "His skull was smashed with something heavy, like a lead pipe."

The inspector nodded gravely. "Now, hypothetically speaking, let's say some hired torch burns down a guy's designated property for cash. But the guy stiffs him out of the fee." He steepled his long skinny fingers, making the case. "Firebugs are brooders. They wouldn't let something like that go. They want revenge. Usually its burning whatever else the guy owns if they can find it."

"There's your firebug!" Bill yelled, pointing desperately at Mother. "Investigate her! Poor Jenkins probably struck his head trying to get out of a burning house, torched by her."

Mother pursed her lips but she didn't raise her voice. "You would've known Mr. Jenkins sold insurance when he was booked into your halfway house. No doubt the arrival of an insurance man out here made you suspicious." She looked at Bill. "So you came back to see if you were right, thinking we'd all gone to the church supper and the house was empty. When Jenkins started to torch the cottage, you struck him and when I came downstairs you panicked and ran. Perhaps you did hope to blame it on me." She shook her head at such perfidy.

"Where's your evidence?" Bill swayed, a diseased elm struck by lightning.

"Would fingerprints on the poker do?" Mother nodded towards the fireplace. "It was lying on the floor when I came downstairs last night. I nearly tripped. So I picked up the nasty sooty thing with my hanky but then I saw the flames and I guess I just carried it on outside."

Bill made a surprisingly agile lunge for the front door and threw it open. Lined across the porch, arms folded across their chests were the volunteers from last night's fire.

"We've got our families up here, Mister," one of them said grimly. "What kinda game do you think you were playing at?"

"Is that really the poker from the other cottage?" Dad asked Mother when they'd all gone away, Bill in handcuffs.

"Certainly not, dear. But there weren't any lead pipes lying around. There didn't seem to be anything else Bill could've hit him with and one poker is much like another."

"I'm sorry for not believing in you, Vere," Dad began in a small voice stroking Mother's hand as they sat side by side on the sofa. He was Arthur now, grabbing a last chance at Camelot. And now that Mother had blown her cover, they didn't need a daughter in the middle.

I went upstairs to write them a note, wondering if she'd always been this able to cope and I, caught in protecting her from herself, had been too blind to see it? Looking back I could see now there were lots of small indicators that she was alive and kicking in both of her worlds. So maybe I'd just wanted to feel needed. Anyway, my sister Janice was right. Guinevere and her Bill had to sort out their lives on their own, whatever length those lives might turn out to be. I decided to use the remainder of the two weeks to find an apartment in town. The condos across from the fire station were a good possibility.

But first I'd go back to town and put new batteries in their smoke detectors.

EB AND FLO

Ebenezer cheated with two on the side,
And Florence was tired of being denied.
She strychnined his tea
And dumped him at sea.
Now Eb just goes out with the tide.

Joy Hewitt Mann

THE INHERITANCE

by Barbara Fradkin

The sense of loss was so acute it brought tears to his eyes. This is ridiculous, Daniel Elliott told himself. He hadn't cried at his mother's funeral, nor in the long weeks of sorting through her belongings, selling the house, and haggling with his brothers and their lawyers over the disposition of her meagre estate. But now, standing on this pathetic piece of abandoned land and looking at the cottage he had once loved, he wanted to weep like a child.

It was so small! Not the magnificently sprawling castle nor the broad raging river of his youth, but a ramshackle clapboard hut tacked together by an unskilled weekend handyman, and a murky, weed-choked creek that oozed westward towards the lake. The Sherwood forest of his youth, complete with imagined wolves and wild boars, was a tiny copse of threadbare cedar and birch, overrun by a tangled underbrush of ferns and saplings.

The properties on either side seemed to press in, shabby rectangles of patio and lawn extending down to a riverfront of imported sand. Faded 'For Sale' signs hung on both properties – testimony to the changes in lifestyle and economics from the sixties to the nineties, as well as to the flight westward of the English Montrealers who had once made the Laurentian mountains their summer playground. Desirable properties near ski slopes or lakes were being snapped up by international developers and French Quebeckers, but modest cottages like these, built in the fifties by working class families hoping for a touch of clean country living, would sit unnoticed for years.

Daniel had known this when he accepted the property as his share of the settlement, leaving his two older brothers equal shares in the city house they had all grown up in. Neither of them had wanted the cottage. John, the eldest, had called it a worthless piece of scrub, and Howard, one year younger than John but lightyears removed in temperament, had said it held too many bad memories for him. But for Daniel, the youngest, who had last been there as an imaginative boy of twelve, enchantment had tinged the memories with gold.

Pushing his way through the thistles and goldenrod that had once been a path, Daniel felt that loss most acutely. He was not a boy of twelve, running freely through the trees, hunting frogs along the shore and sharing ghost stories under the stars. He was a tired and disheartened man of forty-four, no longer on the brink of life but mired in its depths, worn down by a shabby divorce, a doomed custody battle, a stagnant civil service career, and the protracted grief of losing his mother cell by cell to brain cancer. He had counted on this cottage to transport him back in time, not to act as a mirror to his own disintegration.

He stood for ten minutes at the edge of the river, assessing the damage. The cottage itself was beyond salvation; the roof had collapsed, the windows and door had been stolen, and weeds grew up through the gaping holes in the walls. The clearing between the cottage and the lake, where once they had had bonfires and picnics, was overrun with wild raspberry bushes, and all along the river's edge, bulrushes and water lilies had reclaimed the shore. The little mountain stream running down the side of the property, where his father had chilled his beer and his brothers and he had raced miniature boats, was completely obscured by brush.

As he contemplated the wilderness, he felt his bleakness begin to lift. This land was his. There was a challenge and a rebellious beauty about it, as if nature were mocking man's attempt to tame her. He would not tame her, but perhaps in compromise and collaboration with her, he could make something beautiful they could both enjoy.

They say back-breaking labour restores the soul, he thought. Luckily for me, I have nothing else to do with my two-week vacation.

It was a week before he ventured into the stand of trees between the cottage and the road. He had pitched a tent, rented a dumpster and torn apart the cottage plank by plank. Then the raspberry bushes had been uprooted, the soil ploughed and a few of the healthier maple saplings transplanted in their place. His hands were blistered, his legs and arms scratched and his muscles stiff, but his spirits sang.

Each day new ideas came to him. He would leave the lilies and rushes at the riverbank, and he would build a boardwalk and deck out over the water from which to swim and launch a canoe. He would build a little cedar A-frame where the old cottage had been, with a small, natural stone patio overlooking the water. One room was all he really needed – now that it seemed he might spend the foreseeable future alone – one room plus a loft for Michael and Lisa on those weekends they visited.

He put off tackling the woods. He told himself it was because its thick impenetrable brush presented such a daunting task, but that was only half true. When they were children, his brother John had regaled Howard and him with tales of blood-curdling screams and ghostly apparitions that haunted the woods at night, and neither he nor Howard had dared venture in since. Even now the memory sent a tiny shiver down his spine. But looking at the woods and marsh around the stream through adult eyes, he saw they would have to be tamed. He didn't remember it being so swampy in the old days, and when he woke up one morning to discover the floor of his tent wet, he decided to find out why.

Armed with a scythe and hand saw, he began to battle his way through the underbrush into the heart of the thicket. All morning he chopped and pulled and carted brush back to the dumpster, slogging ankle deep in mud and ferns, until he finally found the reason. A beaver dam. Behind it, the stream had backed up, flooded the surrounding land and created a dozen little rivulets that trickled down the slope around the dam. Ferns and water grass grew in profusion, further blocking the water's progress. Daniel pondered the problem. If he let nature – and the beavers – have their way, half his land would be a marsh. But if he cleared the dam, tore out the undergrowth and reinforced the banks with natural stones, the stream would tumble over the stones past the A-frame with pastoral perfection. How could nature object to that?

The beaver dam was uninhabited, as far as he could tell, and proved easy to dismantle. As he shovelled up the last of the muck and branches from the bottom of the pool, he noticed a curiously shaped beige branch amidst the tangle of black in his wheelbarrow. He picked it up and examined it more closely in the sunlight. He ran his hand over its hard, pitted surface and poked at its bulbous ends. A bone, he decided.

Probably the leg of a large animal – a cow or deer, maybe even a horse – buried long ago.

He put the bone aside and gave it no further thought until the next day. Down on his hands and knees in the mud by the stream, pulling out ferns and small shrubs, he gripped another hard shaft. Beige and pitted, bulbous in shape again, but shorter and thinner than the other. Another animal, he decided. I've stumbled on some farm dog's long-forgotten cache. But even as he thought it, he felt a strange compulsion. It was just a faint urging at first, which forced him to forget the ferns and pick up the shovel in earnest, but by the end it was nearer to panic. The sun was setting, casting a swath of peach across the river, by the time he unearthed his final discovery. A blackened, misshapen sphere whose shape, even caked with mud, reminded him of only one thing.

A human skull.

Back in the security and convenience of his Ottawa apartment, he washed each bone carefully with a soft brush and laid them out on his tiny dining table to dry. He allowed a brief smile to lighten his mood. Francine would have had a fit, so there were some advantages to divorce after all.

While the bones dried, he rummaged through his sparse collection of books, mainly cheap paperback thrillers and obsolete college texts, until he found the diagram of the human skeleton he remembered from an undergraduate biology text. He had no training in bones, no idea what he was doing, and a strong feeling he should call the police, but he wanted to be sure of a few basic facts. First, were the bones indeed human? Was it one body or several, child or adult? He'd look fairly stupid dragging in the Sûreté de Quebec to look at a pile of cow bones.

It took half the night and some fairly wild guesses, but in a process rather like assembling a jigsaw puzzle, he finally identified two thigh bones, half a dozen curved bones which were probably ribs, a shoulder blade cracked in two, and a few bones which might be arms. Several were broken in two, the splintered edges worn smooth by time. Using his own femur as a guide, he decided the person was an adult but quite a bit shorter than his own six feet. The round, smooth surface of the skull was split by three radiating cracks and one cheek bone was crushed, but the shape was unmistakeably human. Without question, his next step had to be the police.

He stared at the skull awhile and his heart began to race. How had the body come to be buried there in the first place? And how had the skull become cracked? The soil where it had lain was soft and supple, a gentle grave in which to lie. It was as if someone had smashed it.

He put the skull down hastily. What someone? When? And whose skull was it?

The name Lucille Dubois popped into his head, catching him by surprise and shooting a current of fear down his spine. He hadn't thought of her in nearly thirty years, despite the uproar surrounding her disappearance that last summer he'd been there. Everyone had thought she'd run away, and his oldest brother John had been blamed. 'Big city bad boy turns the head of innocent Catholic farm girl.' John had always vehemently denied the charge, saying it had been all over between them for weeks, but even back then, at seventeen, he had a reputation for treating girls as throw-aways. And although Howard had been too shy to pursue his own girls, he would often trail in John's wake and try to pick up the pieces.

Daniel remembered vividly the Summer of Lucille, the chubby, pony-tailed farm girl suddenly transformed to womanhood and drawing his brothers like moths to a flame. It had been a summer full of slammed doors and swearing at the Elliott house, of flaring rages and manic highs and, after Lucille disappeared, of dark silences, accusations and tears. Daniel remembered Lucille's father storming across the road to their cottage, reeking of whiskey and purple with rage. Everyone was convinced that, had he laid hands on either Howard or John that day, he would have killed them.

Police and volunteers had combed the countryside for miles around, and nearby bus and train stations had been checked, but no trace of her had ever been found. Now Daniel looked at the skull before him. Surely, if Lucille had been murdered and buried in the woods, her body would have been discovered in that search.

But what if it hadn't been? Remembering the rages and jealousies of that summer, his hands began to shake. What if one of his brothers had killed her? Smashed her head with a rock in a fit of jealousy and pain, not meaning to kill her, not even knowing what he was doing, but suddenly discovering she was dead?

He clutched his head in his hands and took deep breaths. One step at a time, he told himself. He didn't know it was Lucille, didn't even know if the person had been murdered. But he couldn't call the police until he knew.

The Dubois farmhouse too was smaller and shabbier than he remembered it, perched at the top of the hill, its paint peeling from the dingy white siding and its Victorian wrap-around veranda buckling with age. All around it, the fields which had once rippled with corn tassels were overrun with scrub. Daniel approached on foot the way he used to, coming up the path from the woods below. As a child, it had seemed a long hike from his cottage, across the road, through the woods and up the hill to the farm, and he was surprised that now it took him only fifteen minutes. A bizarre sense of déjà vu gripped him as he stepped onto the veranda. How many times had he stood here in trepidation as a small boy, wanting to play with Lucille's little sister, Berthe, but terrified he'd see her father instead?

He found himself hesitating to knock, just as he had as a child, then scolded himself. The farm was probably deserted anyway and if not, old man Dubois would be a frail shell of the Goliath he remembered.

There was no answer to his first knock, nor to his second, and he was just turning away when the door cracked open two inches. Large, dark-circled eyes peered through the gap.

"Hi, um – Bonjour. Je regrette . . . Parlez-vous anglais? I used to live down by the river years ago and I – "

"Danny?" It was a whisper, breathless with shock.

He stared. "Berthe?"

Clutching her frayed brown cardigan to her throat, the woman stepped back, letting the door list silently open. In the dim interior light, her face was carved in gaunt angles, the eyes too big, the jaw too sharp, and the lips a thin, tight line. Her gray hair, lightly peppered with brown, hung in a single braid down her back.

Daniel found himself at a loss for words. Berthe, the summer playmate of his youth, had remained forever twelve in his mind, her honey pigtails askew, her face smudged with dirt and her eyes always dancing with some new plan for mischief. This haunted shadow held no trace of her.

She swallowed. "Danny! What . . . ? I didn't expect – It's been years!"

He held up his hands in weak apology. "I'm sorry just to drop in like this unannounced. I wasn't even sure anybody would be here. But my mother died this spring and I – "

"Oh, I'm sorry," she interjected, coming to life. "Would you like some . . . ? I can't offer you much, I don't – Well, I didn't know you were coming. But tea?"

"Tea, sure." The prospect of the comforting ritual filled him with relief as he followed her down the hall into the kitchen, still papered in the green and red teacups of his youth. It was clean, almost Spartan, and she stood at its centre rubbing her arms at some imagined chill and flitting her gaze furtively around the room as if to ensure that nothing would betray her. But the only personal touch was a heavy black typewriter on the table amid stacks of papers.

He pulled back a rickety wooden chair and sat down at the table. "I came up to check on our property and I just decided to drop by. For old times' sake. I didn't mean to scare you."

Berthe fluttered around the kitchen, filling the kettle and finding cups. "I remember your mother. She made me feel very welcome at your place. Always a big smile on her face and a little treat. She probably just wanted to make it up to us, because we didn't have a mother, but to me back then, she seemed like Santa Claus. I wanted to go live at your house."

He glanced through the doors for signs of life but there were none. No coats on pegs, no boots. Nothing but bleakness. Faded curtains shrouded the windows as if to shut out the world. Then, through the doorway at the end of the hall, he thought he could discern the vague outline of a chair. Perhaps a rocking chair, or a wheelchair.

"Your father," he ventured. "Is he still alive?"

The kettle began to whistle, startling her. Convulsively she shook her head and turned to fuss with the tea. "Papa died last month. Another stroke. He had one fifteen years ago, and ever since . . . It's a terrible way to go, for a tough, proud man like that. Confined to a wheelchair, hardly able to lift a spoon."

"And you took care of him all these years? Never left here?"

She leaned against the counter and folded her arms over her thin chest. Her eyes were flat. "Is the world out there such a wonderful place, Danny? Have you done so well?"

"No, but . . . " He was still groping. Berthe had always been the smart one in the family, drinking up his stories of Montreal and dreaming of a writer's garret on Rue St. Denis. His eyes, roving across the barren room to the darkened hall, must have reflected his confusion, for she turned away abruptly.

"I don't need much anymore. I grow my own vegetables and I do some freelance writing for the new local weekly, "Le Patriote" – mostly short stories, gardening columns. I sold a bit of the lakefront to help Papa and me out, and with his pension it was more than we needed."

Daniel thought of himself, newly installed in his bachelor apartment and driven crazy by the silence. "Don't you ever get lonely?"

"I see the neighbours. And I take care of Mrs. Lavigne; she's old now and her children moved to Joliette. But we didn't get out much – Papa didn't like people to see him the way he was – and after a while you don't miss it."

"And . . . Lucille?" He held his breath. "Did she ever come back?"

Her back stiffened and for a moment as she poured the milk he thought she wouldn't answer. "Lucille's gone."

"But do you know where she went? Did you ever hear from her?"

"Never."

He felt a chill. "Not one word?"

She shook her head. "I finally put an ad – a little story, really, about Papa's death – in "Le Patriote" last week. I was hoping she might call. But whatever happened back then . . ." She turned back to him, the cups trembling in her hands. "Papa was never the same after she left. It killed him. To lose his wife, and then Lucille." She set the cups down on the table and pulled up a chair beside him. "You should have seen him, Danny, at night by the window, holding her picture and crying huge, rolling tears. I tried to help . . . But I wasn't Lucille, pretty, girlish, teasing him to make him laugh. After Mama died, only Lucille could make him laugh."

Daniel had been eight when Mme. Dubois drowned, and had only fleeting memories of the crashing thunder, the sheeting rain, and the men soaked from long hours searching the lake. But Lucille's disappearance was vividly seared in his mind. He picked up his cup of tea and blew on it to buy himself time as he considered his next probe. He didn't know Berthe anymore and he wasn't sure how fragile she might have become.

"I remember how upset your father was on the day she left," he began casually. "He snapped our screen door right off its hinges and I thought he was going to kill my brother John."

"It wasn't even John's fault. If it was anybody's, it was Howard's. Howard broke her heart, not John."

"What!" He had been trying to keep the conversation casual, but he couldn't hide the astonishment in his voice. No one had ever assumed Howard could hold a candle to John, with women or with any other conquest. Least of all Howard himself. "What happened?"

She was toying with her teacup, turning it in slow, measured circles on the scarred table top. "She gave up on John, said he was nothing but a brute, but she thought Howard was such a romantic. They were going to run away together, because they knew Papa would never permit them to see each other. And your mother – " She hesitated, a sudden flush adding life to her cheeks. "Well, she was kind to us, but she never really saw Lucille as anything more than a cheap country girl. At least that's what Lucille told me. She was so upset she just couldn't get away fast enough. I remember sitting on her bed the evening she left, watching her pack and put on her make-up. They were going to meet at midnight at the bottom of the path, and they were going to hitchhike to Montreal, maybe even go west to Vancouver. I watched her go, running through the corn that was almost as tall as her. But I guess Howard never met her. It must have broken her heart, and she never came back."

"But why? Broken hearts heal. People get on with their lives."

"It wasn't that. The humiliation of crawling back to Papa would be too great."

"Humiliation? But you said he loved her."

She pulled her sweater tightly around her, as if it were armour against him. "Of course he loved her. He would lay down his life for her. But he was a proud man. On the day she left, they had a terrible argument. She said some dreadful things, and he was so hurt that he never allowed me to mention her name again."

"What dreadful things? About what?"

"About love." She hesitated. "I was young, but I knew she was cruel. She said he didn't know the meaning of the word."

At the mention of Lucille's name, dead silence fell. Through the phone wires, Daniel heard his brother's erratic breath, and he could almost picture him bent over his study desk, pinching his nose to fend off a migraine.

"Lucille. I haven't thought about her in years."

"Well, this whole experience has been like a trip into the past," Daniel replied. "I saw her sister Berthe yesterday, and we got to talking. Lucille came up."

"How is Lucille? Fat and fertile?"

"No. Still missing, apparently."

"Really?" Howard's tone sounded too studied. "I never expected her to stay away so long."

The skull lay before Daniel on the dining table, its gaping eyes like a mute rebuke. She didn't, he thought with a chill. "Howard, what happened between the two of you?"

Howard laughed, a dusty, brittle rasp like the old manuscripts he pored over day after day. "Lots in my imagination. Not much in real life. And it has ever been thus," he added with the sort of woeful literary flourish that had become his trademark. In love affairs, Howard had fared even worse than Daniel, who at least had two children to show for his painful fifteen years of marriage. Howard had nursed a fierce but futile passion for his best friend's wife for nearly twenty years. But, always the English professor, he cloaked his pain in poetry, hoping to sound clever but really trying to keep the world's pity at bay. And also, Daniel suspected, to be as completely different from his brother John as he could possibly be.

"That's not what Berthe said," Daniel replied, ignoring the self-pity. "She said you and Lucille were planning to run away together and that on the night she disappeared, she was supposed to meet you at the bottom of the path. But you never showed up."

"Oh, what an interesting spin on the truth. So much more palatable than my own version. The truth is, Daniel, it was she who never showed up, while I, playing the lovesick fool, waited till dawn in the frigid Laurentian cold."

"But she never showed up?"

"No."

"And you heard nothing, saw nothing?"

"Other than the usual four-letter words bellowing from the Elliott household, courtesy of John? No, Daniel. Why?"

"I just wonder what really happened to her. She's never been heard from since. Didn't you ever wonder what happened?"

"Not really. I know perfectly well what happened."

For a moment Daniel wasn't sure he'd heard correctly. His pulse surged. "What?"

"A sordid, commonplace tale, best left in the past."

Wrestling back his impatience, Daniel tried to keep his tone chatty. "But all her family was frantic. The police were all over. Why didn't you at least tell them?"

"Because Lucille had clearly made her choice and it didn't include her family. She had been desperate to get away somewhere where her family could not touch her, so desperate that she was almost willing to exploit the yearnings of a painfully shy and love-smitten sixteen-year-old to accomplish her goals. Of course I didn't know that then. I thought she . . ." He sighed, and Daniel pictured him rubbing his hands through his thinning hair, as if to reassure himself, for the millionth time, that there was some left. "Anyway, she obviously thought better of it. She'd become rather obsessed with God and sin and redemption, and I'd like to think that's what stopped her. Not her utter lack of interest in me. But whatever the reason, she ran off without me and slipped anonymously into the big city with no ties to the past. But do you think I was going to admit to all this, with big brother John celebrating my humiliation in the background? He said he'd turned her down himself."

"You mean she asked him to run away with her too?"

"So he claimed. You see how complete my humiliation would have been? And she knew what weaknesses to exploit in both of us. With me, she claimed true love. But with John – not the most starry-eyed among us, you'll admit – she used the pregnancy ruse. Claimed she was going to have his baby."

"And you didn't believe her?"

"It didn't matter what I believed. John said she wasn't a virgin and there was quote 'no way she was pinning that on him' unquote."

"Could she in fact have been pregnant?"

"To satisfy your puerile curiosity on that score, Daniel, you'll have to ask John. I was sixteen. What did I know about such mysteries? I never even slept with her."

Like most baby boom English Montrealers, the three Elliott brothers had scattered westward in pursuit of careers – Daniel to the Federal civil service in Ottawa, Howard to the University of Toronto, while John had taken his brash entrepreneurial spirit all the way to

Calgary. But Daniel acknowledged that it was the spiritual and temperamental distance more than the physical distance that kept him and John apart, and he did not feel as free to pick up the phone and reminisce about the past with John as he had with Howard. John had always treated him as a thing of little consequence, ignored at the dinner table and brushed aside in the daily clamour of needs. In the end, as Daniel traced his fingers over the cracks in Lucille's skull and imagined the power of the blow needed to cause them, only the strength of his moral dilemma forced him to call.

"What's up, Danny Boy?" John said as soon as his secretary had announced him. 'Hello, how are you?' would have been a waste of time. His voice was deafening, even through three thousand kilometres of cable.

"I've been doing some work up at the cottage – "

"Yeah?"

"And I got to talking to Berthe Dubois – "

"Yeah?"

"You know, Lucille's sister – "

"Yeah?" In the background Daniel heard paper rustling. His brother always did at least two things at once, a talent which had made him a millionaire in Calgary's boom days. But any hope that Daniel might be able to approach the subject obliquely was fast disappearing.

He plunged in. "Was Lucille pregnant?"

For the first time there was silence. Even the rustling stopped. Then John chuckled, a smoker's rumble which ended in a cough. "Why, has she got some curly-haired thirty-two year-old kid with a great left-handed pitch?"

"No. She never came back."

"I'm not surprised. She wanted out in a big way."

"Why? Was she pregnant?"

"Maybe, but if she was, it happened before I came along. I can tell you she'd seen plenty of action before me. She was so loose a guy could get lost in there. I only slept with her twice, but right away she started getting serious, wanted me to take her back to Montreal, said she had to get away from the farm. And when I said no, she laid this pregnancy on me. Would you believe it, Danny Boy?"

"But if she wasn't pregnant, why was she so anxious to leave?"

"Sick to death of the old man, that's my guess."

Daniel frowned as he considered this and tried to articulate his boyhood impressions of Dubois. "You mean his drinking? His temper?" "That, yeah. Plus he was probably having a go at her himself."

Afterwards Daniel paced his tiny apartment, weighing the facts. John was ruthless; he would squash anyone who got in his way without a qualm. He was also very possessive and had a vicious temper which Daniel had often seen him unleash on Howard as they grew up. But had Lucille fired up his passions enough for murder? She seemed to have roused Howard more than John and if Howard became enraged, anything was possible. Whereas John attacked a threat head on, Howard deflected his rage onto something smaller or weaker, like Daniel. Or Lucille.

No, he thought, pushing the idea out of his mind. Howard had nothing to gain by killing Lucille. He loved her; she was going to run away with him. And John had already told her he wasn't interested. What motive was there for either of them?

None, he concluded firmly, and turned with relief to other possibilities. John had said there were other men before him, maybe even her own father. Old man Dubois – the drunken Goliath of his childhood nightmares. A man widowed in the prime of life, raising two daughters alone, living an isolated rural existence away from proper sexual outlets but also from prying eyes. What had Berthe said? That Lucille had always had a special relationship with her father, had been the one to cheer him up and make him laugh? And that when she disappeared –

Daniel stopped abruptly, remembering Berthe in that shrouded mausoleum of a house, her sweater clutched around her, her nerves jumping at every sound. A vice gripped his chest, pressing in. His heart thumped against it. When Lucille disappeared, Berthe had tried to take her place. To cheer her father up and take away the grief. All these years! Why had she stayed? What hold did he have over her, to transform the feisty tomboy Daniel had known into this reclusive wraith?

As if by some perverse quirk of nature, it was a glorious, blue-skied, sun-filled August day when Daniel drove back to his land to face Berthe. Weaving the car along back highways and country lanes, he wrestled with his doubts. Not about what had happened to Lucille – for he was fairly certain he knew – only about whether or not to tell Berthe. Lucille had argued with her father on the evening of her death, and whether he had acted in a drunken rage or in calculated retribution, he had killed her to prevent her from leaving. But he was dead now, and whatever private bitterness Berthe might harbour towards him, she seemed to cling to his memory almost in desperation and to live in the hope that someday Lucille might come back. What purpose would it serve to tell her that both were an illusion? That her father was a murderer and that Lucille was never coming back?

Before he confronted her with such shattering news, he had to be sure. He needed to check the burial spot one more time, to ensure there was nothing he had overlooked in his less than rational flight after finding the skull. As he rounded the last curve in the gravel road, he caught a brief flash of someone running across the road from his land and disappearing up the path. A rusty red Chevette was parked on the property beside his and he felt a surge of curiosity. Perhaps someone had bought the place. He pulled his car off the road into the small driveway which he had reclaimed from the thistles, and climbed out. All was quiet. Not a sign of life from next door or across the road. Shrugging, he headed for the thicket. The ground was less soggy now, and he could hear the gurgle of water tumbling over stones and roots. But even before the stream came into view, he sensed something wrong. Something disturbed and out of place. A second later he stopped in his tracks.

Ahead of him sat a box, perched at the edge of the stream where the beaver dam and the body had been. Its sides were rotting and blackened from the mud which still clung in chunks. With growing unease, he approached and peered inside to see a tiny, carefully arranged skeleton of a human child. Almost dwarfing it, nestled against its tiny ribcage lay a handmade wooden cross.

Branches and raspberry canes tore at his clothes as he flailed his way out of the thicket and raced for his car in a blind panic to get off the land. Once inside, he locked all the doors and dropped his forehead onto the steering wheel. His heart pummelled against his chest. Fighting nausea, he forced himself to think. Someone had used his land as a burial ground, not just once but twice. And unlike Lucille, the baby had been given the rudiments of a Christian burial. Someone who loved it and cared about its soul had buried it. Then today someone who knew exactly where the baby was had returned and dug it up again. Why? Who?

Daniel sucked air into his lungs as a horrible possibility occurred to him. What if Lucille had been pregnant, not that summer, but earlier? Or what if Berthe . . . ?

It had to be Berthe!

His fingers shook so hard he could barely get the key into the ignition. Revving the car, he bolted forward in a shower of gravel and spun the car up the hillside at the next intersection. The aging Mazda rocked and swayed over the rutted country road, past fields shoulder high in corn, until the steep gables of the faded Victorian farmhouse came into view at the crest of the hill. He caught a brief flash of movement near the barn as a pale figure rushed towards the house, but when the car slid to a halt on the pebble drive, there was no sign of life. He knew she was there. She had seen him and she had run for cover. Hiding from him? What was she afraid he would find out?

He pounded on the front door. "Berthe! Open up! I'm not going away."

No response. He waited. Pounded. "Berthe!"

The chirp of crickets, nothing more.

"Berthe, I'll stand out here and scream at everyone who goes by about the baby."

The door yanked open. Her eyes were like saucers. "What!?"

He barged past her into the house. "The dead baby, the one that's buried on my land."

"Buried . . . ? What baby?"

"You know damn well. You dug it up!"

"Daniel, I – What are you talking about?"

He forced himself to calm down and be patient with her. After all these years of locking this secret in the deepest, darkest part of her psyche, how could he expect her not to be blinded by the harsh light he had suddenly cast upon it? He reached to take her thin hands in his, but she recoiled.

"Berthe, I'm sorry. I don't mean to upset you. It must have been awful for you, pregnant, scared, having your baby all alone – "

Shock whipped colour back into her cheeks. "I never had a baby."

"Lucille, then. Lucille had a baby and buried it."

"I don't believe it! She would never – "

"She would if she was afraid of your father. If it was his baby."

She clutched her throat, eyes wide. He softened. "I know what your father did to you, Berthe. And to Lucille."

She turned from him, whipping her head back and forth. "Papa – Papa needed us."

"He used you. Berthe, you saw Lucille's baby."

"I never saw a baby!"

"You dug it up."

"I didn't, Daniel. I never heard of a baby!"

He stared at her in confusion. If she hadn't dug up the baby, why had she run from him and refused to open the door? And, he thought with his throat growing dry, if Berthe hadn't dug up the baby, who had?

The same horror and confusion was mirrored in her own eyes as she reached out to grip his arm. She swallowed twice before words came. "Show me this baby."

The red Chevette was still parked at the next cottage, but he saw no flickers of movement in the woods as he led Berthe towards the graves. When they neared the crate, she stumbled forward and fell to her knees in the mud beside it. She bent her head, frail shoulders shaking and tears falling onto the sodden wood. Daniel knelt helpless by her side. Why was he even putting her through this? How would he ever tell her about Lucille?

"Oh Seigneur," she moaned. "She was telling the truth!"

"Lucille? The truth about what?"

"She begged me to leave with her. She said Papa was a murderer and she couldn't stay in the same house with him. But I never thought . . ."

His heart lurched. "Never thought what?"

She laid her hand on the wooden crate. "This was Papa's box. He got lots of them from Joliette to ship his vegetables in. Only this one – "

"You think your father killed Lucille's baby and buried it here?"

She bowed her head, tears streaming. Then she looked around her for the first time, her desperate eyes flitting over the mangled underbrush and the tiny coffin. Midday sun dappled through the boughs overhead, splashing sunlight onto the upturned earth. Gradually her tears stopped. "No, Daniel. Lucille buried this baby, not Papa. The crucifix, the care. Papa would never do this."

He searched for a gentle way to guide her to the truth. "But you said it was your father's crate. You said Lucille called him a murderer."

"But this crucifix – that summer, before she ran away, Lucille was making it. She never told me why. I see now it was for the baby."

"But the baby was already dead, Berthe. It would have been dead and buried before the summer."

"It's not possible. How did the crucifix get here?"

He knew the answer but now, on the brink of revealing it, he couldn't find words. Behind him, a twig snapped and he whirled around. Nothing. Just his raw nerves, conjuring up ghosts. He braced himself. "Your father put it there, Berthe. When he buried Lucille."

She recoiled from him. "Buried! You're crazy! Why!"

"I dug up her bones, Berthe. Right here where this baby is. He killed her."

She had turned to paste, her eyes lolling. "No! Papa worshipped Lucille. He would never kill her! She ran away."

"She was going to, but I think your father stopped her that night."

She scrambled to get away from him, floundering in the mud and shaking her head. He turned to catch her. And stopped in his tracks.

Standing in front of them was a woman sheathed in a too-tight floral sundress and streaked in mud from head to toe. Even after thirty years and twice as many pounds, her identity was undeniable. Berthe found her voice first.

"Lucille!"

Shock and estrangement froze them both in place a moment before Lucille rushed forward and pulled Berthe into her arms. Incomprehensible fragments of French tumbled out amid their sobs.

"I've been keeping a check on you," Lucille babbled, suddenly switching to English. "When I read that Papa had died, I decided I could come back."

Berthe pulled away. "But why never a letter! Never a call!"

"You took his side when I wanted you to come with me. And my life was hard when I got to Montreal. It was . . . well, I'm not proud of it and I did not think you would understand. But I kept a subscription to "Le Patriote" – I even saw some of your columns – so I knew you were all right. And later I heard he had a stroke and was paralyzed. I decided as long as he couldn't hurt you, maybe it was better for you not to know."

"To know what?"

"My God!" Daniel cried. "It was you I saw running from my land. You dug up the baby!" His first reaction was a surge of relief, for if Lucille was still alive, his brothers could not be murderers. But his second was chilling fear. If the body was not Lucille . . .

Lucille blew her nose and shoved a clump of brassy hair from her eyes. Black rivers of mascara streaked her cheeks. "I have been coming by, getting up the nerve to come see Berthe ever since I saw the story in "Le Patriote". Then I saw someone was clearing up your property and I was afraid the graves had been destroyed. Now that Papa is dead, I want them to have a proper grave."

"Them! Who else? Another baby!" Berthe sagged against a tree as if her legs had given out. Emotion fled her face. She looked as if she had absorbed too many shocks for one day. Even Lucille, fighting to control her own emotions, seemed to notice.

"Not more babies, but something else," she replied reluctantly.

The truth struck Daniel like an epiphany as more pieces fell into place. "That's why you disappeared! You found the other body, didn't you?"

Lucille's eyes flitted towards him before returning to Berthe. Slowly she nodded. "I went down to give my baby a blanket and a crucifix. Papa had said she was stillborn and I tried not to think about her but it bothered me that she had no last rites or burial mass. So one night that summer I sneaked down and dug her up. That's when I found the body."

Berthe had gone white as a sheet. "What body?"

Lucille swallowed. Her thick jowls quivered as she groped for words. "I was eight when Papa first came to my room. He told me it was the way big girls showed their Papas they loved them." She shrugged as if to apologize for her naivete. "I was just a farm girl, going to school with the nuns. One day I started to bleed and I got scared and told Mama everything. She got really angry at me, slapped me and called me dirty. Then she and Papa had a huge fight. I remember the yelling, and Papa saying he loved me and would do what he wanted in his own house. Then she disappeared and I thought she killed herself. Papa's story about her going out on the main lake and the storm coming up didn't make sense. Mama was a good swimmer, and she grew up on that lake. I thought she hated me so much for stealing Papa that she . . . But – " She faltered and with shaking hands reached up to her neck and pulled out a tiny crucifix on a gold chain.

Berthe gasped. "Mama's crucifix!"

Lucille nodded. "When I found it there with the bones, I knew she died trying to protect me. So I ran away. I'm sorry, I should have stayed to protect you, but I thought maybe it was just me he wanted, and he'd leave you alone. But I should have protected you."

Good God, thought Daniel as he looked at the two trembling sisters before him. Please let the worst of it be over. No more past to haunt us, no more skeletons to unearth. But then Berthe pulled her sweater more tightly around her and flickered a ghost of that smile Daniel had once known.

"I was all right. That first stroke he had? I pushed him down the stairs."

WIDOW'S WEEDS

by Sue Pike

It was minus 37 degrees the night in February when my only son, Blake, froze to death. He and his wife had driven up from the city earlier that day, leaving their car at the end of the ploughed road and skiing the final three kilometers along the shore to the cottage. The last Tess saw of him was when he went outside around midnight to bring in an armload of firewood.

The coroner ruled the death was accidental, probably caused by the victim losing his footing on the deck and stumbling over the low railing to the frozen lake below. The sheer drop would have broken his bones, but it was the bitter cold that killed him.

I was in the city when it happened and only later heard how some trappers checking their lines early the next morning had noticed bush wolves gathered around something near the shore. They frightened the animals off and one man stayed with the body while the other two wakened Tess to phone for help.

I never saw the convoy of snowmobiles speeding across the lake or the paramedics strapping his body to the sleigh. But I picture it often enough. In my mind's eye I'm standing on the deck looking down. I see Blake with his legs and arms flung out like a rag doll tossed to the ice by a petulant child; his skin is translucent, bruised and torn, his face slicked over with a fine coat of crystals.

I was picturing it five months later on a warm July afternoon as I walked along the narrow road that winds behind the three family cottages on our point. So absorbed was I that I didn't even hear the car until it was nearly on top of me. I only just managed to scramble to the verge before the left front wheel skidded to a stop exactly where my foot had been seconds earlier.

Tess.

My daughter-in-law lowered the window part way and pushed her sunglasses over her forehead.

"Sorry, Isabel. Did I frighten you?" She tilted her head to one side and smiled up at me, and I caught a glimpse of casually elegant riding breeches and a crisp cotton shirt. So it's to be the Princess of Wales today, I thought.

I leaned onto the door and my own sixty-nine year old face glared back at me from the lower half of the tinted window, all pouches and creases under a crooked Tilley hat.

"You're driving way too fast for this winding road, Tess." We'd had this discussion before. "One of these days you're going to kill someone."

"Oh let's not go into that again." Her voice was unperturbed and smooth as the pebbles under my feet. "I'm just anxious to get to the cottage. This is the first I've been able to get up here since Blake had his accident and there's so much to do." She waved a pale hand in the direction of the lake.

I stared at her but said nothing.

"I've been incredibly busy. Settling the estate and dealing with lawyers and accountants. It's all quite daunting."

'Daunting' had a British lilt to it. Very Lady Di.

The last time I'd seen Tess was at my son's funeral. She was Jackie Kennedy on that occasion, the brave young widow greeting mourners in a trim little suit and veiled hat. The only thing missing was a small son to salute the casket, but they hadn't been married long enough for that, would never have been married long enough for that, if I knew Tess.

I suppose I was hoping for some change in her since then, some mark of Blake's death written on the perfect planes of her face, but she was as bland and beautiful as ever. Tendrils of fair hair floated down from a loose knot to cling damply to her neck. Her eyes, the colour of blue willow china, were clear and untroubled.

"By the way," she splayed the fingers of her left hand against the steering wheel and began to maneuver the rings into perfect alignment. "I'm thinking of selling the cottage. It's too much upkeep for me to manage by myself."

She looked up at me through her lashes but I kept still.

"My financial advisor tells me this would be a good time to put it on the market. He thinks I can get quite a lot of money for it. Especially if we can sever the property into lots."

"Lots?" My heart lurched. "But you can't do that. This is family land. Blake would never have allowed any of the old property to be broken up."

"Well I'm sorry, Isabel, but Blake's portion is mine now. And anyway, he was coming around to the idea. We talked about it quite often." She blew some wisps of hair out of her eyes. "In any case, he's not here anymore, is he?"

"How many lots?" I was having difficulty getting my breath.

"Lots of lots." She laughed. "Well, as many as will fit, I guess. I know one developer in the city who says twelve building sites would make the deal viable." Tess took a lipstick from her purse and pulled the rear view mirror around so she could apply a fresh coat. She made a little moue with her mouth, blotted it and then flipped the tissue out the window where it fluttered to my feet.

I clutched the edge of the glass hard and forced air into my lungs. My inhaler was in my pocket but I was damned if I'd resort to it in front of her.

"Well, I must go," she turned away and I could feel the window pushing against my hands and then, just as suddenly, it stopped and I was able to unclench my fingers and step back to the verge. "By the way, would you be a darling, and tell Alastair I'm here? I promised I'd let him know the minute I arrived."

Pebbles and dust shot away from the spinning tires and it took every bit of my strength to remain standing until the car was out of sight. Then my knees buckled and I sank down among the buttercups and daisies, wheezing and cursing Tess and the deadly emphysema that sapped my strength and numbered my days on this piece of land I loved so much.

I found my daughter kneeling on the deck of her cottage. She had the porch door off its hinges and was prying the screen from the frame.

"Raccoons!" Lindy sat back on her heels when she saw me. "The kids left a package of cookies lying out last night and the beggars decided to break in for a snack." She wrenched the last of the torn screening away and began to measure a new length from a fresh roll lying at her feet. I picked up the wire cutters from the picnic table and handed them to her.

"I ran into Tess on the road. Or rather, she almost ran into me." I chuckled, hoping to sound more neutral than I felt.

"Mm. I knew she was coming. She called Alastair last night to ask if he'd come over to help her open up the cottage." She had her back to me, her head bent over the door. "By the way, who is she today?"

"Princess Diana, as near as I can tell," I picked up the staple gun and passed it to her when she had the screen in place. "But why Alastair? Being a cottage handyman is hardly his strong suit. Why not hire someone from the village?"

Lindy's shoulders stiffened but she said nothing. I dragged an old wooden Muskoka chair closer to where she was working. The sun was moving behind the cottage now but it was still hot in the shade and my heart was juddering in my chest. I tried to relax, listening to the rhythmic clump of staples biting into wood.

When Lindy finally put her tools down, I patted the seat of the chair beside me. She sank into it and we sat still for a moment looking down at the lake where five teenagers in swimsuits were splashing around. I recognized my two granddaughters and the Crawford kids.

"You haven't wanted to talk about Blake and what happened to him and I've respected that." I turned to her. "But now we must, Lindy. It's important."

"I know, Mom. It's just . . . " Lindy began.

"Hi, all." Tess climbed the steps to the deck and leaned against the railing. She'd changed out of the jodhpurs and into a high-waisted, low-necked blue dress that reached almost to her ankles. Her hair was down and tumbling in tiny curls about her shoulders. A Jane Austen character, I thought, or perhaps one of the Brontes.

"Aren't you a quaint pair, sitting out here in your old camp clothes." Tess leaned closer, studying each of us in turn. "But look at you! You're letting your skin turn to leather. I'll bet neither one of you has been wearing those sunscreen samples I gave you last summer."

I didn't dare glance at Lindy. Tess had sold cosmetics to help put herself through university. When she married Blake she tried to unload some products on her new in-laws, but found us disappointing customers.

Tess sighed and leaned back again. "And I see you've forgotten to give Alastair my message, Isabel." She smiled at me indulgently then, as if she'd always suspected I was senile. "Never mind, I'll roust him out myself."

She flitted away on her fine leather slippers and we could hear laughter coming from the living room. After a while she reappeared tugging Alastair behind her by his fingertips. I thought he looked extremely foolish and would have told him so except at that moment he had the grace to extricate himself and lean down to give me a kiss.

"Isabel! I had no idea you were here. Can I get you a cold drink?"

But Tess was having none of that. "She knows where the refrigerator is." She reclaimed the fingers and began tugging him off the deck and up the path to her cottage. "We have work to do and if you're very good, I'll give you a cold drink when you're finished."

Alastair shrugged a little sheepishly in our direction before allowing himself to be borne out of sight.

"Don't start." Lindy gave me a warning look.

But I'd been quiet long enough. "What is going on, Lindy? It's not just Blake, is it? What about you and Alastair?"

She took a deep breath. "Does Alastair like being married to a woman who's so consumed with rage over the way her little brother was allowed to freeze to death because his wife didn't happen to notice he was gone?" Her bitterness was frightening. "I'd say probably not, wouldn't you?"

I waited.

"She terrifies me, Mom. She's like that praying mantis Dad found on the woodpile when we were kids. Do you remember? The female was eating the male while he was still copulating with her."

I remembered Rob explaining that people were sometimes like that. Perhaps Blake forgot.

"And now Tess has Alastair over there." Lindy said. "God! I feel the way Maggie must have felt when Tess first started putting the moves on Blake. Poor Maggie!" She shifted back in her seat. "To have that fey creature sitting in on Blake's Nineteenth Century Poetry class all that year, hanging on his every word, waylaying him in the parking lot to discuss the symbolism in Keats and Shelley. She was so clever and so incredibly gorgeous. And just needy enough to appeal to his male ego."

"Yes but Maggie and Blake were having a bad time right about then." I had to try and make sense of it, for myself as well as Lindy. "Maggie had just had the second miscarriage and she was crying all the time. It seems to me that Blake just allowed himself to be flattered for a bit and then it was too late." I watched a blue heron swoop along the bay and land at the foot of a dead pine tree on the other shore. "But surely Alastair's not attracted to Tess. He's way too smart not to see through her."

"And Blake wasn't smart? Give me a break!" Lindy snorted. "She has this talent for helplessness that men find appealing. If I tried it, Alastair would think I'd flipped. He'd tell me to buck up, like a good girl. But with Tess, he falls all over himself to help her out."

"What do you mean? Has she done this before?"

"Mm. It started right after Blake's funeral. She wanted Alastair to sort through some papers. It made sense at first, with Blake and Alastair in the same faculty. But then it was household things. Would he look at the furnace, that sort of thing."

"The furnace!" I tried to picture my elegant son-in-law squinting at a furnace. If it didn't have a sonnet inscribed on it, I couldn't imagine what he would make of it.

"I know." Lindy tossed her head impatiently. "I'm sure he's never noticed we even have such a beast."

We sat quietly for a while, looking across the water, each lost in our own thoughts. I reached over and took her hand.

"There's something else," I said. "Tess spoke to me when we met on the road. She wants to sell and she's hoping to get permission to sever their twenty acres into building lots. She says she and Blake had talked about doing it before he died."

"Bullshit!" Lindy's hand flew out of mine as she leapt to her feet. Her eyes were wild. "That is total crap! I talked to Blake just a week before he died and he told me then how important the cottage and family land were to him. He sounded depressed and I had the feeling he thought this was the only stable thing in his life."

"You talked to him?" I leaned forward. I didn't think either of us had talked to him since he left Maggie. We were too angry and too proud.

"It wasn't a happy conversation and I didn't want you to know he was feeling so bad." She was pacing the deck now, her arms hugging her chest. "But I know damned well he'd never have sold his part of the property. It was our grandfather's for God's sake!"

She sank back into the chair and hugged her knees to her chest. "Alastair thinks I'm being paranoid about Tess." She had her voice under control now. "He believes her story about what happened the night Blake died. He believes she fell asleep and didn't realize Blake was still outside. But Tess would need to get up in the night to put more wood in the stove, just to keep herself from freezing. When I confronted her at the funeral, she did her little-girl-crushed routine and Alastair was appalled and horrified at my lack of tact and sympathy. I don't know when I've seen him so angry."

There was a pause and then she continued in a voice so low I had to lean toward her to hear.

"I never told either one of you I called Tess later. She blustered for a bit, then admitted she'd gone outside that night to get logs for the stove. Said she was furious with Blake for leaving her alone to cope. They'd apparently had a fight and he stormed out in a snit. She thought he was just out walking off his anger. Walking! My God. There was at least twenty inches of snow on the ground and it was one of the coldest nights that winter."

I closed my eyes and I could see Blake again, broken and helpless at the foot of the cliff. Only this time his eyes were open, waiting, watching as his blood turned to ice.

"I couldn't understand what they were doing here in the first place." Lindy said. "Blake and Maggie used to ski in all the time. But Tess? She never struck me as the outdoors type."

"Maybe she was being Amelia Earhart that weekend. The plucky little adventuress." I said, but I knew that wasn't it.

There was a pause and then Lindy began to speak again, her voice tight and agitated.

"Remember last Wednesday, when Alastair took the kids to town?" She went on without waiting for an answer. "I waited until they were off the point and then went over to Blake's cottage to look around. The shutters from the windows overlooking the deck were piled under the cabin. Blake had painted all the shutters last summer but when I dragged those four out into the light they had new scratches on them, as if someone had tried to pry them off. Only whoever did it, didn't have proper tools. It looked like they'd used a piece of wood or something."

I held up my hand to stop her. "But that could have been anyone, prowlers perhaps," I cried.

"I thought of that, but why just their cottage and not yours or mine? And serious thieves would come by snowmobile. That would imply some intention on their part and if that were so, wouldn't they have brought crow bars or something? Whatever was used left splinters and bark behind in the scratches and whoever did it wasn't successful. None of the hooks are ripped out of the wood."

Lindy looked over at me then, her face taut and flushed.

"And something else was weird. All the other shutters were still fastened on and just those four had been removed and put under the cottage. How? Who could have taken them off? Tess says she hasn't been up here since that weekend."

I was silent, thinking, imagining the unimaginable.

"What if it was Blake trying to get back into the cottage?" she said. "What if she locked him out. She might have been trying to teach him a lesson. A lesson he'd never forget."

"She might have pushed him off the deck, I suppose, when he became disoriented." My voice shocked me. It sounded rational except what I was saying was beyond anything I could ever have imagined.

Lindy came over to kneel in front of my chair and hug me to her.

"Oh Mom. We must be crazy to be thinking these things." She tried her best to smile. "Surely it can't be as bad as we're imagining."

She didn't look sure of anything though, I thought, as I walked slowly back along the road to the place where it overlooked Blake's cottage. I stood looking down at the deck and out of the corner of my eye I thought I saw his body falling to the ice again. But it was only Alastair and Tess sitting close together on the old wooden glider. She had a hand on his knee and he was talking earnestly to her, his face flushed and animated.

I puffed some of the powdered medicine into my struggling lungs and then turned back toward my own place, remembering as I walked, how things had once been on this point.

When Lindy and Alastair got married seventeen years ago and then Blake and Maggie the next year, Rob and I had the peninsula surveyed and severed into three twenty acre lots. Blake and Maggie had built a winterized home at the neck of the peninsula and we transferred the middle portion with the old family place to Lindy and Alastair. Then, just the year before he died, Rob and I built a small log cottage at the very tip of the point, on a sheer granite cliff high above the lake.

I sank into my favourite chair with a glass of iced tea and a couple of pills and waited for them to take the edge off the pain in my chest.

In the morning I filled the hummingbird feeder and watered the tiger lily plants surrounding the clearing where I park my car. Then I hunted through the bathroom drawers until I found the sunscreen Tess had given me last year and I had never used. I applied a good thick layer and then sat in the soft scented air until I thought she would be awake.

"I wondered if you could come for coffee. I think we have some things to discuss." That was all I said and she agreed to be there at eleven.

When the visit was over I slumped back in my chair and dozed for a while.

The pain in my chest was nearly gone when I woke but there was still something bothering me. For the first time, I hadn't been able to tell who Tess was playing today.

I got out of my chair and looked down at the figure lying on the rocks below. The loose white shift had rucked up over her legs and suntan lotion glistened on the soles of her bare feet. It was the little ringlet of daisies fallen from her head and bobbing gently in the shallow water that gave it away.

Ophelia, I thought. Of course! And I went inside to find detergent and a cloth to wash the oil from the deck.

HUNTING LESSONS

Bring out the pretzels, bring out the beer,
Bring out the cold cuts –
For hunting season's here.

Bring out the rifle, bring out the gear,
Bring out the old pal –
Who cheated you last year.

Bring out the bullets, force out a tear,
Bring out the Oscar –
"I thought he was a deer!"

Joy Hewitt Mann

GETTING RID OF COTTAGE PESTS

by Rosemary Aubert

I've always been the kind of person to give things a chance to prove themselves. Which is one of the reasons I married Sam and one of the reasons I didn't argue when he said he wanted to buy a cottage. People like Sam – the impulsive sort – make decisions in a hurry. Not me. I wait.

When I first started going up to the country, I hated how you had to be killing something or thinking about killing something all the time.

It started with the garden. Sam spent four hundred dollars at the nursery in the city and carted everything up with us the first warm weekend of spring. He said if I was going to give myself the opportunity to learn to love the country, there was no better way to begin than gardening. "You'll enjoy it," he said. "It'll be just like the balcony."

Only it wasn't. The impatiens and pansies I planted every year in the window boxes on the balcony of our highrise were dainty and lovely. But even in early spring, the garden at the cottage was overrun with weeds, some tall and thick with a single tiny yellow flower at the top, like a large man with a small head.

I tugged and hacked. The plants seemed a lot stronger than me. But in the end, I had a big pile of dead ones.

"Good girl," Sam said, "I knew you could do it. Just try to go a little faster. We've got a lot of planting to do." He handed me a rake and hoe. I was already totally exhausted, but country life is about endurance and I figured a city person like me could use a little more of what Sam called "stamina."

My rake, grabbing clumps of thick, brown dirt, scraped across a nest of beetles. They scrambled in all directions.

I shuddered. Sam, watching from beside the stump of a tree he'd just felled, wiped the edge of his ax on the leg of his jeans and ran his finger along it, testing it for the next whack. Then he smiled. "That's it," he said, "get 'em running. The more pests we get rid of, the better."

Luckily, he had gone to wash up and wasn't there when my hoe cut a worm in half and I finally lost it and burst into tears. Getting a grip on myself, I brushed the earth back over the halves and went in to cook supper.

The garden wasn't much of a success. Even though Sam sprayed everything with what he called "a damn good dose" of insecticide, the leaves of the spindly plants were riddled with holes and bites.

"Animals," Sam said. He took me by the hand and walked me around the garden. "You're not paying attention," he announced. "Look at this." He put his hand at the back of my neck and bent my head until my eyes were trained on the dirt at my feet. I saw a hole, about the size of a dollar coin. "Chipmunks . . . "

"How cute!" I moved away from his grasp and bent down to get a better look. But before I could see an actual chipmunk, Sam grabbed a handful of soil and shoved it into the opening. "That'll fix the bastards," he said.

As the weeks went on, the window boxes in the city thrived. Sometimes we'd eat breakfast on the balcony, looking out over the city, so calm and peaceful in the early morning haze of summer. "This place bores me to tears," Sam observed staring out over the sea of sunlit rooftops.

Come Friday, it would be back to cottage country. One night as we were rounding the last curve in the road before our drive, we saw one of the local farmers beside the road waving his arms. Sam slammed on the brakes and screeched to a stop. "Wolves," the local said. "Seen a bunch of them. Watch out."

Sam nodded wisely. He liked to pretend he was as sparing with words as his country neighbours.

I guess it must have been about the end of July that I looked out the window after serving lunch and saw that something was swimming in the river that ran past the picture windows of the cottage. It was moving steadily and quickly, making a V in the water so wide that it reached the bank on either side.

"Beavers," Sam told me.

"How beautiful – "

"You won't say that when they start chomping on the timbers of the house – "

I laughed at his joke. Then I caught a glimpse of Sam's face. I wasn't surprised when, that afternoon, he made a deal with another local man to put traps under the water along the shore. "I told the trapper he can keep any pelts he catches. That's what I love about the country," Sam said. "Tradition. There's still people around who know where to sell a good beaver pelt."

"It breaks my heart . . . "

"Don't start," Sam said. "A person has to be tough in this world. It's us against them. *Mano a mano*. You can't feel sorry for the enemy."

When we got back to the city, he bought me a present, a tiny orange kitten with a sweet pink nose, a little pink tongue and eyes the blue of baby eyes. "You can bring her up to the cottage every weekend to keep you company. In fact," Sam said with a smile, "you can bring her on our vacation."

"Vacation?"

"Yes. I've arranged for us to spend the whole month of August at the cottage."

"Why didn't you ask me first?"

"I wanted it to be a surprise." He gave me a little kiss and I kissed him back. Sam often arranged our vacations. He hadn't done badly so far. I wasn't crazy about spending more time in the country, but then, what could I say? I hadn't objected to buying the cottage or to spending the weekends or to working on the garden and the grounds. It was a little late to complain. "You can take up a few hobbies – write something or paint. You'd like that . . . " he said, and he kissed me again.

I named my kitten Baby, and it was lucky I had her, or I would have died of boredom during our vacation. Except for the uncommunicative farmers and the shy wives I sometimes saw with them, there wasn't anybody else around. When I suggested to Sam that we go into town he said, "There's nothing there. And gas costs money, you know. Besides, once you get used to it, you'll see that you're happier just staying here at the cottage. My little woman will turn into a country girl."

Yeah, sure. I thought. But I kept my mouth shut. You can't decide whether a thing is working out in less than a month.

But Baby showed signs of turning into a country cat. Every time I opened the door, she ran out. She'd doubled in size, and it seemed as if her running speed increased every day.

About a week before we were supposed to head back home from vacation, Baby got away and disappeared behind the cottage. I went chasing after her.

"You get back here," my husband shouted. "It's dangerous out there – "

I ignored him. Behind our cottage was a ridge of rock covered with thick vegetation. Vines sucked at my ankles, but I just kept climbing. Behind me, Sam gave up shouting. I heard the door of the cottage slam once, then slam again.

I was out of breath when I finally caught up with Baby. And my heart was pounding. But when I saw what she was doing, I stopped breathing altogether.

She was standing in a clearing on top of the rock ridge. Every hair on her little body was standing on end. Her back was arched. She was hissing. She was hissing at a wolf. *Mano a mano.*

I don't know what either of them intended. Before I could move, I heard a loud crack and saw the wolf explode in a cloud of red mist and black fuzz.

I heard two screaming sounds mixed together – the cat sound of Baby, who had run up my leg and into my arms, and the human sound of me.

Then I heard another human sound. A laugh.

I turned. Sam was standing at the base of the rock ridge with a long-barrelled gun in his hand.

That night, I was too upset to cook supper. So Sam took me to a restaurant – not a real restaurant, but that truck stop on the highway that leads back to the city. After supper, I asked Sam to just keep driving. To take us home. He smiled and reached down to cover my hand with his. "You know," he said, "you've just got to stick it out. It's going to be okay. I'm going to take care of everything. I'll protect you just the way I protected Baby from the wolf . . . "

I watched the scenery slip past. You could still see every bush and tree, the big straight trunks like the bars of a jail.

"Why don't you let me drive for a while?" I asked Sam.

He smiled and slowly shook his head. "You'll drive us right home; we won't even go back for our stuff," he joked. When I didn't answer he said, "Today was a bad day, that's all. I want you to promise you'll give this place one more chance."

I looked out at the sun sinking behind the trees. I expected it to look as red as the blood of the wolf, but it was a pearly orange glow. "Okay," I said.

Two nights later as we were going to bed, Sam told me he had another surprise for me.

"What?"

He didn't answer right away. Baby came up and snuggled down between us in the bed. Sam reached down and stroked her thick fur. She licked his hand. Then she gave it a little bite. Sam pushed her away – hard. She scurried out of the room. "I've given notice on our apartment in the city and made arrangements to have all our belongings moved up here," Sam said. Then he started to stroke my hair the same way he'd stroked the cat's.

You think I'm going to give up our life in the city just like that? Without even discussing it? I was shocked. But I kept quiet. Just in case this was a trick or a joke.

"You promised," Sam whispered. "You said you'd give living here a chance." He dropped his hand from my head to my shoulder and rubbed my neck with his long fingers. "Listen, we can be happy here alone together." He rubbed harder. "And it'll give you a chance to toughen up a bit. You'll learn that when something is your enemy, you have to defeat it. You can't be soft. If you're afraid of your enemy, you can never sleep at night. But if you know you have the wherewithal to deal with it, you'll always be safe."

He fell asleep before I could answer.

At first, I cried. Then I thought about what he said. Sometimes an enemy sneaks up on you, like that wolf. The safer you feel, the more in danger you are. That's a mistake. Maybe Sam had made the same mistake.

I went over everything in my mind. There was the ax Sam had used to cut down the trees around the garden. There was the big can of insecticide in the basement. There was the farmer who made deals to set traps. There was the long-barrelled gun.

I listened to the deep, even sound of my husband's breathing, and I knew he was right. You can't feel sorry for your enemy. You can never be safe if you do.

It occurred to me as I drifted to sleep that one good thing about the country is, nobody knows your business. A person could have an accident and not be seen around for a while – or again. Who'd know? Plus, there was one other thing Sam was right about. It *is* possible to live happily if a woman sets her mind to it. Especially if she lives exactly where she wants and only has to provide for herself – and one tiny orange cat.

UP THE POLE

by Liz Palmer

"God, it's going to be a cold Thanksgiving." Joan Gordon held her hands out towards the glowing woodstove in her neighbour's log cabin. "They're forecasting snow tonight."

"The end of a lousy summer." Doug Withers dipped a battered metal cup into the pot of cider simmering on the stove, and poured it into a mug. "Here."

"Mmm . . . thanks." Joan breathed in the warm, rich smell of cinnamon and apple. "What do you mean 'a lousy summer'?"

"Your dear protégé, Victor Simpson. What did you think I meant?"

"Oh heavens, Doug, don't start that again. I can't stand it." Why couldn't he accept what had happened? "Get it into your head. The land was for sale and Victor bought it. At least he's made the nature club welcome, despite your continual harassment."

"You're all so damned naive." Doug grabbed his backpack and slammed it onto a chair. "As soon as we've gone for the winter he'll have the surveyors in planning his development."

"You can't know this. You're making it up."

"Joan, nobody puts a high-tension power line in for one cottage."

"I knew it would come down to the hydro. But most people aren't like you. Most of us want electricity."

"You don't have a line of hydro poles less than a hundred yards from your cottage. I chose to live in the woods without electricity and now I have to look out at that." He flung his arm towards the window. "It makes me damned mad."

And bitter, mused Joan. Almost as though the electricity had warped his personality. "Anyway," she began, "there must be laws against development in the Rideau . . . "

"But Rock Lake isn't part of the Rideau system." Doug interrupted, his voice rising. "Can't you see? He's only subject to local planning and he's got money. We all know what that means."

Joan got up. "I'm not interested in more arguments, Doug, I only came over to say goodbye. I'm closing the cottage after the Thanksgiving brunch tomorrow."

"We can say goodbye there." A smug look spread over Doug's face.

"*You* are going to Victor's party? Why?"

"I've an announcement to make." Doug opened the backpack and started to stow away the warm clothes and camera equipment which were laid out on the table. "It's going to wreck your precious Victor's plans."

"Oh for heavens sake, Doug. If you're going to say something to ruin the party, don't come. Because," – it was time she spoke plainly – "people won't thank you for it. We all like Victor and you haven't exactly endeared yourself to anyone this summer."

Doug stopped packing and turned towards her. "They were as suspicious as I until you persuaded them he was okay."

Joan clamped her mouth shut. She'd tried before to make him see reason but his mind was set. She turned to go.

"Joan. Wait. I want to show you something. You're going to be thrilled, and if you *are* right about Victor he will be too."

Joan stopped. She couldn't resist the excitement she heard in Doug's voice. "What have you found?"

"I'll show you." Two strides took him across the room to the desk under the window. "Come and see." He fumbled in an envelope stuffed with papers and fished out three photos.

They were all pictures of a small yellowish bird.

Joan picked one up. "This is it?"

"It's a blue-winged warbler, Joan. It's incredible to find one this far north. I've been watching it all summer. See this." He pointed a calloused finger at one picture. "It's sitting on a nest! They've been known to breed down in southern Ontario but here . . . " The words bubbled out of him, reminding Joan of the old Doug.

"Are you sure? The pictures aren't really clear, Doug, and there are a lot of small yellow birds about."

"I'm sure. Look closely. See the male here. See how blue the wings look and you can just see the wing bars. And the yellow head. I guess the colour hasn't come out perfectly. It's more . . . " he looked round the cabin, "kind of between my chainsaw and the gloves."

Joan glanced at the bright yellow chainsaw and the shiny beige gloves draped over the handle.

"Like a goldfinch, you mean?"

"Mm, with a tinge of green. And see how neat the nest is snugged into the long grass. It's where you'd expect to find one. I want to get more close-ups of it before the snow. I should have gone earlier but I had to go into Elgin for film. Still, if the light isn't good enough when I get there I'll stay. I can cover the nest and get the shots in the morning."

"But Doug," Joan hated to dampen his enthusiasm, "lots of warblers build nests in places like that."

"You'll see. I've asked the Ministry to make this a protected area." He put the photos back into the envelope and stuffed it into the desk drawer. "They're waiting for more information before meeting with me. And I know your 'dear Victor' won't be happy about this, because I've some information about him in that envelope that shows him for what he is." He patted the desk drawer, his face twisting. "Maybe I'll be the hero then."

Joan trudged down the hill. She found it increasingly hard to remember how much fun they all used to have. How Doug would take the boys off exploring so she and Mike could have time alone and how helpful he'd been the summer Mike died. He'd started the nature club too. Under his leadership they'd built a network of trails on the Merrill property.

When the land came on the market the club had tried desperately to raise the money and Joan had lobbied hard to get the council to declare it a conservation area. It wasn't Victor's fault they hadn't succeeded. What's more, Victor had been the first to suggest they keep using the trails. Joan climbed over the stile onto the path.

"Joan."

She jerked her head up. "Victor! You startled me." She looked at the tall grey-haired man in front of her, trying to see him as an underhanded developer.

He began to laugh. "You're staring at me and shaking your head. Have I got mud on my face or something?"

"Oh, sorry, Victor." Joan pulled herself together. "I've just come from Doug's."

"Ah. You're looking for my horns."

"Don't be silly. You know what I think." She touched his arm sympathetically, glad that she had at least convinced the rest of the club to accept him. "Did you know Doug is planning to come to your party tomorrow?"

"Bearing an olive branch?"

"Not exactly, but he may have some exciting news."

"Oh? What sort of news?" Victor looked up the hill towards Doug's cabin.

"I shouldn't be talking about it. It's Doug's discovery. He's going to try to get more pictures before it snows."

"There he goes now." Victor put his binoculars to his eyes. "He's got his backpack and a . . . " He stopped.

"A what?"

"Hm? Just a walking stick."

It wasn't what he was going to say. The thought popped into Joan's head. She squinted up the hill, but without her glasses Doug looked like an ant in the distance.

Victor tucked the binoculars into his pocket. "I'm heading home before the flakes fly. I've got my nephew down for the weekend."

"Roddy? How lovely." Joan hurried along beside him trying to match his stride. "He made a big hit with everyone this summer. It's come to something, though, when we have to have a thirteen-year-old remind us that nowadays the Three R's mean Reduce, ReUse and Recycle. Did he do well on his project?"

"It's not finished until he's done the follow-up. I warn you he's come to check on you all." Victor laughed. "He has to see whether you've really reformed or whether you slipped back as soon as he left." They reached the fork in the path and Victor stopped. "He'll probably be down to rifle through your garbage before the weekend's over. He's already gone through mine."

"And you failed?"

"Only by a mayonnaise jar!"

They parted, laughing, and Joan made her way down to her cottage wondering if she should sort her recyclables into separate piles before Roddy appeared.

Victor walked briskly until he reached the row of cedars leading up to his place. He looked back through the fading light. It wasn't dark enough yet to risk going to Doug's cabin – he might be seen. But any news that would excite Doug Withers was almost certain to interfere with his own plans and he'd like to be forewarned. He turned and strode on up the hill. He'd have to take a chance on Doug still being out when he got back from dropping Roddy off at the Community Centre that evening.

And why was Doug carrying an insulated pole? Victor had recognized it straight away, with its distinctive red stripes. One had gone missing during the summer along with a few other things. The hydro workers had blamed local teens, but nothing had been proved. Obviously Doug had taken it. And what would he need it for today? Victor's pace quickened. He could guess. He ran up the stairs to the wide deck overhanging the lake. Doug was aiming to knock out the power supply and ruin the party tomorrow.

The first flakes of snow landed softly, melting against Victor's warm skin. He wiped his face on the sleeve of his fleece jacket and removed his boots before lifting the latch of Doug's unlocked cabin.

He slipped through the door and stopped to listen. Nothing. No humming fridge, no clicking of expanding or contracting metal baseboard heaters. No machinery sounds at all.

Taking a small flashlight from his pocket and shielding the beam with one hand, he shone it slowly around the room. Good. Doug might spurn modern conveniences but he was conventional enough to have a desk.

The wooden floor felt cold beneath Victor's socked feet as he crossed the room. What could he do if Doug had found some rare plant or animal? Who could he get at in Environment? Who did he know with influence?

Damned conservationists. His hand clenched on the flashlight. If Doug hadn't delayed the hydro installation with his court battles, the property would have been divided into parcels and sold by now. And he, Victor, would be receiving thanks from his creditors instead of threatening letters.

Putting the light down on the desk, he opened the drawer. Tucked inside he found a bulky envelope with a Ministry of the Environment return address.

Victor dumped out the contents. Photos of birds, a map, a letter to the Minister and some folded papers. He skimmed the letter. A request from Doug asking the Minister to stop any development on the land until a study of the blue-winged warbler nesting there had been undertaken.

"Interfering bastard." Victor slammed the letter down onto the desk and spread out the map. An area about half a mile up from his cottage was shaded in red. Right over the planned access road. If he couldn't put that in, he'd lose the five lots on the back of the property and all his profit.

He unfolded the other papers.

They were headed: 'The Ross MacPherson Agency – Private Investigators.' Beneath the bold black printing was typed: 'Report on Victor Simpson. Mr. Simpson originates from Nova Scotia where he has on two occasions developed properties after leading local cottagers to believe he was only interested in preserving the land . . . '

Victor shook with rage. If Doug showed this at the party tomorrow, together with the information about the bird, the community would swing round to support him. Another delay would be financially disastrous.

What could he do? Get rid of the evidence. He shoved the map into his pocket, stuffed the rest of the papers back into the envelope and pushed the envelope into the woodstove. A quick twist of the dampers, and the papers flared up.

Outside, the ground was already white. Victor climbed quickly up the hill through the swirling snow. He had to locate the nest and get rid of it.

With no written evidence and no nest, Doug's accusations could be shrugged off. People were tired of his ranting.

Victor was almost at the top when he glimpsed a light through the snow. It had to be Doug returning. He stopped and waited for a few minutes, but the light stayed put.

Keeping his eye on it, Victor crept forward, moving from tree to tree, thankful for the wind which masked any noise he made. Then there were no more trees ahead. He'd reached the hydro right-of-way.

The light appeared to be suspended above the ground. Victor edged towards it keeping within the shadow of the trees. The wind dropped, the snow eased and there was Doug not thirty feet away, half-way up the hydro pole. The light fixed to his helmet shone on the transformer above him. Checking the impulse to confront him, Victor watched as Doug reached up with the insulated pole and disconnected the fuse. He then hung the pole over the now dead line and climbed down.

At the bottom he switched off the light and Victor could no longer see what he was doing. But he could hear, and Doug wasn't trying to move quietly.

As soon as the sounds had faded down the right-of-way, Victor headed for the pole and shone his light on the ground around it. A pair of spurs, a climbing belt and two insulated gloves lay in the snow.

Victor didn't hesitate. He buckled on the belt, strapped the spurs to his feet, slipped his hands into the gloves and scaled the pole. He smiled to himself as he lifted the insulated pole from the dead line. Doug was in for a surprise. Bracing his feet against the pole he reached up and reconnected the fuse. A flash of light arced through the sky further down the line.

Something had been touching the wire.

"But the fact is, Mrs. Gordon," the policeman said, "Mr. Withers was electrocuted while interfering with a high tension power line."

Joan guessed the policeman's opinion of Doug's mental capacity from the tone of his voice. "Could he have had some sort of breakdown?" she asked.

"That's what we're hoping to find out from you. We found nothing in his cottage to indicate anything abnormal about his state of mind and it seems you might have been the last person to talk to him. How did he appear to you?" The constable sat down at her kitchen table and opened his notebook. He seemed especially interested in Doug's dislike of Victor.

"An unreasonable hatred, would you say, Mrs. Gordon?"

Joan had to admit it was.

"Almost obsessive?" When Joan nodded he closed his notebook and stood up. "We have heard Mr. Withers liked to throw obstacles in the way of Mr. Simpson whenever he could."

Joan was unable to refute this. Perhaps he had been a bit insane, she thought, closing the door behind the policeman. One thing she was sure of . . . nothing would induce her to live near a power line. Doug had been fine until the hydro went in. Or had he?

Had he, in fact, been changing very slowly and she had been too concerned with her own affairs to notice? Would it have made a difference if she'd seen more of him? She couldn't help him now but what she could do for him was to follow up on his research.

She decided to stop at his cabin on her way to the brunch and pick up the envelope he'd shown her. She would announce his find at the party and pass round the photos. And the papers concerning Victor that Doug had said were in the envelope. What should she do with them?

Doug's cabin felt cold and forlorn. Colder than outside where the sun was fast melting the snow. Joan glanced across the room to the woodstove. Odd that Doug had opened the dampers instead of banking up the fire. Almost as though he knew he wouldn't be back. She hurried over to the desk.

Hoping Doug wouldn't have minded, she opened the drawer. No envelope. Puzzled, she shuffled through the other papers. It wasn't there. He must have taken it out again as soon as she'd gone, and put it somewhere else. Quickly she searched the room. Nothing. Surely he wouldn't have taken it with him? But where else could it be?

Leaving the cabin she hurried up the hill towards the Merrill property. This was the way Doug had come yesterday. What had been in his mind? Excitement because he'd located a bird rarely seen in these parts, or excitement because he thought it would be a blow to Victor? Joan wanted it to have been the former. She tried to focus on his enthusiasm when he'd shown her the photos but the picture of his twisted face as they'd parted kept intruding.

She trudged on into the hydro right-of-way. Every time Doug had wanted to walk the trails he'd had to cross this power line. It must have driven him mad.

Joan leaned against the first pole, to catch her breath, and looked down the line. She'd have to pass that old pine he'd fallen from. Now she'd never know if he'd really been concerned about nesting ospreys when he fought to delay the felling of the tree, or if, even then, he was planning to use it against Victor.

What could have possessed him to try and mess with live wires? He hadn't been stupid.

Joan bowed her head and stared unseeing at the scuffled leaves and churned up snow around her feet. A wave of guilt washed over her. He must have been ill and she hadn't noticed.

She shook herself. Now was not the time for soul searching. If she didn't get to the brunch soon, Victor would have a search party out.

A row of bright red blobs beneath the junipers caught her eye as she hurried down the line. Poison ivy leaves? Doug was always the one who rooted it out from the trails. Now who would do it?

Joan slowed down, frowning to herself. There was something in the back of her mind . . . Something nagging at her. She stopped abruptly and turned back up the hill.

Poison ivy doesn't grow in straight lines.

When she reached the juniper bushes she could see at once that what she'd thought were red leaves were, in reality, parts of a red and white striped pole.

Joan didn't take it out. She knew what it was. Despite his promise, Doug hadn't returned the things he'd stolen from the hydro workers. And he'd used this insulated pole to turn off the power, or so he thought, and tucked it beneath the juniper bush to be retrieved later. This scenario made much more sense to Joan. And the belt and spurs were there too, pushed further back under the branches. At least he hadn't been stupid enough to meddle with a live wire, only careless.

As she scurried back down the hill Joan tried to picture what had happened. Once Doug thought the power was off he must have hidden the things, gone down the line and climbed the tree. Then, according to the policeman, he'd put a branch on the line and apparently tried to cut the wire.

It looked as though he thought the hydro company would be fooled into thinking the branch had broken it. But, in that case, he'd need to put the power back on. So why hide the pole and things before he was finished with them?

The big pine loomed up before her. Beneath it the snow hadn't yet melted. It lay dirty and churned up where many feet had trampled. This was where Doug had fallen. Hate had killed him. As she stared sadly down, she thought of the snow round the hydro pole. It had the same scuffled look. Had Doug walked round and round trying to make up his mind? She shook her head. No, that wasn't in character – but then this was a Doug she hadn't known.

Going on down the right-of-way, Joan soon reached Victor's lane. She picked her way along the winding path, past Victor's new red pick-up and on to the wide wooden steps of the verandah.

What would have happened had Doug been successful in cutting the line, she wondered? A small inconvenience to Victor and then almost certain arrest for Doug. Because Hydro wouldn't have been fooled. And then what? Jail? No, more likely a psychiatric ward.

A wave of sound engulfed her as the patio door opened.

"Joan. You're so late. Come on up." Victor beckoned to her from the doorway. "We've been worrying about you. Roddy went down to check your garbage but you'd already left."

"Sorry, Victor. I needed to take a walk." Joan let Victor take her arm and usher her into the room.

"Your hands feel cold. Let me fetch you a glass of mulled wine."

"Joan." Sharon Foss pounced on her. "Isn't it dreadful? Poor Doug."

"The wire cutters were still in his hand when he fell." Arthur Garland joined in excitedly.

Sibylla Watson turned round. "I knew something like this would happen."

Joan sidled away. She found it unpleasant to see her normally caring neighbours sinking to the level of tabloid gossips. As soon as she could, she'd introduce the subject of Doug's find. Even without proof it should generate some intelligent discussion.

Crossing to the bar Joan accepted a steaming drink from Victor. He looked strained, she thought, burying her nose in the glass.

A sudden sadness washed over her as she inhaled the cinnamon scent. Only yesterday afternoon she'd sat drinking hot cider with Doug and now he was gone.

She looked up at Victor and saw he'd gone very pale. She turned. Roddy was coming towards them, a look of triumph on his face.

"Got you, Uncle Vic," he crowed, waving a pair of gloves in the air. "I re-checked the garbage and look what I found. And there's nothing wrong with them."

"How dare you!" Victor shouted, slamming his tumbler down on the bar with such force the glass shattered. Blood spurted from his hand. Everyone stared in stunned silence.

No one was more stunned than Joan. Those were Doug's gloves. She'd got it all wrong. Doug hadn't hidden the things at all. Victor had – after he'd switched the power back on – and he must have forgotten he was wearing the gloves. Everything made sense that way. No wonder the snow around the pole looked so scuffled. Doug hadn't been the only one to walk there.

She moved swiftly. Taking the gloves from Roddy she soothed his shock. "Your Uncle's upset over the tragedy, Roddy." Then turning back to the frozen Victor she began to give orders while her mind grappled with the staggering knowledge.

"Sharon, iodine from the bathroom cabinet, please." She took Victor to the sink and ran his hand under the cold tap. He must have seen the insulated pole yesterday when he looked at Doug through his binoculars. If only she'd kept her mouth shut about Doug's news. Obviously Victor had gone into the cabin and taken the envelope. And burned it, she thought, remembering the open dampers on the stove. She'd been wrong about Victor and Doug had paid for it.

"Sibylla, make Victor some tea. He's still suffering from shock. He feels responsible for Doug's death, *don't you*, Victor?" She looked from Victor to the shiny beige gloves she'd last seen draped over Doug's chainsaw. She felt his hand tense under hers.

What should she do? Would the police be able to prove anything? Surely Victor couldn't have known Doug was touching the line, could he? She folded some paper towels into a pad and pressed it over the cut. And then it came to her. A way she could make amends.

"Victor," she spoke to everyone, but looked at Victor. "Victor knew Doug hated the hydro line. Doug wouldn't believe him when he said he wasn't going to develop the land and so today he wanted to give Doug a surprise. You see," she took the iodine from Sharon, "yesterday I confided Doug's secret to Victor."

Victor kept his eyes on hers.

"I told him about *all* the papers Doug showed me." Joan stared steadily back at him. He need never know she hadn't seen the ones pertaining to him. "I was to bring them today, but they seem to have disappeared. But," she looked round the room, "it won't affect the announcement. Would you like to make it, Victor? Or shall I?"

Victor stared at her, his face expressionless.

"Okay, I'll go on then. Doug had located the nesting site of a bird rare to this area and thought the area should be protected. In view of Doug's death, Victor would like to designate the whole property The Doug Withers Conservation Area."

The audible gasp from Victor was put down to the sting of the iodine.

KANATA TIMES October 29th
Prominent Local Woman Victim of Hit-and-Run

Mrs. Joan Gordon, well known for her charitable works, was killed last night while crossing Hazeldean road. The driver did not stop. Gordon was returning from her weekly volunteer session at the Youth Centre. Police are looking for a late model, red Chevrolet pick-up truck with Nova Scotia licence plates . . .

MEA CULPA

by Jane Tun

Marilyn tossed a pillow on the end of the ramshackle dock, stepped out of her thongs and sat down. Minnows scattered as she submerged her feet in the calm green waters of Feather Lake. Somewhere in the small woods bracketing the cottage, a woodpecker tapped an energetic search for grubs. She raised her face to the morning sun and felt the early June heat sink into her bones.

She gazed over her shoulder at the faded, redwood cottage on the crest of the slope. The peeling shutters and sagging steps testified to the years of neglect but it didn't matter. The shabby exterior hid a solid structure that the empty years had not weakened.

Strange to think that the cottage belonged to her now. She thought of the tight-mouthed lawyer who'd informed her of her father's death. He'd expected her to be upset that her father had left his savings and the house in Ottawa to a distant cousin. She hadn't told the lawyer she'd expected nothing at all. Her initial surprise at inheriting the cottage, which she'd assumed long since sold, had given way instantly to a bitter understanding. Her father meant the cottage to be a painful reminder of her sister and what had happened here so long ago.

She didn't need a reminder. The past was always with her.

She gazed at the cottage and considered again the idea that had obsessed her since the meeting with the lawyer. Her recent divorce had left her financially secure. She had funds enough to renovate the cottage. Even to winterize it. Even to . . .

" . . . live here year-round." Startled to hear the thought spoken aloud, she inhaled sharply. Well, why not?

Over the last few years, dissatisfaction with her life as a trophy wife had seeped into her. She was tired of the endless business parties. Tired of the vain, idle women who were her only company. Tired of their lecherous husbands with their crude advances.

If she were ever to have a new life, a good life, she had to face her mistakes and try to move on. To become someone worthwhile, someone real. At least in her own eyes.

Her family would never know. It was too late to beg their forgiveness but maybe, in time, she might find some measure of peace. Here, where she first lost her way.

A sense of anticipation filled her.

"I could paint again," she murmured to the breeze. "I could."

The idea spread to fill her mind with an eager excitement she had thought never to feel again.

"Yes!" She laughed softly and scrambled to her feet.

She bent to retrieve the pillow and almost tumbled into the water when footsteps rattled the loose boards of the narrow dock. Surprised, she straightened and turned to see a stranger approaching.

His smile was polite, friendly, but a certain stiffness in his heavy build sent spider-feet scurrying down her spine. Where had he come from?

She edged back until her heels hung over the end of the dock. Should she jump? She hadn't swum for years and had never been very skilled in the water.

Before she could decide, he stopped in front of her and thrust out a muscular arm. Marilyn gasped and instinctively threw up her hands in defence. Comprehension flashed across his face. He dropped his hand and stepped back.

"God, I'm sorry. I didn't mean to frighten you."

Marilyn stared. As her heartbeat steadied, she slowly straightened. The man blocking her way was tall, with broad shoulders, a prominent Adam's apple, opaque brown eyes, receding hair and an apologetic expression on his unremarkable face. Nothing about his manner suggested danger. Relief banished her fright.

"That's okay," she stammered. "I thought I was alone on the lake."

She gestured to the family cottages across the water. "Normally, the other cottagers don't arrive until the end of the month, when school lets out." She paused. "Where are you staying?"

He angled his head toward the small woods separating Marilyn's property from the next cottage.

"My name's Brad. And you're right about the other cottages being empty. That's why I was surprised when I heard your car last night. I came over to say hello and introduce myself. I should have realized I'd startle you. My apologies."

Marilyn recovered her poise. The man seemed harmless enough despite his size. It pleased her that his gaze hadn't once swept her body in that speculative way she'd grown to hate. Her lush figure, of which she'd been so proud when she was young and naive, acted as a beacon to the kind of men who didn't care about a woman's mind. She'd met too many of them.

She shook his hand. "I'm Marilyn."

They exchanged pleasantries for a few moments, then she followed him off the dock. She didn't mention her divorce, in case he took that as an invitation. Other men had. When he veered away toward the woods she merely nodded goodbye and retreated into the cottage.

She didn't see him stop at the treeline and stare back at her.

After three overcast days of brisk wind and chilly temperatures, the kind of weather that made cottage owners glower, the inside of the cottage sparkled. The lawn was cut, the bushes trimmed and the gutters emptied of their sodden burden of dead leaves. Ignoring her exhaustion, Marilyn glowed with satisfaction and pride of ownership. She'd been right not to sell the cottage. The past would be no harder to deal with here than anywhere else.

And what better place? Before that thought could resurrect painful memories, she thrust it away. She wasn't ready yet.

When the next morning dawned cool but clear, she settled on the lawn with her neglected easel and paints. Her bare feet dug into the soft grass as the pine-scented breeze toyed with her flannel shirt. Three hours later she stepped back and cast a critical eye on her work. The greens of the water weren't quite right but the painting was better than she dared hope. She stared at the slightly ruffled face of Feather Lake. Her eyes lost focus and for the first time, she allowed her imagination to plunge beneath the innocent surface, down to the cold depths. What had it been like to . . .

"Marilyn. Are you all right?"

Jolted, she whirled to see Brad striding toward her. Something in his face told her he'd called her name several times before his voice pierced her consciousness. Though she wasn't sorry to be rescued from her contemplation of the watery depths, she didn't really want company. Still, he was her neighbour. She smiled when he reached her.

"Am I interrupting?"

"Not at all," she assured him. "I was just . . . doodling." She stepped aside and gestured shyly at the easel.

He examined the painting. She watched his surprised expression change to a frown when he lifted his head to peer intently at Feather Lake. She was startled when he turned and looked directly into her eyes.

"That's very good. You've captured the sunlight dancing on the surface of the water and yet, one senses the cold darkness deep below. How did you do that?"

It was Marilyn's turn to frown. She studied her work. He was right.

"I don't know," she admitted. For just a moment her throat closed and she felt the weight of the water pressing her down, down. Sudden darkness whirled in her head.

She must have made a sound or swayed. The next thing she knew Brad's arm was around her waist. He led her up the slope to the cottage and eased her into a wicker chair on the porch, then backed away immediately. Concern and curiosity filled his face.

"Are you going to be all right? What happened to you?"

Marilyn admitted only that she'd been working hard and hadn't bothered much with food. He shook his head in rebuke.

"Come over for dinner tonight. I'll feed you a proper meal."

Her suggestion that they eat at her cottage instead was brushed aside.

"Another time," he insisted, "when you've recovered from your bout of housecleaning. Lie down for a rest. I'll expect you around seven."

Unable to explain her reluctance to enter his cottage, she finally agreed.

Later, she told herself he was right. She'd slept deeply for several hours and felt much better. Stronger. Though she hadn't realized it until now, visiting the neighboring cottage was a necessary step if she were ever to bury the past. She told herself she could handle it. Straightening her shoulders, she saluted herself in the mirror and set out to keep her dinner date.

Pausing at the edge of the treeline, she was dismayed by the frisson of dread that sliced through her at the sight of the green clapboard building. Nothing had changed. Yellow lace curtains hung in the windows. Marigolds grew in the circle of earth around the flagpole. Motionless in the still air, the rusty swing set waited patiently for long-ago playmates. Almost she could hear the laughing, childish voices from the past.

The sun slid behind a cloud and for a moment, the cottage seemed malevolent, almost . . . expectant. Her pulse thundered in her ears. Marilyn shivered and half-turned to retrace her steps. Then the cloud moved on and the impulse to flee gradually passed.

Berating herself for the unwelcome attack of nerves, she left the deep shade beneath the trees and approached the cottage. At the screen door she stopped and peered into the dim interior.

"Anyone home?"

A voice answered from somewhere inside. "Come on in, Marilyn."

Marilyn forced herself to open the door. As she stepped inside her gaze sped around the kitchen. Goosebumps puckered her skin. For a moment, she felt she'd stepped back in time.

The same maple chairs circled the same table. The cupboards looked freshly painted with the same cream-colored glossy paint she remembered. Swaying, she felt the blood rush from her face and reached out to grip the worn counter.

After twelve years, she hadn't expected to be confronted with the past in such detail. Strange, almost eerie, that nothing had been changed, at least not in the kitchen. Hearing footsteps approaching from the hall, she inhaled deeply and turned to greet her host.

"Hi, neighbour. You're just in time to – what's wrong? You look as if you've seen a ghost."

"No. It's nothing." When his eyebrows rose in disbelief, she stammered, "You'll think I'm silly. It's just that, well, nothing's changed."

His eyes narrowed. "Are you saying you've been here before?"

Oh yes, God forgive her, she'd been here before. She cleared her throat and nodded.

"Really? I assumed you were new to Feather Lake. Would you like to see the whole cottage? Take a sentimental journey into the past?" He held out his hand.

Marilyn stepped back. When he frowned at her abrupt movement, she forced herself to laugh lightly.

"Uh, no thanks. Another time." She gestured at the table. "What can I do to help?"

She breathed a sigh of relief when he followed her lead and didn't mention her reaction to the cottage again. By the time she'd tossed a salad together and Brad had whipped the potatoes and grilled the chops, her nerves had subsided. While they ate he recounted interesting stories of his travels and to her surprise, Marilyn heard herself countering with amusing anecdotes from her single days as a stewardess. He listened with flattering attention and didn't make a single pass. That night, as she curled up in her own bed, Marilyn wondered if she had finally found a friend, a real friend, someone who wanted nothing from her.

"Tell me about your family," Brad said the next afternoon. He spoke for the first time since he'd dropped into the chair beside her on the lawn.

Marilyn sipped the lemonade he'd brought. "They're all gone now. My mother died about almost eleven years ago, my father three months ago."

"Were you an only child?"

"No, I had an older sister," she said, after a long moment. "She died a month before my mother."

"I'm sorry. I didn't mean to resurrect sad memories." Brad leaned forward. "Do you want to talk about it?"

"Yes." Her impulsive reply surprised Marilyn. She caught her breath. It was true. She'd never discussed her sister's death with anyone but now she felt a compulsion to talk. Maybe the death of the last of her family had created a need in her. Or was it Brad's obvious interest?

"She drowned. Here in Feather Lake. I was told there were no witnesses and the water was calm. The oars were found in the bottom of the boat, along with her life jacket." Marilyn swallowed. "I've always wondered if she committed suicide."

Brad inhaled sharply. He studied her face, an unreadable expression in his eyes. For just a moment, remembering they were alone on the lake, Marilyn tensed. But he didn't touch her and her alarm faded.

"That's terrible. Why would she do that?"

"She . . . lost her fiancé and was very upset. But no one had any idea that she might take her own life. It was a terrible shock. I guess she really loved him."

She glanced at Brad. His face looked remote, his jaw tight and his eyes staring into the distance. He seemed to have forgotten her presence.

"Mostly I try not to think about it." She sighed a long, quavering breath. "The trouble is, sometimes I feel so guilty."

His head snapped toward her.

"Guilty? Why?"

Marilyn stiffened, disconcerted by his suddenly alert expression. She wished she'd never mentioned the tragedy. Faking a self-deprecating shrug, she shook her head.

"No reason. I only meant that I feel I should have been able to help her somehow. I should have known."

"You couldn't have known."

Marilyn nodded, as if in agreement. If he knew the whole story, he wouldn't be so quick to reassure her.

She answered his knock late the following morning and found him shifting from foot to foot. He looked nervous and exhilarated at once. And determined, as if he'd made a decision but wasn't yet comfortable with it. He didn't give her time to ponder the impression. At his insistence, she followed him down the slope of the lawn. To her surprise, an ancient, flat-bottomed rowboat bobbed gently at the end of the dock.

"Brad, what are you up to?"

He swept an extravagant arm toward the boat. "We're going to eat lunch on Nameless Island."

"Today? In that old boat?"

"It's seaworthy." His smile flashed on and off like a dying light-bulb. "Indulge me. Please."

Disconcerted by his strange mood, Marilyn hesitated and glanced around. The air was still, the clear sky an anemic blue. The birds had gone into hiding. The surroundings appeared somehow odd, out of focus.

The bizarre thought suddenly seemed silly. Why not a picnic? It might be fun and Brad's mysterious impatience intrigued her. She peered into the boat. At the sight of a wicker basket, a large cooler and a blanket stored under the seat, she smiled widely and clambered aboard.

Brad climbed in after her, untied the boat and began to row with long, powerful strokes. Relaxing, Marilyn trailed her fingers in the cold water and settled back to enjoy the excursion to the tiny island at the far end of Feather Lake.

When they had pulled the boat to shore, Brad spread out the blanket on the narrow strip of sand and emptied the basket. While Marilyn unpacked plastic containers of sandwiches and salad and a luscious cherry cheesecake, he produced a bottle of white wine. By the time they'd finished the almost silent meal, Marilyn was wondering why he'd suggested the picnic at all.

He'd eaten very little and didn't appear to be enjoying himself. Instead, he seemed almost agitated.

It occurred to her that the romantic setting, might be the staging for a seduction scene. She dismissed the thought. Though she'd known him less than a week, she felt certain this man wasn't like the others. Her virtue was in no danger.

When Marilyn declared she could eat no more, Brad cleared his throat several times, but seemed unable to find the words he wanted. Marilyn began to feel uneasy.

"What is it?" she asked.

Ignoring her question, he leaned across the blanket and topped up her wine glass, then stood. She looked up in surprise.

"Pardon me, I'll just be a minute." He turned and disappeared into the small grove of trees.

For a few seconds, Marilyn stared after him. When it occurred to her that he'd gone to answer the call of nature, she giggled and realized she was a little high. Well, it didn't matter. She wasn't the designated rower.

But what in the world was on his mind?

She pulled up her legs and wrapped her arms around them. For the first time since they'd reached the island, she noticed the changes in the sky. A low bank of churning black clouds was moving toward them from the west. In an hour, no more, the storm would reach them. Wild grasses began to rustle in the freshening breeze. Small waves harassed the shore. She sniffed and tasted the water in the air and remembered how quickly the lake's mood could change.

Whatever was on Brad's mind, it would have to wait until they were safely at home. Getting to her knees she gathered the empty food containers and lifted the lid of the picnic basket. And froze.

A photograph rested at the bottom of the basket.

She blinked in recognition. The faded photo portrayed her family and their closest neighbours, enjoying a long-ago gathering on the front lawn of the cottage. On the left, her sister and her fiance, their arms entwined, their faces bright with smiles. Separated from the happy couple by the two sets of parents, she saw herself, standing a little apart and looking stiff and resentful.

Marilyn's heart began to thud against her ribs. Her stomach clenched and something sour crept up her throat.

A movement in front of her brought her head up. Brad towered over her, his expression grim, his hands hanging in tight fists at his sides. Unconsciously, her hands rose in a gesture of appeal, the plastic containers dropping unnoticed to the sand.

A full minute passed. Neither moved. Neither spoke. She could see a muscle throbbing in his jaw. Finally, she could bear it no longer.

"Brad? Where did you get this picture?"

His answer was a scowl. His hands opened and closed, opened and closed.

The approaching storm forgotten, Marilyn inched back. Why was he so angry?

"You're nothing but a slut, aren't you?"

"No!" she cried, shocked at the unexpected attack.

"Yes." His harsh contradiction sent a quiver of fear down her spine.

Was he a madman? Shaking her head violently, Marilyn tried to stand but her legs wouldn't support her. She sat down hard and pulled her knees protectively to her body. Only one other person had ever called her a slut to her face. But she couldn't think about that now.

"Tell me how your sister came to lose her fiancé."

"What?" Marilyn's mouth dropped open.

He forced the words through tightly-clenched teeth. "Tell me what happened to Alison and Trent Phillips."

Marilyn sucked in her breath. How did he know her sister's name? And Trent's? She knew she hadn't mentioned either.

For an instant, she pictured the tall, handsome Trent Phillips, whose family had owned the cottage next door twelve years earlier. Trent Phillips, the only man who had preferred the quiet, delicate Alison to her voluptuous, younger sister. The man who had laughed at her immature attempt to seduce him. She shuddered, remembering her humiliation when he'd repulsed her in the Phillips' kitchen. In the kitchen where she'd eaten dinner with Brad two days before.

"I don't know what you mean," she said, as defiantly as she could.

"Yes, you do. Trent was arrested for attempted rape."

"He was found guilty," she blurted. "He betrayed my sister. That's probably why she killed herself. He was a horrible man."

"Shut up!" Brad's nostrils flared as he visibly struggled for control. Finally he asked through clenched teeth, "Who charged him with sexual assault?"

Marilyn opened her mouth to lie, then changed her mind. He already knew. How could he know?

"I did."

In the silence that followed, Marilyn became aware of the strident call of the gulls and the rising wind.

When he finally spoke, his voice sounded utterly drained.

"You lied. He was a good man. He loved your sister. How could you do such a terrible thing?"

Marilyn's throat closed up. She wanted to tell him she hadn't lied but she knew he wouldn't believe her. Just as Alison hadn't. Just as their families hadn't. But the jury had believed and pronounced him guilty.

Brad looked away, as if he could no longer bear the sight of her. "Trent had no interest in a tramp like you. That's what you couldn't stand. He was the one man who didn't drool over you, the one man who had the good taste to prefer your sister. You were jealous. So you lied. And he went to prison."

Marilyn didn't speak. She hadn't been a tramp but the rest was true. Since the year her figure had blossomed, men had circled her like bees at a honey pot. She'd gained a reputation she hadn't deserved. And so she'd been drawn to Alison's fiance, the one man who treated her like a person. But she'd wanted more. When Trent rejected her insistent advances, she'd retaliated with furious lies.

Brad's next words were little more than a hiss, but the wind blew them back to her.

"Then Trent died. When she heard, your sister killed herself."

Marilyn felt her insides shrivel.

"Trent's . . . dead?"

Brad nodded slowly, still without looking at her.

"He died in prison, trying to protect a young man being attacked by three thugs in the laundry room. One of them threw Trent against the metal vat. His skull cracked. He died before he reached the hospital." Ragged pain roughened his voice. "It happened just a week before he was due to be released."

"I didn't know," Marilyn mumbled. "No one told me." Her fingers plucked mindlessly at the blanket. Her family had turned away from her after the trial. Neither her parents nor her sister had ever spoken to her again. She hadn't learned of Alison's death until after the funeral, when a distant cousin who hadn't known of the estrangement, called to offer her sympathies. At last Marilyn understood why Alison hadn't waited out Trent's sentence.

For the first time, she thought, really thought, about what she'd done. She'd been jealous of her sister and angry with Trent for his indifference and his scorn. Young and miserable, she'd wanted to punish them both, to break them up. But her family hadn't believed her accusation. Rather than back down, she'd called the police. Things had escalated from there. She'd been almost as stunned as her family and his parents when the judge sentenced him to a year in prison.

But still, she'd kept the truth to herself. A year hadn't seemed such a very long time. If her family had taken her side, she would have dropped the charges. She would have.

Recognizing that for another lie, she covered her face with her hands and began to rock back and forth. The years since the trial flashed through her mind. The terrible loneliness; the hasty marriage she'd known wouldn't work; the guilt that haunted her dreams. And she hadn't even known about Trent's death.

"A little late for that, don't you think?" Contempt and a deep sadness had replaced the anger in his voice.

Marilyn dropped her hands and lifted her stricken face.

"Who are you?" she asked.

"Brad Phillips."

For a few heartbeats, she waited for more. Then memory flooded through her. Brad Phillips, Trent's older brother. A man she'd never met. Brad Phillips. Of course. She remembered the picture in the basket. Finally, it all made sense. Fear rippled down her back, to be replaced by a feeling of inevitability, then resignation. It was time to pay for her mistake.

"Are you going to kill me?" She waited for his reply, a part of her astounded at her calm acceptance of the idea. Twelve unhappy years couldn't compensate for two lives.

He grimaced, then his face seemed to crumple. "No."

Their gazes locked.

"But you planned to. Here, on the island."

"Yes. When you told me yesterday about your family, I suspected, but I never expected to see you here of all places. Last night I searched my cottage and found the picture. Then I knew for sure. I've hated you for so long, I thought I could kill you." He lifted his hands and stared at them. "I intended to kill you." He paused. "But I can't." He paused again. "I wish I could."

She nodded and almost smiled at the realization that he'd intended the picnic to be her last meal. Neither spoke for several minutes. Then they both looked up at the sky. The rain-swollen clouds were overhead, turning afternoon into dusk. Wind whistled in her ears and whipped her hair around her face. When Brad held out his hand she shrank back.

"Get up," he said curtly. "The storm's almost here. We've got to get moving."

She hesitated. Cursing, he grabbed her hand, pulled her to her feet and shoved her toward the boat. She clambered in and moved awkwardly to the bench furthest from the rower's seat. Brad snatched up the flapping blanket and other items, thrusting everything at Marilyn. Avoiding his eyes, she shoved the remains of their picnic under the middle bench. A moment later, he'd locked the oars in place and begun to row against the choppy waves.

The clouds spilled over.

Marilyn clutched the edge of her seat, as much to combat the roiling emotions within her as to keep her balance in the rocking boat. Trent Phillips was dead. Dead in the prison where her lies had sent him. Her sister was dead. Dead in the very water tossing beneath the boat.

And both deaths were her fault.

She lifted her head to the sky. Tears poured down her face, mingled with the rain and filled her mouth. The wind snatched at her cries and threw them back in her face. Her body shook with the pain of her grief and guilt.

Brad rowed.

Finally, limp and empty, she became aware of the wet and the wind.

She gazed around. They'd reached the middle of the lake. She could just make out her cottage through the rain. It looked impossibly far away.

She turned her head to find Brad watching her as he pulled with long strokes at the oars. She looked away and down. As he fought the wind and waves, Marilyn studied the angry water. What had Alison felt when she plunged into the beckoning depths? Anguish? Fear?

Peace?

Marilyn shuddered as dread expanded within her. Then she lifted her head and gazed with longing at the distant cottage. A long moment later, she closed her eyes, inhaled a deep breath and straightened. Turning to the man facing her, she asked him to stop rowing. Looking puzzled, he did as she asked.

"I'm not a very good swimmer," she announced, more to herself than to him. "But I might make it."

He didn't reply, but his eyes widened as he caught her meaning. He looked almost comically surprised.

Quickly, before she could lose her courage, she gathered her wet hair and tied it behind her head with a lacing from her shoe. Tucking her socks into her sneakers, she set them neatly under her seat. Finally, taking care not to capsize the small boat, she lowered herself over the side. The cold, dark water embraced her.

Before loosing her grip on the edge of the boat, she looked up once more at Trent's brother. He leaned toward her and extended his hand.

"You don't need to do this," he said. The desolation in his face had eased. A hint of approval moved in his eyes.

"Yes, I do."

He searched her face for a long moment and seemed about to argue. Finally, he gave a silent nod.

"I'm sorry," she said. "For everything."

She let go of the boat and began to swim toward the distant shore.

SEPTEMBER MOURN

by Audrey Jessup

I lay awake most of the night worrying about the three men in my cottage.

"We'd like to get away from the regular routine," Luke had said. "Have a weekend just for the guys, you know. Me and Roger and his cousin, Gordy. You know, he came to the last Sports Day. We thought we'd have a few drinks, tell a few stories, maybe pretend to fish a bit. You know."

Actually, I didn't know. A weekend 'just for the guys' had never appealed to me more than being with Marion. Drinking and smoking and telling lies was not my idea of a good time.

At school Luke hung around more with the Phys. Ed. teachers than with the rest of us in the Science Department. Roger was the swimming coach, and I didn't much like the way he would roll his eyes as he described the girls in their swimsuits. In fact most of their conversation in the staff room seemed to be of the "Have you heard the one about the girl who . . . " or "Jeez, that new Home Ec. teacher can switch my oven on any time" variety and after they'd had their daily guffaw, they'd slip outside for a smoke between classes. It was the thought of the smoking which kept me awake.

In my imagination I saw the three men staggering off to bed befuddled with drink, leaving a cigarette perched on the edge of a saucer because there weren't any ashtrays. The cigarette fell to the floor, burning into the carpet and setting fire to the curtains. Flames raced through the wooden walls and Luke and his buddies, trapped in the bedrooms, were overcome with smoke before they could escape. The scene became more horrendous as the night progressed, and I could hardly wait to get out the next morning to buy a smoke detector to take up to the cottage.

I had my shopping finished by ten o'clock and I started the long drive.

I wasn't looking forward to going back. I'd only been twice this year. In the spring I'd gone to open up, check the roof, hook up the water, and kick out any little critters who had taken up residence, but I left as soon as I'd finished the chores.

I'd tried spending the July 1st weekend there but I didn't last beyond the Saturday. It was too lonely without Marion. Every time I looked out the window I could see her on the beach, keeled over the bow of the canoe, clutching her chest. Without a telephone to call for help, I'd had to cope on my own. I didn't care what people said about doing everything I could, it hadn't been enough, and now a year later I still could hardly stand the sight of the place.

If Luke Gansey hadn't asked me if he and his friends could have the cottage for the weekend, I would probably have closed it up, even if it was only September. I didn't much like Luke's buddies, but in view of the way I felt about the place now, there didn't seem much point in refusing.

Luke had been there before. We had lent him the cottage for his honeymoon. He was a student teacher then and his bride, Louise, was a secretary at Marion's school. They didn't have much money so Marion suggested we let them have the cottage for a couple of weeks. They said they enjoyed it. Well, who wouldn't under those circumstances? They didn't mind that there were no neighbours.

We'd had them back once for a weekend after Louise became pregnant but it hadn't been a big success. Luke was not too pleased about the baby because it would mean losing Louise's salary, and when he wasn't snapping at her, he was sulking.

Now he was permanently on staff, he associated more with the younger teachers and, apart from department business, he and I didn't have a lot to do with one another.

As I turned at Shawville I caught the yeasty scent of fresh bread from the bakery where Marion and I had always stopped. The aroma filled the car but I kept on going.

Some of Marion's drawings and paintings were still at the cottage and I had cleaned out the stationwagon so I could bring them back with me. Marion had always used the holidays to paint. When she died she left almost a whole summer's worth of work which I hadn't done anything about. I knew it shouldn't be left there another winter. I had put off moving the paintings because I knew it would make me feel as if I were removing traces of her presence, and traces were all I had left.

I slowed down going through the little village, where every second house had an old car up on blocks in the driveway. It was 15 kilometres away from the cottage, and the general store was the closest place with a telephone.

As I turned down the access road to our cottage, I thought for the thousandth time, if only I could have reached a phone sooner to have an ambulance meet us on the highway, Marion might have been saved.

Luke's big grey stationwagon almost filled our parking area. When I backed in my small silver wagon, it looked like a baby whale snuggling up to its mother.

It wouldn't take me long to install the smoke detector and drop off the other things, then I'd collect Marion's work and be on my way.

From the parking lot, I looked down at the cottage roof. There was no smoke from the chimney, but it hadn't been cold last night so they probably hadn't bothered with a fire.

I had cut a zig-zag path so the slope down to the house wouldn't be too severe. Even so, I'd had to put Marion in a wheelbarrow to get her up the hill to the car. She had tried to insist she could walk, but I didn't want her making any unnecessary effort. Her face was grey as it was.

I got the stuff from the back seat and headed down the hill. There was no sign of Luke and his buddies. The canoe was still pulled up on shore, so they weren't doing any fishing. Maybe they'd flaked out after lunch.

I knocked at the door. "Anyone home?" Even if it was my cottage, I didn't think I should just barge in.

There was no answer.

When there was still no response after a second knock, I walked in. The door opens right into the living room and I was really pissed off when I saw dirty glasses and bags of chips and pretzels scattered all over the place. It smelled funny, too. At the far end of the room, I could see the kitchen table piled with used dishes. Those lazy bums mustn't have washed up since they'd arrived. Marion and I always kept things clean and tidy. Even when she was painting, the place was never a mess like this. I wondered if I should write a note to say I hoped they'd leave the cottage in good shape when they left. I'd certainly have to come back next weekend to make sure they had.

I fetched the stepladder from the storage cupboard. I figured I'd put the smoke alarm between the living room and the kitchen. Those seemed the most likely places for people to be smoking. I pushed the couch to one side so I could set up the ladder and I had one foot on the first step when I heard the bedroom door open behind me.

The bathroom and two bedrooms are off a small hallway two-thirds of the way down the left-hand wall of the living room.

Luke was standing in front of the bedroom door, zipping up his jeans. His hair was rumpled and his chin was dark with stubble. He didn't look like a man having a nap after lunch. He looked like a man getting up for the first time that day.

"I thought I heard someone out here," he said, frowning at me. "I didn't think you were planning to come up this weekend, Ray."

"I wasn't," I said. "But I got to thinking that you would probably all be enjoying a smoke in the evening and how I didn't have any ashtrays, so I brought some up. And I thought while I was at it, I might as well bring up the smoke detector I've been meaning to install. I'll be on my way as soon as I get it up."

I turned back to the stepladder but as I lifted my foot the bedroom door opened again.

"Hello, Mr. Berman." Wanda Price, Grade 11, leaned against the doorjamb in sheer pink pyjamas and pink slippers with bunny faces and ears. "Have you come up to join the party?" She giggled. "Did you bring a chick?"

I could feel my face and neck going red as I looked from Wanda to Luke.

Luke grabbed Wanda's arm. "Will you get back in there. I told you to keep quiet."

"Ooh. You're hurting me, Lukey," Wanda pouted. "I was only trying to be friendly. After all, everyone knows Mr. Berman hasn't been getting any for the last year. I thought he might . . . "

"For God's sake, get in there and keep quiet." Luke roughly pushed the girl back into the bedroom.

My hands were still gripping the sides of the ladder and my shoulders felt as if there were an iron bar across them.

"You'd better also tell her to get dressed," I said. My tongue seemed suddenly too big for my mouth.

I managed to wait until Luke had closed the door before saying any more, my rage mounting with every second as I thought of how he had defiled the bedroom that had been mine and Marion's.

"So this is your 'weekend with the boys,' is it? You lied to me so you could bring one of your students up to my cottage. So you could break the law on my property."

"Hold it, Ray," Luke said, "Wanda's over sixteen, you know. She's no beginner. She really came on to me."

I had to clench my fists to stop myself attacking him. "You bastard. So she's sixteen, and that makes everything okay? She's still your student. And you still have a wife and three kids. Get your stuff together and get the hell out of here."

I kicked the stepladder out of the way and it fell over, the metal ringing against the counter as it went down.

"What's going on? You need help, Luke?" Roger came out of the second bedroom with Gordy crowding behind him. Someone in the bedroom giggled.

"Christ Almighty," I yelled. "Who else have you got in there? Open that door."

Gordy and Roger looked at Luke. Luke shrugged and walked over to the kitchen table where he picked up a half-empty bottle of coke and drank. Mr. Cool himself while I churned inside.

Roger came through into the living room. Gordy turned his head and grunted over his shoulder, "You'd better come on out."

I didn't know these girls. One looked only about fourteen, a pretty little blonde with long hair. She stood there swaying and leaning against her friend. The second girl was taller and darker, but she didn't look much older. Her grey eyes had a dreamy, unfocussed look. They were both wearing short nighties and they both smiled at me tentatively before the little blonde burst into giggles.

"Don't tell me these two are sixteen," I said. "What have you been giving them? I thought I could smell marijuana when I came in."

Wanda came out of the bedroom, dressed in purple flowered leggings and a tight electric blue angora sweater.

"Did you meet my friends?" she said to me with a gap-toothed smile. "This is Diane," indicating the blonde, "and this is Demi . . . like Demi Moore, you know. You probably saw them in school. They're in Miss Weatherby's class."

I looked at Gordy and Roger, two middle-aged men beginning to go to seed. "Miss Weatherby's class. Grade 10." My stomach heaved and I thought I might throw up. "Get them dressed and out of here."

Gordy and Roger looked again at Luke, who was leaning against the table still holding the half-empty coke bottle. He shrugged again and jerked his head towards the bedroom to indicate they should do as I suggested. They both shot hostile glances in my direction but they shuffled the girls ahead of them back into the bedroom.

"Go and help them, Wanda," said Luke.

She pouted at him. "But I wanted to tell Mr. Berman how much I like his wife's paintings." She looked at me with an ingratiating smile. "She was really pretty when she was young, wasn't she? I was looking at the photo album . . . "

I could feel the hairs on the back of my neck bristling. This little tramp had been pawing through our belongings. I felt as if my chest was going to explode.

Luke pointed the coke bottle at Wanda. "Go and help them, I said."

"Gee, you're starting to sound just like a schoolteacher," Wanda muttered. But she went.

"It's too bad you didn't sound more like a schoolteacher earlier," I said. "You're finished in teaching. You and Roger. You know that, don't you?"

Luke lazily pushed himself away from the table. He was thin and athletic-looking, nearly 6'0" to my 5'7". I knew most of the female teachers thought him quite good-looking with his thick brown hair and heavy-lidded brown eyes, but now I looked carefully, I could see the ugly twist to his thin lips.

"How do you figure that, Ray?" He raised one eyebrow and I could have smashed his face in right then and there.

"You don't think you'll be staying after I tell the principal and the school board, do you? To say nothing of the police. Sex with minors is a criminal offence."

Luke laughed. "Where did you get so gutsy all of a sudden?" he said. "You haven't stood up for anything since I started teaching at Deacon High eight years ago. You've let them promote two less experienced teachers over your head. You've let them give you lousy timetables. You've let the administration walk all over you with the worst classes and rotten schedules without saying 'Boo.' You always said it wasn't worth a hassle. And now you're thinking of just walking in and dropping yourself right into the middle of the biggest hassle of your life. Get real, Ray."

"I'm prepared to take that chance."

"Are you sure about that? You accuse us and we'll deny it. We'll find witnesses to say we were somewhere else. You know how nasty people can be. They'll be only too ready to believe it when we hint that you've gone a bit peculiar since Marion died."

I turned away from that smug self-confident face and went over to the window. Luke was right. I had accepted all sorts of situations rather than argue, either with the administration or other teachers. When I came to D.H.S. I had vowed I wouldn't get involved in anything which didn't actually concern my students. I had avoided joining any staff activities, and I refused to fight over classes and timetables. It was easier just to go along. That way I could keep my distance.

"I'm pretty sure we can convince the girls it would be in their best interests not to talk," Luke said. "And then you have no proof. I even think if the chips were down and salaries and pensions were going to fly out the window, we could manage to persuade our wives to vouch for us being at home all weekend."

The bedroom door opened once more and Wanda shepherded Diane and Demi out, with the two men coming behind carrying their bags. I knew Roger was married and had children. I wasn't sure about Gordy. But Luke and Roger were in positions of trust with children. My stomach clenched again.

"What's he going to do?" Roger asked Luke.

"Well, we were discussing that," Luke said, placing the coke bottle on the table, "and I think Ray has just about decided to follow his usual course and do nothing."

After an initial reaction of surprise and relief, Roger looked at me with a knowing smile. Gordy behind him snorted. Sour saliva rose in my throat as the pair of them smirked at me over the heads of the girls. Diane suddenly leaned sideways and started to slide down the wall.

"Get the girls out to the car," Luke said. "I'll be with you in a minute."

Roger bent down and seized Diane under the arms, half carrying her out.

"Goodbye, Mr. Berman," cooed Wanda as she headed for the door. "It was real nice of you to invite us."

Luke laughed. When the others had gone, he turned to me again. "There's your other problem. Wanda probably thinks you invited us all up here, so she'd say you must have known all about it."

I took a deep breath, trying to keep my voice steady. "You could be pulled over on the highway," I said. "They're doing safety checks this weekend. How will you explain Diane?"

Luke narrowed his eyes as he looked at me. "Too bad there isn't a phone so you could alert them," he said. "But I think we could cope. Diane's my daughter, and she ate something at the cottage which disagreed with her so we're rushing her into town for attention. I think that would do it, don't you?" He smiled, and turned away. "I'll just get my stuff and be on my way."

He went into the bedroom and a moment later came out with a sports bag. As he opened the cottage door he laughed. "Louise will be just thrilled when I tell her I was lonesome for her so I came home early."

My head was bursting and my legs felt unsteady. I lurched over to the kitchen table and pushed the dirty dishes to one side so I could sit down and hold my throbbing head in my hands. What was I going to do? Everything Luke had said about me was true. I'd lost the habit of standing up and fighting.

I'd learned my lesson at my previous school. I had reported a colleague for dipping into the union funds. The colleague had been dismissed, all right, but I had been shunned by the rest of the staff for blowing the whistle. People I thought were good friends became reluctant to associate with me. I learned then that professional associations close ranks around members accused of wrongdoing and they strongly resent the accuser. I had found the feeling of isolation so bad, I applied for a transfer.

Marion thought when I moved to D.H.S. I would forget the miserable experience and participate in the staff life once again.

"You can't sit in a corner in the staffroom like a stick," she kept telling me. "For God's sake, get involved."

But I couldn't forget and I didn't get involved. It was the only serious disagreement we had in our whole married life. Even for her, I couldn't make myself that vulnerable again.

So what was I thinking of now, saying I was going to report Luke and Roger to the principal, and even the police? It was going to be the same can of worms, and I didn't know whether I could stand going through that again.

But the thought that those three perverts would get away with this, and perhaps even do it again, made my skin crawl. Would it really matter if I had to leave this job, too, because the rest of the staff treated me as if it were my fault, as if I were the traitor to the profession? I was due to retire in five years anyway. I'd lose a bit of pension but that didn't matter as much now Marion was gone. It was the long, lonely days without a job ... without the students ... without Marion ... how would I fill my time? This last summer had seemed endless.

And how would I convince people my story was true, anyway? I didn't doubt that Luke, and presumably Roger and Gordy also, would be able to persuade their spouses to back them up. Wanda would probably go along with them and, among them all, they'd probably be able to cajole or frighten Diane and Demi into keeping quiet.

As I pushed myself up from the table, my glance roved over the debris and suddenly I felt my rage mount again. One of those girls had been using Marion's favourite mug. A stain of bright red lipstick dribbled down into the pale blue forget-me-nots. In fury, I hurled the mug against the fireplace, where it shattered into tiny pieces. Those bastards had spoiled everything they touched. They'd made me wish I could just walk out and never see the cottage again.

But they wouldn't get away with it. I wouldn't let them get away with it. I flung open all the windows in the living room. The cool September air would help take away some of their rotten smell. I had to brace myself to go in the bedroom and I kept my eyes turned away from the tumbled bed. The room stank of Wanda's pungent perfume. I threw open the windows there and marched into the other bedroom to do the same.

I thought perhaps I would burn all the bed linen, but I didn't want to tackle it right then.

I unfolded a big green garbage bag and went around the living room and kitchen furiously tossing in all the coke bottles, Kentucky Fried Chicken boxes, chip bags, and half-eaten pieces of pizza, while all the time my brain worried at the problem of what to do.

One thing I'd brought with me I hadn't mentioned to Luke: a cellular telephone. I'd planned on leaving it for them in case there was an emergency. When Marion had her heart attack, I'd have mortgaged my soul to have had one. Could I phone the police to stop the car on the highway? Would they do that on my say-so? Or would they first have to come up and check me out to see I wasn't just some nutcase?

I filled the sink with soapy water and put all the dirty dishes and cutlery to soak while I finished gathering the garbage. I knew the police would stop a car to deliver a message if there was an emergency in the family. Maybe I could make up some story like that. Quickly I ran the small vacuum round. I didn't want to come back and find the place crawling with ants.

There had been worse things crawling around my cottage this weekend, though, and it was up to me to get rid of them.

After I'd washed the dishes I piled them on the draining board. I'd wash them again when I came up next weekend. Maybe put some disinfectant in the water.

I could tell the police my cottage had been vandalized and I'd seen this grey stationwagon driving away with three girls in the back. But if by any chance the police missed the car, they'd come up to see me and I'd have nothing to show. There was no physical damage. No, the emergency story would be better. Too bad I didn't have Luke's licence number.

Suddenly I realized I was trying to distance myself again, trying not to get involved. Why was I so worried about telling the truth, anyway? Wasn't that what I had bragged to Luke I was going to do? My policy of not making waves had become so ingrained I was having a hard time being up front.

The police were sympathetic. I gave my name and address and told them there was a grey stationwagon on the highway with three men and three underage girls in it and I thought at least one of the girls had overdosed on drugs. I told them the driver was Luke Gansey and he had spent last night at my cottage. I had arrived after lunch and I was really worried about the girl. No, I didn't have the car licence, but how many grey stationwagons could there be on the road with three young girls in the back?

I felt much better once I'd made the call and knew the police were going to be on the lookout for Luke's car. They said they'd get on it right away. I was certain once they saw Diane and Demi, they'd realize both these kids were on some kind of drugs. And when they saw that, surely they would ask questions.

I had got myself involved, taken a stand . . . and it felt good.

I was so cheered up I decided I could face stripping the beds. I piled all the linen in a bundle to deal with next week. At least the beds would have a chance to air.

I closed the windows, checked all the lights and taps, and locked the door. I'd drop the bag of garbage off at the dump.

As I trudged up the path to the parking lot, I thought again of Marion. I was sure she would approve of what I'd done and what I planned to do. If only we'd had a phone a year ago.

As I reached the top of the hill level with the parking lot, a sudden puff of wind brought me the heavy scent of Wanda's perfume.

"Hi, there, Mr. Berman."

She looked like an exotic flower nodding out at me over the silver car door, with her bright fuschia lips and her eyes heavily mascaraed under turquoise eyelids that matched her sweater.

"Mr. Gansey said you'd be glad to drive us all into town. He thought, like, maybe they wouldn't go straight back." She nodded her head towards the back seat. "Diane and Demi are having a nap, but I figured you'd like me to stay awake and talk to you." She smiled at me toothily. "It's not, like, a really *interesting* ride back, is it?"

IT'S IN THE BAG

I'll buy an ax
for Cousin Max,
some rope for Auntie Sue,
this rifle here
that has no peer
will be for Uncle Lou,
the nice garotte
that I just bought
will suit my sister Jill,
and for her brat,
my nephew Nat,
I'll buy a little pill.

I'll buy a dirk
for in-law Kirk,
poison for Cousin Lee,
and peanut cake
for Uncle Jake
who has an allergy.

Such is their fate
'less they vacate
my cottage – it's no hotel.
I won't deny
I'm hot to try
The Shopping List from Hell!

Joy Hewitt Mann

CONSPICUOUS PRESUMPTION

by Pat Wilson and Kris Wood

"Pass me another couple of Rolaids, will you Honey Bun?"

I watched Miffi reach into the glove compartment and pull out the bottle. She shook it and commented, "It's nearly empty, Miley . . . you'd better slow down on them."

Slow down? I snorted to myself. Slow down? Any slower than this and we'd be parked. The radio announcer said for the three hundred and forty-ninth time in the last hour, "Well, folks, cottage country traffic is tied up as usual; expect a few minor delays on your way north." Minor delays! Six hours on the road, and never once over 32 kliks an hour. I glanced at the temperature gauge – still normal, but I kept an eye on it anyway. The poor old Beamer wasn't used to this kind of driving. I popped the Rolaids and hoped the burning in my stomach didn't presage a full-blown ulcer attack. Did they have hospitals up here? Emergency centres . . . doctors?

Not for the first time, I began to wonder whether a weekend cheering up Sherm was worth it. I glanced over at Miffi. Somehow, I couldn't picture my Passion Flower in the wilderness that Sherm had chosen to hide in. Not that she didn't look the part. In fact, she was the spitting image of an outdoors girl (page 356 in the L.L. Bean Catalogue). Trust my Honeypie to look her best – even for a trip to the lake.

I checked my image in the rear view mirror. I didn't look so bad myself either, I thought. Certainly not like a lawyer today, although the all-wool hiking socks itched like hell. I cranked up the air-conditioning another notch.

I reached out and stroked Miffi's knee. She was perfection.

Everything I had ever dreamed of in a wife. My precious little Miffi-Babe. I was so proud of the way she looked when we walked into a room together. It still gave me a thrill to see all those other guys drooling. Even after four, no almost five, years. I'd do anything to keep her happy.

The problem was my Miffi-Jewel's happiness didn't come cheap. That damn New York market – still bearish (Stern's Market Watch Report). Down 23 points today alone! I felt a familiar clutch of fear around my heart. Mentally counting to four, I took in a deep breath, held it while I counted to four again, and let it out for a count of eight. ("Take Control of that Anxiety", Tape 3, Side 1). I could feel myself relax. I wasn't going to think about money this weekend. I was going to enjoy being at Sherm's cottage and nothing more.

"Not far now, Sweet Cheeks," I said as cheerfully as I could. "Just think how pleased poor old Sherm's going to be to see us." I couldn't believe he'd been up here for two months already, hiding out while his divorce went through. "Sandra's been giving him hell. She'll clean him out if she gets the chance. Just between you and me, Sugar Lips, I think she wants to get him mad enough to take a poke at her. Then she'll sue him sideways to Sunday. That is, if she doesn't take a poke right back at him." Sandra could flatten him, too. I told him it was a mistake marrying another lawyer, especially one who made the All Women's Wrestling Team. Poor old Sherm. He was really scared of Sandra. I tried to imagine hiding away up here. Not just hiding, but roughing it, too. Not even a Stair-master or a hot tub.

As a matter of fact, I had a sinking feeling that Sherm didn't even have electricity up here, but I wasn't about to tell Miffi that. My Tweetie Bird had taken enough persuading just to get this far. I sure hoped she wouldn't let Sherm see how much she hated leaving the city lights. If I was going to get that partnership I deserved, and yes, I'll admit it, really needed, a lot depended on keeping Sherm on my side. I didn't want him getting upset by my Miffi-cookie. He was a tad anti-female already, thanks to Sandra. If Sherm got upset, I could say goodbye to the partnership. No Rosenfield on the letterhead. No step up the corporate ladder. My heart began to pound. Wait. I couldn't let myself get worked up like this. I counted to four, breathing in slowly.

If only I could be sure of the partnership. I needed that partnership.

I glanced at my Honeycake again. Geez, she was beautiful. Sometimes I had to pinch myself to believe she was mine. My heart clutched again. She wouldn't be mine much longer if I didn't get that partnership. It didn't take a genius to figure that out. My sweet Miffi-Bunny hated being the only wife in our group who wasn't married to a partner of some kind or other. Even the time share in Nassau (Golden Dreams Vacations) hadn't made it up to her. No – only a partnership would do.

I checked my Rolex. At this rate, it would be sunset before we reached Sherm's cottage on Lake Winnikashapo. I felt a trickle of disquiet. Would I be able to find the turn in the dark?

A cold nose in my ear told me that Tink (Fanchon's Tinkerbell of Red Feather), was getting a little antsy too. "Soon, soon," I whispered. She woofed softly and settled her little furry butt back onto the arm rest.

Suddenly, I saw the sign for Lake Winnikashapo. We'd made it! I wrenched the Beamer out of the bumper-to-bumper parking lot called Highway 11, and down a side road that within minutes deteriorated into a cart track. The trees closed in on each side, and at that moment, the sun slipped behind the hill. Miffi stopped singing Tink's go-to-sleep puppy song. I knew she hated the dark. "Don't worry, Rosebud," I said. "Sherm's map shows the cottage just over this ridge. Aha! This must be the driveway." The cart track became a hiking trail.

I wasn't sure that the Beamer was meant for this kind of road, but there was no way that I'd ever get Miffi to walk from this point. "Sit tight, Sugar Plum," I cautioned. "No little rock or rut can stop Maserati Miles," (thanks to Dudley's Defensive Driving Diploma Course). I turned to her and smiled reassuringly. The Beamer came to a sudden, grinding halt. Miffi screamed. Tink landed in a yelping heap between my feet. "What the . . . !" I yelled. It was Sherm's Jeep (Grand Cherokee, 4x4, Limited Edition 5.2 litre V-8). "What the hell is that doing in the middle of the road?"

I threw the Beamer into reverse. It was stuck! The Beamer's bumper (good for up to 35 km/hr impact), had wedged itself under the bumper of Sherm's Jeep.

Thank goodness we were going too slowly for the dual-airbags to deploy. I shuddered to think how my Miffikins would have reacted to 16 cubic feet of compressed air on her perfect maquillage (Helena Rubenstein and Estee Lauder).

Actually, I felt sick at the thought. My perfect little Angel-face scarred for life? Why had I brought such a delicate flower to this God-forsaken hole? If only I could pull a Uey and get us out of here. Back to good old Toronto. To heck with the partnership, Sherm, everything.

What was I thinking to take my Miffi-pie to this unknown territory. I knew how she felt about the unknown. She didn't even like shopping anyplace else other than Saks Fifth Avenue and Holt Renfrew.

I pulled myself together. Miffy was fine. Just a little scared by the sudden bump. I had to get a grip. Breathe, I told myself sternly. I couldn't back out now – I needed Sherm and that partnership. I had to keep Sherm sweet.

Besides, we were stuck. I decided to put a brave face on it for the sake of my Miffi-kitten.

"Well, Peachblossom, I think we're here." Tink jumped out, glad to relieve herself behind the nearest bush. (Both my girls were shy). I could see that Miffi wasn't so sure. "Come on, Sweet Cakes," I urged her. "Sherm's sure to have the wine on ice." That moved her.

The cottage loomed in front of us, its windows dark. Why hadn't Sherm at least turned on a light or two? No wonder I hadn't seen the Jeep. Who the hell could see anything in this kind of dark? Not even a streetlight or two. I didn't know how Sherm could stand it up here.

Where the hell was he?

I stood uncertainly in the dark. This just wasn't like Sherm. He was always right there, ready to glad-hand everyone in the room. "The quintessential host" according to McLean's ("Up and Coming Bay Street Boys", June '95).

It was quiet – too quiet. I could feel my heart begin to triphammer in my chest. What I wouldn't give to hear a familiar siren or two, but nothing. Just the rustle of wind in the leaves and the lapping of waves on a beach somewhere. Suddenly, I was aware of silent dark shapes swooping across the clearing – bats? I had to get out of here!

Before the panic overwhelmed me, I shook my head. "I am strong. I am bold. I am an oak," I told myself. ("Self-Talk to Success", Tape 4, Side 2). My Golden Treasure depended on me to be her oak. That's how things worked for us Rosenfields. Miles the oak and Miffi the tender flowering vine, twining her exquisite tendrils around my heart. I pulled myself upright, feeling the oak power surging through my veins. (Tape 5, Side 1).

"Sherm! Hey, Sherm," I yelled. My voice echoed back from the trees. "Leave everything, Precious Pet," I said. "Let's go find Sherm. He'll give me a hand with the Beamer." Single file, with Tink in the lead, we started for the cottage.

Tink's excited yapping ended suddenly with an agonized yelp! Miffi leapt forward like a thoroughbred racehorse at the starting gate, shoving me aside. I fell into a clump of prickly bushes just as I heard her bloodcurdling scream. My heart froze. My Honey Bee was in danger! Ignoring the thorns tearing at my manly flesh, I rushed to the rescue.

My sweetest Miffi-lamb was standing under a wriggling Tink, who swung just inches above her outstretched hands. Pulling myself up to my full five foot five inches, I managed to untangle Tink's little paws from some sort of netting. What the hell was it? I looked up. Dangling right in front of my nose was a loop of rope. It didn't take a hangman to recognize a noose! If Tink had been a person, she would have been throttled by now.

For one mad moment, I wondered if the isolation had affected Sherm's brain. A trap! A lethal trap. Right where people would be walking. Right where *I* would be walking. Was Sherm trying to kill me? My brain did a quick right-hemisphere lateral sweep ("Mind Power – It's Yours Today", Chapter 12). And came up with a startling idea: was someone trying to kill *Sherm*?

Someone who didn't know we were coming. Someone who hated Sherm. Someone like Sandra!

I grabbed the rope and yanked it down before my little Cream Puff saw it. I'd have to warn Sherm when I saw him. If I saw him.

Tink jumped out of my arms, none the worse from the experience, but Miffi, my poor Miffi. With a tear-stained face, she held up her broken nail for my inspection. I kissed it tenderly, and assured her the other nine (Nicola's Nifty Nails), still looked wonderful. "Come on," I said, shoving the loop of rope down into the nearby bushes, nearly ripping off my arm in the process. "There's a path here. Maybe old Sherm's in back. Maybe he's got the barbecue all fired up. Maybe he didn't hear us come in."

But, the back of the cottage was equally deserted. By now, I was beginning to suspect the worst. No Sherm. And it wasn't as if he was a novice at this outdoor stuff. After all, at Kamp Hard Drive (the Komplete Komputer Kamp for Kids), Sherm had been a whiz at all the survival-in-the-woods games. I'd had trouble just getting myself into a canoe, but the Shermster had won every Woodcraft badge going. He'd even got the Best Hard Drive Camper award that I'd been working for all summer. Which wasn't fair, since I was the one who could make a computer sit up and whistle Dixie.

Yeah, old Sherm had always beaten me to the punch. Deep down, I guess I kinda envied Sherm. His getting a partnership like that, way before I had any hope of one. Just because Sandra's uncle (Brewer, Brewer and Sheldon), knew old man Weinberg. It still teed me off.

Still, things weren't looking so hot for Sherm right now. The divorce wasn't going to be any bed-of-roses. And I was breathing down his neck client-wise. What a stroke of luck, glomming onto the Birks account. There was no getting away from it. I was a shoo-in for a partnership. And I woulda got it long before now if Sherm hadn't stolen my thunder. Sherm was going to have to step aside because the Miler was coming through! That is, if Sherm was still around.

For a moment, I pictured a Sherm-free world. I'd be a partner; my Miffi-Puff would be Partner's Wife Numero Uno; my stock portfolio would double with the added Partner's shares.

What was I thinking! I shook my head to clear away the self-serving thoughts. Sherm was my buddy. We went way back together. If he needed me, I was here for him.

Behind the cottage, the small clearing and path to the lake were dark and uninviting. "Wait here," I told Miffi. She nodded, grateful for an opportunity to examine the extent of the damage to her nail. I stepped warily into the clearing. And tripped over an ax. Not just any ax, but a big ax. I picked it up. It was heavy . . . and there, on the shiny head . . . something dark and shiny. Blood? It had to be blood!

Without thinking, I tossed the ax into the bushes. And immediately wished I hadn't. Why had I picked it up? It was stupid to touch things at the scene of crime. It didn't take a Bay Street lawyer to know that. Hey, my brain was playing tricks on me. There wasn't any crime. I was way out of line.

Or was I? A noose, a bloody ax. A bloody ax with my fingerprints on it. Steeling myself, I rummaged in the bushes and found the ax. Quickly, I ran my handkerchief (Hermes100% pure silk) down the shaft. Just in case. I wasn't sure in case of what, but whatever happened, I wasn't going to explain to anyone why my fingerprints were on the ax. I tossed it back in the bushes.

Where was Sherm? Could something terrible have happened to him? Could Sandra, his almost-by-now ex, have carried out the wild threats she made at Marvin's son's Bar Mitzvah reception? Her voice echoed in my brain. "I'll kill you, Sherman Silverstein," she'd screamed into the surprised faces of Sherm and Angie Levy (Bryn Mawr '86), as they lay entangled in the pile of coats on Gloria and Marvin's bed. I shook my head angrily. No, not Sherm, not the Shermster, not the Sherm who broke the Sigma Beta Beta record for crushing beer cans in his armpits. Nothing could happen to Sherm.

My suspicions about Sandra had to be totally off-the-wall. But I couldn't get them out of my mind. After all, people did do nutso things all the time ("History of Serial Killers in the Civilized World", PBS).

I glanced over at Miffi. She was sniffing pitifully. I knew that I was moments away from those delicate little sniffs turning into a full-scale Niagara of tears. At this point, only a hot bath and a cold drink were going to reconcile Miffi to life in the wilds. But it was going to take a lot more than that to make me forget the noose and the bloodstained ax. I decided to keep my suspicions to myself. No need to upset my Pussywillow any more.

I peered around, trying to see in the growing darkness. I was really uneasy. A bat swooped down across the clearing. I must have jumped a mile, and I could hear my heart pounding. I wished I'd brought along my blood-pressure monitor (Pulse Master 2000). At this rate, I might not survive to make partner.

And if anything happened to Sherm . . . I mentally shook my head. Nah. Nothing had happened to the Shermster. Still and all, without Sherm, someone would have to fill his space in the firm. Not that anyone could, of course. Except, well . . . me.

I glanced over to where I had thrown the ax. I should stay and look for Sherm. But my Miffi-peach was unhappy. I was torn. Bottom line, all I wanted to do was to get the hell out of here and get my Sweet Pea back to civilization.

A huge full moon was rising in the night sky. Sweet Pea saw the lake wrapped in evening mist. Her baby blues (Optimal Optics), widened in delight, and with a squeal, she tripped down the path. Even in my distress, I had to admire her firm tush (thanks to Thighs R Us). Tink, close at her heels, yapped excitedly. Not for the first time, I marvelled at the resilience of my girls. Swallowing my own fear and apprehension, I followed them. Perhaps Sherm was in the boathouse.

With a shudder, I wondered what sort of shape he'd be in. Why hadn't he called out when we arrived? I had a terrible feeling we would never hear Sherm's voice again.

Suddenly, the hush of the evening was rent by a series of hideous cries . . . barely human, and yet, not quite animal. My mind flashed to images of Freddie Kruger. Sherm! Was Sherm being tortured somewhere? I wouldn't put anything past Sandra. God knows what kind of tricks she'd learned at that fitness club of hers (Go Figure – for NOW women). I'd seen that mean look in her eyes when she first met my Angel-cake. Jealous, of course. The woman was capable of anything. Poor old Sherm didn't have a prayer.

Miffi threw herself into my arms. I could feel her delicate body (Slimfast and Lean Cuisine), trembling against mine. Tink began to bark wildly and went into her pointer stance (not easy for a Yorkshire Terrier). There was something in the water.

Holding Miffi's hand, I crept to the end of the dock. There, floating on the water like an aquatic baked alaska, was a hat. Not just any hat, but a genuine Tilley hat. I knelt down and fished it out. It was identical to the one on my own head. Turning it upside down, I quickly found the secret pocket. Inside, damp, but still readable, a card: Sherman Silverstein, Attorney-at-Law.

Things were looking pretty bad for old Sherm. It didn't take a rocket surgeon to figure out that a noose, a bloody ax, a cry in the night and a floating hat spelled trouble.

I had to face it – Sherm was history.

For a moment, I was stumped. I admit it. I didn't have a clue who would be the best people to get for the funeral. Me, the Miler, the guy who always knew the best place to get anything. There was no doubt I'd be called upon to organize the funeral. Who else was there to do it? Sandra would be locked up where she belonged.

Maybe not a funeral, considering the circumstances, I thought. A memorial service. That would be classier. I'd give the eulogy. After all, we'd been like brothers, almost. And my Miffi-sweet looked wonderful in black. She cried really well, too. Just big pearl drops sliding down her alabaster cheeks and dripping slowly off her delicate chin onto her silk blouse. I could see it all now.

As Sherm's best buddy, and as a new partner in the firm, I'd arrange the whole thing. It would be the best. I ought to get started on the arrangements right away. I could use my Cell. Were there Repeaters this far north? I wondered who would know the best funeral home in the city?

Poor old Sherm. I was going to miss him. I'd have to have his office redecorated. Get rid of all that leather and mahogany and hunting stuff. Get a decorator (Christoph's Classic Business Spaces). Tell him to make that office say, "Miles." Something in black and chrome. Yeah.

But all that could wait. Right now, I just wanted to take my Tootsie

Pie and my Tink and head back to the city where we belonged. I could call the police, the Mounties, the sheriff, or whoever the hell you called, from the safety of our own little home (Melrose Towers, Penthouse Suite).

I could tell from the tears that trembled on Miffi's eyelashes (Antoines' of New York), that she was nearing the end of her endurance. There was nothing I could do for Sherm now. It was time to take care of the living.

At this point, I became aware of two things: one, the irritating whine of mosquitoes around my head. No doubt, the scent of fresh city blood had called them out in droves. I tenderly brushed one from my Lamb Chop's palpitating cleavage (L.A. Silicone Services), almost forgetting my growing anxiety. And two: a steady "thunk, creak . . . thunk, creak . . . thunk, creak" sound, growing louder, drawing nearer across the water.

In a flash, I knew what it was. Sandra was coming for us! Planning to get rid of any witnesses to her heinous crime!

"Come on, sweetheart," I urged, trying to keep the panic out of my voice. "Let's go back to the Beamer for your nail-file." I knew the broken nail was still bothering my Baby Lamb. Miffi smiled gratefully at my sensitivity (Day Two of the Togetherness Weekend), and she and Tink started up the dock. I don't think they realized what was happening.

I hoped they never would. My sweet Miffi-puff was going to make one helluva partner's wife. I didn't want the terrible trauma of Sherm's death spoiling it for my Miffikins. And I wasn't going to let Sandra get rid of the only people who could testify against her. Especially my Candybar. I knew Sandra would love to take a whack at my Precious Jewel. Maiming her. Disfiguring her lovely face. And Sandra didn't like me much, either.

"Run," I urged Miffibits, using my best oak voice. I gave her a gentle push, ignoring the horror in her eyes. Never before had I asked her to do such a thing. Gamely, she began a hop-skipping trot up the path.

I was close behind her, too unnerved even to admire the view. We had to get out of there! I bet Sandra could run like the wind. Those wiry women who do their own gardening terrify the life out of me.

The same blood-curdling cry halted me in my tracks. The last echoes had hardly died away when I heard Sherm's best courtroom voice booming across the water. "Hey, Rosenfields, did you hear the loons? What a sound, eh? Don't hear that in the city, eh? Welcome to good old Lake Winnikashapo." Out of the mist appeared Sherm, skillfully rowing a wooden craft. Thunk, creak . . . thunk, creak . . . thunk, creak.

"Just been catchin' us some supper," he yelled cheerfully. The boat bumped the dock gently and Sherm threw me a rope. I was too stunned to catch it. Sherm! Alive! It was all too much to take in.

"How was the traffic? A killer, I'll bet." Sherm retrieved the rope and skillfully tied it to the rusted mooring ring. "Oh great. You found my hat. Lost the darn thing getting into the boat." He reached out and took the hat which I still clutched tightly.

Sherm! Alive! He wasn't going to be vacating his corner office. I wasn't going to be made partner right away. Miffi wasn't going to be a partner's wife.

"Bring me the ax, willya?" he said. "It's just on the path back there. I was using it to cut bait. It'll take the heads off these babies." He held up three small fish. Still, I couldn't move.

Sherm! Alive! I wasn't going to find the best funeral home in the city. I wouldn't be giving the eulogy.

Sherm started handing me things: a tackle box, bait bucket, fishing rod, life jacket and seat cushions. "Great place, eh? I've made all sorts of improvements. Did you see my hammock? Put it up myself . . . on that big tree just as you come in. Hope you folks didn't run into it. I didn't have time to finish stringing it up and I think there're a couple of loops of rope still hanging down. I used all those great knots I learned at good old Hard Drive." He handed me an oar.

Sherm? Alive? My hand clenched the smooth satiny surface of the oar. Through the mists of my confusion and disappointment, I glanced at the brand (Barkley Sound). Sherm bought only the best, too. It felt good in my hand.

Sherm bent over to get the other oar out of the boat. His great winking backside mocked my unbelieving eyes.

Sherm. Alive. A vision of his corner office – sans hunting prints and leather – flashed through my mind. Chrome and glass. I couldn't let it go.

And my Cupcake, my Precious Pearl . . . so tenuously mine, and slipping away from me with every dropping point on the Dow-Jones. The Partnership. The stock options. No longer certainties with the demise of Sherm, but just possibilities. And not great ones at that.

I remembered the pain when Sherm was handed the Award for Best Hard Drive Camper. My hand tightened on the oar. Sherm turned towards me, his bald spot gleaming in the moonlight.

Even Sherm would have argued it was justifiable homicide.

PARTNER-IN-CRIME

I've had enough of leaky boats
and bailing for my life,
I didn't know the risk I took
when I became your wife.
I've had it up to here with mice
and one fat porcupine
who moved into the cottage
and trashed everything that's "mine".

I'm scared to death of flying things
that want to drink my blood
and almost broke my neck last week
when I slipped in the mud.
And every time I empty "it",
that thing you call the can,
my aching back starts killing me.
Is that part of your plan?

This cutting wood has done me in,
I want to stop and die,
but I'm so busy staying alive
I haven't time to try.
You're finishing me by slow degrees
with water, mud, and tree.
You picked a great accomplice –
this cottage is killing me.

Joy Hewitt Mann

AUGUST IS THE LAMB OF WINTER

by Michelle Marcotte

On summer weekends our cottage bursts with teenagers. As soon as I arrive with my two daughters, a stream of boys beats a path to our door. They come laden with beer, accompanied by the pounding beat of music and their own racing blood, hot on the scent of my two beauties. I'm not worried; I've taught my girls to be patient, to observe the boys' hearts and know their own. Somehow, I've convinced them to wait for a summer love hot enough to last through the winter of their lives. I want them to avoid my mistake. So, when I see them skillfully play at love, testing and observing while avoiding entanglements like matadors, I am so proud of them.

Their hearts are not cold, they are just careful because they know what we are capable of.

But while they sort out the boys and their own hearts, I have to canoe into the lake for some peace, and to examine my memories. Today, I paddled to Lily Bay. I like the lilies. Their roots are buried deep in the mud, where, I suppose, ours are too. I paddle out here often, to thank God for my life and gifts she has given me. Each time before I leave, I look at my reflection in the bay, and to see if under the lilypads, I can see his face.

I knew when I first took him to the lake, that he had what I needed. Frightened of the prospect, I wanted him in my private place where the heat of the day would warm his heart and the summer night could cloak our first touch.

In the Ottawa Valley, lakes swim from one to another through beaver marshes of dead trees and bulrushes. Loons call and dive to hunt and evade. They are my only black and white memory of that time.

The cottage belonged to my mother. It was poorly furnished then, with lumpy chairs and single beds. A topographical map to guide fishermen and canoeists was its sole decoration. It was not furnished for love. But the lake, the trees and rocks made furnishings and decorations enough for me. I tramped with him through the bush showing him my favorite places and things. I explained how fallen trees provide for new growth in the life and death of the forest.

I still love the woods, I draw strength from sunlight filtering through the green leaves of summer. The musty smell of the forest excites me. He trod woodenly on wild flowers and lichen. He did not see the Blue Jay gliding among the trees. He sweated and swatted flies I did not feel.

We swam together at noon. As my cold lake enveloped me I felt washed clean as baptism. And it was as fearful as baptism. He ducked me under until my bubble of air left me, then he finally let me rise, calling me baby in answer to my fear. He was just playing, he said, and kissed my fear away. Pushing up my bra, he cupped my breasts and circled my cold nipples. I knew it was my time; I wanted him. I reached for him, but he pulled away to sun on the dock with his head turned from me.

All afternoon I tried to amuse him, beguile him and make him sweet on me with the care I took of him. We paddled to where the water lilies of summer bob on quiet bay waters. Their virginal faces brushed our canoe with delicate pink lips. But he was bored, he did not like the cold depths of the lake or the sounds of the forest. And in truth, he did not seem to like me.

But at least the night seemed right. Alive with stars unseen in the city, the sky spread as dense as time. The heat of the day had escaped through starholes and a chill settled softly on the full, dark shapes of evergreens.

I wanted his love, the romance of seduction that first night. It seemed he was my only chance. I playfully cajoled him to love me, teased and tugged him bare chested down the pine needle path that cushioned our silent footfall to the dock. My flannel nightgown floated behind me like a white sheet in the breeze.

We stood toe to toe on the rough wood, smelling the trees and each other. I felt his desire rising, but as I touched him the August night showed herself, distracted me with gold, glistening ribbons in the sky. I stood and let the Northern Lights cut my silhouette, let him see me as I pointed and swayed with their energy. I knew the Northern Lights tell of cold to come, but I understood the beauty in cold, in the winter harshness that becomes an August night. The black lake, the cloak of the sky and the silent guardian evergreens inspired me to slip the nightgown over my head, to let the cool night air kiss my skin as I wanted him to. And we lay on it, flannel on the dock. I kissed him, trembling for love, but struggling against the swift harshness of his touch, the rough pinches and entries of rush.

Should I have understood the warning of the Northern Lights as we lay together that first night? Having first wanted him, I was frightened as he held me down, felt the cold enter me as he did. He slipped in me as easily as a bare foot in a muddy lake bottom, coldly and deeply. But isn't that what the first time always feels like?

It got better. In October, I told him I was pregnant as we walked in the fallen leaves at Kingsmere. He kicked the acorns. I placed his cold hand on my belly and the wind brought tears to my eyes. I stood under an abandoned church arch and said I loved him. God forgive me. Was that a mortal sin? Finally, he said he loved me too.

But, it was a cold winter, dark and lonely. I harboured the baby inside me and wondered if her eyes would be as black as the night, as green as the evergreens or as blue as the lake she came from. And wasn't it just natural to curl inward and hold her, my baby. She held me too and kept me warm.

As he pulled away, I thought it was my fault, that I had made a circle of two and left no room for him. I told myself it was my fault he did not come home, did not join with me in joy or love, or even need.

We stood together at bus stops, staring at the snow and slush without words for each other. I wished for summer warmth and wondered if I had only imagined that some of it had come from him. On winter nights when he did not want me, or when I was punished, I sat by the window and looked at the street. It ran both ways, and I should have too. But I needed one more gift from him.

I tried to please him, naively playing house. But my cleaning was not clean enough; to my dinners he sat silent. Meat loaf. Stuffed peppers. I painted the baby's room yellow. My hard nipples pressed against his back at night did not make him turn my way.

From the beginning our decisions were his to make. My paycheque was deposited into his bank account. It was easier that way, he said. Had I become like the child I was carrying?

In January I saw the Northen Lights again. They danced for me one night. We had argued and I had left our bed. I opened my gown to see the reflection of my full breasts and round baby tummy in the window. Behind the closed door I touched myself. Was I so wrong to want to have my tender nipples suckled before the baby even came? Naked, alone in the baby's room I danced with the Northern Lights. But I was afraid he would catch me, and freeze my baby in ice water with his coldness.

On the weekends we would go out hand in hand. We walked in Sears, the happy couple admired by the sales ladies. We sat in church, where I prayed for redemption. I already knew hell was keeping up appearances. In March he confined me to home. Wasn't that the way it was supposed to be? Confinement was for the good of the baby, to protect me from the harshness of the world in my delicate condition. Or to protect the world from seeing a pregnant woman with a black eye?

The baby came early. It happens. But my baby came early and made me a whore. His tight smile lasted only the day I was in the hospital. Why is it you can break a bone and they keep you in the hospital for days, but give birth and they send you home in 24 hours? He said I had trapped him into marriage with another man's bastard and he owed me nothing.

I know spring comes eventually and patience has its rewards. So, I tried harder. The house was cleaner, the meals were better. Roast chicken. Baked fish. I met him at the door with smiles and seduced him one night with red wine. On top of him at last as my womb caught what he gave me, my breasts squirted milk. Wet from me, he remembered that first night. Witch! he said. He slapped me and made me sleep in the baby's room.

And in spite of this, it was for her that my heart broke. I thought he would love her in time. For how could he resist my baby? Her eyes were mud brown like mine. She had come from the lake and from me. She laughed like the loon calling.

And she was still a newborn when I became pregnant again. I swelled quickly; there was no hiding my unborn from him. Frightened now, I drew a tight circle around the three of us, my baby, my unborn and me. And like the loons we submerged to hide from danger. We swam quietly through our days, careful to avoid attracting attention. Spring came and the leaves unfurled, yellow, green and clear, so open to the light. We walked in the woods, smelled the first sweet, birch leaves and listened as the loose bark tapped in the breeze. I hoped I had survived the darkest time. The spring brought warmth, but it showed the dust on the baseboards and the dirt of my marriage.

I cleaned all summer. I set our mattress to sun and tidied the cupboards. I washed the baseboards. The windows sparkled with sunlight. My affairs were in order. In August I brought him to the lake again. On the cusp of September, one night settled still and cold. I bowed my bruised face to the lake. I threw my hope to the wind and my soul to the dark guardians. And I waited for their answer in my flannel nightgown.

The Northern Lights flashed for me again, calling me, waving me to come. I was forbidden to canoe alone, but I climbed in, intending to paddle to the center of the lake to see their message. But, he had been watching and stopped me. He sat unsteadily, drunkenly, in the canoe, and for the first time, I steered my own path into the night.

Thankfully, the lake is not silent at night. Toads grunt, insects buzz, fish splash and animals hunt. At night you cannot see the ropes of weeds from the lake bottom and you cannot see the sucking mud. The lake gently slapped the canoe, urging me on like a kind horsewoman. In the clear bay, where the lilies floated with faces closed to the night, I finally understood the warning of the Northern Lights. Dip, dip, swing, one strong stroke of my paddle flashed in the yellow light and he fell in the lake, in water deep enough, in mud cold enough.

His struggles tipped the canoe, and I had no fight left in me. I slid peacefully into the lake floating gently with the weeds and flowers while he fought and floundered. I gave myself to the water if she wanted me, but my unborn and my milk-full breasts bobbed to the surface. I floated, facing the Northern Lights, to the dock. Dripping there, I thanked them.

In the morning, when the canoe returned gently to shore, my white flannel nightgown hung on the clothesline, drying in the sun.

HOLDING DOWN THE FORT

by Therese Greenwood

I was a kid again as I stood on the steps of the canteen, inhaling the smells of childhood at the cottage. Noxema and sunscreen on sun-burned skin. French fry grease. Barbecue smoke. The illusion was abetted by the fact that the jetskis were mercifully silent, the only sound a motorboat passing just in front of Poker Island about half a mile from shore.

I was in quest of a chocolate ice cream cone I hoped to enjoy alone as I strolled the beach in a moment of self-indulgent silence. Steve was out on one of his two-hour mountain bike rides and Drew had snuggled up on the couch engrossed in a new comic. If the beach gods were with me, I could nip in to the canteen while none of my relatives was there and avoid another of the long querulous conversations that had been marring our summer vacation.

The beach gods were absent. Aunt Hattie limped in on her cane just as I was paying $1.85 for the single scoop cone that had cost my mother a nickel.

"I thought I saw you sneaking in here," she said. "You've got time to come in here and fill your face but you don't have any time to discuss family business."

"I'm sorry, Aunt Hattie," I said. "But – "

"No buts," she said. "It's not good keeping to yourself all the time, waiting for that fancy-pants husband of yours to finish riding that crazy bicycle. Especially now, when we need you. If the Fort is still good enough for you in the summer, then the family's still good enough for you."

"The Fort" is what we call Fort Allen, a fur trading hamlet that bustled in the days when the river was the area's main transportation route. The hotel which serves triple duty by housing the only canteen, tavern and flophouse for 30 miles is the sole remaining building from the original trading post.

The main industry now is tourism, with summer cottagers paddling their kevlar canoes where the courier de bois once glided along the river. A lot of the Fort's summer residents are like me, descended from fur traders who put down roots here. The cottages have been in the family for generations and so we were all caught up, to one degree or another, with Aunt Hattie's new problem.

"Since I'm here, we might as well have a drink," Aunt Hattie said. "Sit down over there."

She gestured with her cane to one of the tables, plywood planks nailed to thick stubs of wood, and ordered a rye and coke from Bob. Silently he brought it to the table, the glass filled to the brim with ice the way she always drank it in August. Aunt Hattie didn't thank Bob when he put it down.

Bob avoided eye contact while he counted out her change. Expecting no tip, he briskly returned to the other side of the canteen's counter. Leaning forward, his burly forearms against the smooth counter top, he watched from a distance as she sipped her drink.

Aunt Hattie nodded towards Bob. "We can't talk with MacDougalls around," she hissed loudly from the corner of her mouth. "Come over tonight after dinner and we'll figure something out."

"Yes, Aunt Hattie," I said.

The cool evening breeze was coming in from the river when Steve and I paid our command visit to Aunt Hattie's summer home, the pride of Fort Allen's Campbells. Most of the area's cottages were casual clapboard bungalows filled with cast-off furniture. But Aunt Hattie had spent years and every spare penny restoring Grandma Campbell's farmhouse. She had even mounted a wooden plaque on the west wall noting the year she finished the restoration.

Drew hated that place, more museum than cottage. Sand from the beach was strictly forbidden and little boys not much more welcome. Steve and I saw no reason for him to suffer and had sent him off to play with his cousins.

As we walked up Hattie's flagstone steps we could hear music from the hotel next door. That meant Aunt Hattie would not be taking us out to the screened-in porch. Instead, after presenting us with the requisite rye and cokes, she led us into the parlour where a dour Grandma and Grandpa Campbell looked down from their wedding day photograph.

The pine rocker protested as Aunt Hattie lowered herself into it and we took our usual spot on the old love seat reserved for visiting cottagers.

"So," she said. "What are we going to do about Blind Billy?"

It was the question I'd been trying to avoid all summer and Steve tried to save me from it.

"Aunt Hattie, what a beautiful little blanket," Steve said slyly. He got up and walked towards the knitted spread that always covered the antique washstand.

He knew the story of the blanket as well as I did but was hoping to distract Aunt Hattie with a recitation of the family history. He knew she always got caught up in the telling, reliving the glorious old feud.

"It looks very old," Steve said, fingering the blanket and wrinkling his nose at the hint of the mothballs which kept it company every winter.

"Old!" Aunt Hattie harumphed. "That's the crib blanket Grandma Campbell knit for Uncle Harold using those very knitting needles on the cabinet."

Steve picked up the ivory needles that had come all the way from the old country with Grandma Campbell's mother. They were a family treasure which I had never been allowed to touch as a child, even though one had long been missing its tip and the pair would never again produce a family heirloom.

"She finished the blanket the very night Blind Billy was murdered," said Aunt Hattie. "She was just laying down those needles when he was brought home."

"Murder?" asked Steve. "I thought that was never proven."

"Good Lord, I can't believe she'd tell you the story leaving any doubt as to that," said Aunt Hattie, glaring at me. The Campbells believed there were two sides to the story about Blind Billy, our side and the wrong side.

"Maybe you'd better refresh my memory," Steve said.

Then she motioned with her cane, down the beach and past the government dock where Drew was fishing with his cousins, and began the story I had heard every summer of my life.

"Every time I look down that river I think of that miserable son of a bitch," she said. "There's no doubt Blind Billy was a miserable S.O.B. Many's the time I heard my mother, his own daughter, say that.

"He was drunk more than he was sober, and he was a mean drunk. That's why they called him Blind Billy, because when he was blind drunk he'd hit anybody in his reach. It didn't matter if it was the sheriff or his wife. That's why nobody believed Tricky Dicky MacDougall's story.

"It was early in May when Blind Billy and Tricky Dicky went off to do some muskrat trapping. This was in '04. It wasn't like the old days when trapping fur was like coining money, but you could still do good from the trap lines if you knew what was what. Blind Billy knew his stuff but he'd lost his boat that spring. He was too drunk to pull it up on shore one night and it washed out in a storm. Got smashed to pieces. He'd drunk up all the money from the year before so he couldn't buy a new one, and he didn't have time to build another.

"Tricky Dicky didn't know dick-all about trapping 'rats, but he had the best boat in Fort Allen and an eye for the dollar, so they hooked up together. It worked pretty good, until that one day.

"Grandma Campbell started getting worried about dinner time, when they weren't back. Mama was just four years old then, but she remembered that Grandma Campbell had dinner ready at six on the dot because Blind Billy always liked to eat at the same time. She started worrying because she knew he'd taken a bottle with him but no more food than an apple and a bit of cheese, and it wasn't like him to miss dinner.

"By ten o'clock it was dark and still no sign of Blind Billy. But there wasn't much she could do about that. She put the kids to bed, all but Harold, because he wasn't born yet but she stayed up all night by the fire, working on that crib blanket. She was just putting in the last row when she heard the boat pulling up.

"At first Grandma Campbell thought there was no sign of Blind Billy. She could see by the moonlight and she didn't see him sitting up in the boat. But he was in there, lying on the bottom of it. He was dead drunk, Tricky Dicky claimed. He told Grandma that Blind Billy had got to drinking, saying he'd stay out all night raising hell if he felt like it. Then he'd got into one of his rages and started thrashing around and fell out of the boat. Tricky Dicky said he'd hit his head on a rock and knocked himself out and that he, Dicky, had hauled him back into the boat and brought him home.

"They woke Mama up when they put him to bed, although they were trying to be quiet. Mama said she heard Tricky Dicky say, 'I'll do that, Edna. If we wake him up he'll beat the bejesus out of both of us.' Then she heard Dicky lift him onto the bed and leave. Grandma was crying a little bit when she crawled in bed with Mama.

"The next thing Mama knew it was morning and Grandma Campbell was waking her up to tell her Blind Billy was dead, that he'd never woke up. There was no sign that he'd suffered, just a few drops of dried blood under his ear on the side where his head had been hit.

"Mama said it was at the funeral when it all came out, when her oldest brother Earl found out Tricky Dicky was keeping all the trap lines. Dicky said Blind Billy had borrowed money from him and that the traplines were the collateral. That's when people started talking, saying that Tricky Dicky had got Blind Billy drunk and hit him on the head when he was passed out. They figured Billy was already dead when Dicky brought him home and that's why he wouldn't let Grandma Campbell get too close."

"Uncle Earl got mad and said Grandma needed money to live on didn't she? He said Tricky Dicky was taking food right out of the mouths of her kids. But Dicky said Billy was alive when he left him, that he was a drunk who hit his own head, and that was that.

"Grandma Campbell said she'd get by, that being a widow was bad enough without the whole of Fort Allen talking about her husband's boozing, that she'd rather just get on with it. She never complained, not one word. But the bad blood was there."

She stopped there, but we knew the rest of the story. That bad blood was the life's blood of the families who summered in Fort Allen, even though they had long spent their working lives in the city four hours to the south. It dictated who went to barbecues at whose cottage, whose kids played with whose, who could park their visitors' cars in which driveway. Categorizing families by a feud that went back four generations was as much a part of our summers as getting one of the Howards from Dog Lake to turn on the water at the cottage the weekend before May 24th.

The feud had been fueled by the fact that the MacDougalls owned the hotel, bought with money from the trap line. For generations the Campbells had been forced to buy their ice cream cones and rye and cokes from the progeny of a murdering son of a bitch. But tradition also said that the MacDougalls were tight with a dollar and so it seemed part of the natural order that Campbell money ended up in MacDougall hands. The MacDougalls, for their part, insisted that if the Campbells wanted to drink away all their money, it might as well pour into MacDougall pockets.

Now, as we sat in the ghost of Grandma Campbell's living room with the dull throb of the MacDougall's jukebox in the background, Aunt Hattie repeated her original question.

"What are we going to do about Blind Billy? The MacDougalls want to dig him up you know."

I knew, of course. It was the talk of the summer. The MacDougalls were expanding the hotel and had applied for a permit to build a beer patio where the graveyard stood. It meant digging up the six bodies there, five MacDougalls and Blind Billy.

Billy had been laid there to save Grandma Campbell the price of a cemetery plot and the family had not had the money to move him after the feud broke out. He had lain peacefully in the same spot for over 90 years and we had come to regard his gravestone as a constant reminder to the MacDougall family of their patriarch's iniquity.

Now the Campbells were gathering forces, determined to save Blind Billy from another indignity at the hands of the MacDougalls. The law said MacDougalls had to foot the cost of moving the body, but it also said the Campbells had some say in where Billy ended up. And the Campbells were inclined to leave him right where he was if it bothered the MacDougalls.

The feud might have waged on for another four generations, with Drew telling his children to keep away from those thieving MacDougall pups. But I told Aunt Hattie I'd pay for a new stone for Blind Billy in the Highboro cemetery.

The inscription was of her choosing: "The voice of thy brother's blood crieth unto me from the ground." Every time a MacDougall was buried in the Highboro cemetery, the mourners would have to pass by those words. (For their part, the MacDougalls had decided to act like the words weren't directed to them. I suppose they figured if that's what it took to get Bob his beer patio permit, so be it.)

Since I was footing a big chunk of the bill, Aunt Hattie said I had a duty to stick around till the week after Labour Day when they were due to dig up Blind Billy. And so my summer stretched on a bit longer after Steve and Drew had returned to work and school. I had traded my T-shirt and shorts for a sweater and jeans when the day of the exhumation rolled around.

I heard the back hoe before I saw it scraping away at the century of dirt that covered Blind Billy. As I headed up the beach towards the hotel, I could see the tip of the shovel as it thrust out towards the river, then swung back in to scoop away at the grave. When I got closer I could make out the individual MacDougalls standing to the left of the graveyard, facing the Campbells gathered on the right. I joined my cousins in their vigil.

Aunt Hattie stood watch from her screened-in porch, Harold's crib blanket wrapped around her shoulders against the chill creeping into the September air. She stood alone, peering through her binoculars until

Billy's rotting box was unearthed and his remains hermetically sealed for transportation to Morrison's funeral parlour.

Aunt Hattie did not wait to see the fate of the remaining MacDougall boxes. She called her clan to her house and we obediently headed over. Taking off our shoes at the door, we waited in the old kitchen while Hattie poured our rye and cokes. Then we headed into the parlour where Aunt Hattie replaced Harold's blanket in its usual spot.

A while later we heard the MacDougalls move from the gravesite to continue their family celebration in the hotel next door. I pictured them gathered around the cigarette-scarred tables, having a few rounds of draught in honour of Tricky Dicky. When Aunt Hattie and I went back out to the kitchen for more drinks, we could hear them baritoning Loch Lomond.

That's when John Morrison, the funeral director, came in. I'd been expecting John, a convivial man whose family had been burying Campbells and MacDougalls for years. It was tradition around Fort Allen that all bills were handed over in person and no Campbell account with Morrison's had ever been settled by mail.

"Hello John, are you ready for a decent rye?" said Aunt Hattie. She knew he had gone to the hotel first to present the MacDougall bill.

"Don't mind if I do, Hattie," he said.

She prepared him a drink and made some small talk. Then, stubbornly balancing a tray-load of drinks, she hobbled back out to the parlour, leaving me to complete the family business.

"Hello missy," John said to me, scraping forward one of the kitchen chairs. "I thought I'd catch you before you went back to the city." After we sat down at the kitchen table he handed me the bill for Blind Billy's monument.

"There's one more thing," John said, after checking to make sure Aunt Hattie was out of earshot. "I know this sounds weird, but I thought you'd want to know."

"There wasn't much left of Blind Billy after 90 years, just the bones. That's not unusual, I've seen that before. But when we were putting him in the new box, I could hear something sort of clattering around in his skull," Morrison said.

"I thought I'd better take a look and I found this," he said. He handed me a plain white envelope, with the words 'Blind Billy' pencilled just above my name.

Inside was the one-inch tip of Grandma Campbell's ivory knitting needle.

MURDER BY MOONLIGHT

by Marguerite McDonald

Maude's headlights picked up the red Ferrari parked in the narrow roadway. "Uh-oh," she muttered to herself. "Bruno is back."

She inched her car around Bruno Zadorski's vehicle, and gritted her teeth as branches dragged along the driver's side. "Damn that man! I'm going to call the police and have him towed. Enough is enough!" She backed into the parking spot on her own property and looked around.

It was shortly before ten on a moonlit night in late August. The birch trees stood stark white against darker trunks, the leaves shimmered where the moonlight touched them, and the river beyond lay so still it made her catch her breath.

It took only half an hour to drive from Ottawa up into the Gatineau Hills of Quebec, to the silver silence here along a broad stretch of the Gatineau River. And yet the transition rarely failed to soothe her spirit.

From far up the valley, she heard the faint moaning whistle of the Wakefield steam train.

"Lost in contemplation?" The man's voice made Maude jump.

A short, stocky figure stepped out of the shadows.

"Bruno!" she said in a strangled voice.

Bruno Zadorski gave a short bark of a laugh.

Maude's heart thudded, but she kept her voice under control. "When did you get here?"

"This morning. My new play has just opened in Toronto and the critics all agree it's brilliant." The director-producer struck a theatrical pose. "For my reward, five days in the Gatineau Hills. Tuesday I go to San Francisco to work on an opera."

A grey Japanese car pulled up behind Bruno's Ferrari. Their neighbour, Suzanne Pelley, put her head out the window. "Bruno, would you move your car? I don't think I can get past. Winston will be furious. I'm keeping him waiting."

"My dear lady there is plenty of room. Allow me to direct you."

He waved her car well away from his own vehicle and into the bushes on the side of the road. There was a nasty tearing sound and the Subaru emerged with its side mirror gouged and bent.

"You see?" he said. "Nothing to worry about."

"Oh Bruno!" Suzanne Pelley was near tears. "What am I going to tell Winston?" She began to babble. "We're going out to the pub in Chelsea to watch the Ottawa Lynx on the big screen. And I'm late. We'll just make the second game of the double-header." She gave them both a desperate look. "What am I going to do?"

Maude grimaced in sympathy. Major Winston Pelley ran his home like an army unit – and Suzanne clearly hailed from the ranks.

Meanwhile Bruno peered down his nose at Suzanne and made a dismissive gesture. "If you're late, I suggest you get home as soon as possible."

He watched Suzanne's car head down the hill towards her cottage at the water's edge. "I see why the Major does not allow his wife to drive the big classic Cadillac," he said. "She is very stupid."

"Bruno," Maude said, "forget Suzanne. Forget the Cadillac. Your own car is a menace in this roadway. You do the same thing every summer – and I'm not going to stand for it anymore. You have no excuse. There's lots of room in the community parking lot just up the road. If you don't get your vehicle out of here by morning, I'll have someone move it for you."

Bruno laughed again. "You WASPS are so uptight! Relax! Live a little!" And with a wave he crossed the road to his cabin.

Maude ground her teeth. That man!

She climbed the crushed stone path that led toward her own cottage. She loved this odd little property. It was sandwiched between an old railway line that cut through an outcropping of rock, on the west, and a road that angled down the hillside to the river below, on the east.

There were no lights on in the side porch facing her or in her stepson's room beside it. Maude walked through the cottage to the verandah on the other side. Her husband Tom was sprawled in the hammock, his face smooth and relaxed as he read a science journal. His son was thumbing through his collection of classic comic books. Both had the same abundant dark hair, but Damien's was encircled by a headband made from a bandana.

Maude tried to gauge the climate of the room. Her stepson was thirteen and given to dark moods.

"I come home from a twelve-hour work-day and there's no one to greet me when I arrive!" she said with a tentative grin.

Damien leaped to his feet. "Hi, Maude," he said. "Do you want to go for a swim? The water's great!"

"Thanks," Maude said. "I think I'll take my water with a large scotch, if you don't mind." When she saw the enthusiasm drain from his face she cast around for an alternative. "How about around eleven, after I've had something to eat? The moon will still be out."

He thought a moment. "O.K." He nodded. "That's cool."

The phone rang.

"I'll get it!" Damien darted into the kitchen. A moment later, he shouted, "It's for me. I'll take it in my room." He gallumped down the hall.

"A girl?" Maude asked.

"Who knows?" Tom spread his hands. "My son no longer blabs everything that comes into his head, the way he used to. He's just spent an hour sitting in the dark, talking to his friends on the phone, but I have no idea what he's thinking."

Car doors slammed out on the road and irate voices disturbed the quiet. That does it, Maude thought. That Ferrari has got to go. I'm calling the police – first thing in the morning."

The Wakefield tourist train came chugging round the curve of the bay, the antique steam engine giving sharp whistle blasts at every level crossing.

Suddenly, there was a long, angry blast, and the screech of steel brakes against steel. The train ground to a halt behind the cottage. Something was very wrong.

Maude and Tom scrambled down the rocks to the track just as the engineer swung down from the steam engine. The conductor was striding along the right-of-way from the back of the train.

As they made their way forward, the engineer saw them and cried out, "I tried to stop. As soon as I saw it on the track, I tried to stop!"

At that moment, Damien came barrelling down the rockface.

Now they could see the engineer standing near a dark mound on the railway ties. The conductor shone the powerful beam of his flashlight toward it. The light paused just behind the engine's wheel. In that moment, Maude caught a glimpse of mangled flesh and clothing before the light moved on, along the upper torso of a man to his face. There, sightless eyes stared past them into the night sky.

Damien pushed in amongst them to get a better look. "Mr Zadorski!" he gasped. "That's Mr. Zadorski!" And he fainted.

Over the next few hours, Maude kept the nausea and horror she felt under firm control. There was Damien to deal with. She and Tom helped him back to the cottage and put him to bed. She mixed him brandy and hot water and then decided to make another batch for Tom and herself.

Neighbours who'd gone to the track to gawk trickled into the cottage to talk about the shock of it all and to take more glasses of proffered brandy.

Police came to the door with sharply worded questions. Strange how they made you feel *you* were under suspicion, Maude thought.

Tom firmly turned aside their attempts to talk to Damien.

Then a policewoman came to get someone to sit with Bruno's girlfriend. Maude stayed with her until Carole's sister arrived to take her into the city.

Throughout it all, Maude kept clamping down on the image of Bruno's mangled body and his eyes wide open in death.

It was after one before the last of the visitors left.

Tom checked one more time on Damien before they climbed into bed and huddled together under the covers.

"How's he doing now?" Maude asked.

"Still pretty shocked I think. He's stretched out in the dark with headphones on, listening to music." Tom said. "What about Carole? Was she here when the train hit Bruno?"

"No. She'd gone to the airport to meet her mother's plane. She arrived back here at the cottage to find police cars all over the neighbourhood. She was stunned, of course. I felt pretty helpless. There wasn't much I could do except listen."

Tom shook his head. "She was full of chatter and vitality when she came over this morning."

"She was here?"

"Yeah. She wanted to borrow an axe. She made quite an impression on Damien."

"He's probably never met a pretty young actress in the flesh before," Maude said reaching to turn out the light.

"In this case there was a lot of exposed flesh to meet," Tom said. "She was wearing short shorts and a little bikini top. Damien went around with a glazed look for the rest of the day. Then, this afternoon he saw her at the beach. She told him she was a Yankees' fan – and that clinched it. He gave her his baseball cap."

"The cap you brought back from New York? The treasured? The one and only?"

"The very one."

"Actually," Maude said, "I was surprised to see her out here at the cottage. I thought she and Bruno broke up last fall. Remember? He cast someone else for a part she wanted."

She could feel Tom shrug.

"Well, they were definitely back together today." He thought a moment. "Did she have any idea what Bruno was doing lying across the railway tracks?"

"None. Apparently the corporal who talked to her wondered if it might be suicide."

"Well, I suppose it's possible . . . "

"Uh uh! No way," Maude said. "Not now. *Not* when his play is doing so well. Not ever. You need a certain frame of mind for suicide. Bruno Zadorski didn't know the meaning of guilt or self-doubt."

"And we both know he wasn't a big drinker. And I doubt he was into drugs," Tom said. "That leaves two other possibilities."

"I know," Maude said. "Either it was something like a heart attack – or it was murder."

When at last she slept, Maude's dreams were filled with blood and terror.

In the morning, Maude decided the best thing she could do was stick to routine. She went down to the river for her usual morning swim.

Major Winston Pelley was washing his big white Cadillac near his cottage, while his wife hung out a clothesline of T-shirts.

Suzanne straightened her long, skinny body, pushed her cap up off her face, and came over to the fence to talk. She looked paler and more anxious than ever.

"I still feel a little stunned about everything that's happened," she confided to Maude. "I got a call from Bruno's ex-wife last night, after the police went to break the news to Bruno's son."

"How's the boy handling the news?"

"He's away on a wilderness canoe trip. They won't be able to reach him for a couple of days. Andrea was home alone when the police got there."

"I hadn't thought about Andrea Zadorski. But she was married to Bruno for more than ten years. She must have a whole mixture of feelings."

"Yeah. I went over and made her a cup of tea, and we sat at the kitchen table while she drank it. Then she said I should leave. And thank you for coming. I mean, I didn't really mind. It only took me a few minutes to walk over there and everything . . . but there was something strange."

"What's that?"

"Well, she looked as though . . . I know this sounds funny but . . . it was like she couldn't figure out how she felt."

Major Winston Pelley gave his car's bumper one last flick of his polishing cloth. "Tragic thing for our neighbourhood," he said.

"Speaking of neighbourhood," Maude said, "I'm trying to decide whether it would be neighbourly to go and pay a formal sympathy call on Carole after work – or whether to wait until tomorrow. I thought we might try to go together."

"Can't do anything today," said the major. "I've got an important job interview this afternoon." He leaned forward confidentially. "By this time tomorrow, I may be the new executive assistant to the Minister of Defence!"

"How nice for you," Maude said half-heartedly.

Pelley suddenly looked sheepish. "I shouldn't be talking about a promotion at a time like this. Have you heard anything more about Zadorski?"

Maude shook her head. "I may get something later today." Now it was her turn to feel sheepish. "I have an old boyfriend in the Sûreté du Quebec. He's an inspector now."

The major gave her a knowing wink.

"But so far I haven't thought much beyond what I saw last night," Maude said. "You know, it's one thing to deal with accidents and murders in news stories, but this is different. Someone died a horrible death at the edge of my own back yard."

Maude threw herself into her work at the office, but when she did allow herself to think about Bruno's death she was surprised to find herself oppressed by a real sense of loss. Bruno Zadorski could be profoundly irritating, but in a real conversation, ideas sparked off him like strings of firecrackers.

Had someone killed him? She knew Bruno angered many people. There was his arrogance – and his contempt for those who lived around him. There was a troubled relationship with his ex-wife. And who knew what professional and personal jealousies he might have stirred up?

Around noon, Maude called her old flame. "So what do you know about Zadorski's death?" she asked.

"Maude, you know I'm not supposed to tell you anything," he said.

"Come on. You can tell your ol' buddy," Maude coaxed.

"Look, Maude, it's not my case."

"But I bet there's a lot of gossip around the police station."

There was a long silence. Then he said, "You understand that this is completely off the record?"

"My lips are sealed."

"Well, the autopsy results are in. The buzz around here is that he was still alive when the train hit him. But he already had bruises and some hemorrhaging from an injury on the back of his head.

"That means . . . ?"

"They think someone must have whacked him with the proverbial blunt object while he was out walking along the tracks. Either that, or if you wanna stretch things, a couple of guys carried him there. No one found any drag marks near the railway line. Anyway, he was very much alive when the train hit him."

"Would whoever laid him across the tracks know this?" Maude asked.

"Any twelve-year-old knows enough to check for a pulse, Maude. Someone carefully arranged his body across the tracks so the train would do maximum damage. Where I come from that's called first-degree murder."

Later, when she checked with Tom at home, Maude found the police had come by twice to question Damien.

"They seem to think he has something to hide," said a concerned Tom. "What they don't seem to understand is that thirteen-year-olds rarely have anything worthwhile to say to adults. And besides, he's still very shaken by what he saw."

"Do you think we should call a lawyer? I don't like the sound of this."

"Not yet. If they keep coming back, I'll tell them they're harrassing the kid and I'll get some legal advice."

Maude wasn't satisfied. What she needed, she thought, was to find out as much as she could about the people who knew Bruno Zadorski.

She tried Carole several times, but her calls met a solid wall of answering machine messages.

On the way home from work, she detoured to the other end of the beach road to see Bruno's ex-wife Andrea. Maude remembered Andrea from the first summer they'd met. In those days, she'd been stunning: graceful and well-muscled, with the height to carry it off. Since her divorce, she'd been putting on a few pounds a year, and now she was solid flesh.

The big woman began talking the moment Maude appeared at her door. "Good! It's you. I want you to show me where the train hit Bruno. The police say it was near where you live. I want to see for myself."

"I don't want to go back to the railway track, Andrea."

"What's the matter with you? You can't tell me they haven't taken away the body!"

Maude felt her stomach lurch. She swallowed hard. "No, Andrea. It's just not a good idea." She turned back towards the car.

"Well, if you feel that way, I'll give Damien a call. I've known him since he was five. I'll just tell him I want to see him down at your place."

It was perfectly calculated to stop Maude in mid-step. She knew Andrea. Knew she'd be willing to involve the boy.

"Get in the car, Andrea. I'll take you."

Maude led Andrea from the parking area, down the steps cut in the rock to the tracks below. There were stains and chalk marks on the railway ties, but nothing else to indicate the tragedy.

"So that's where the bastard bought it," Andrea said. She hunched down and looked north along the rails as though she were imagining an approaching train. Then she grunted and stood up.

"Well, that puts a stop to his screwing around."

She looked Maude directly in the eyes. "I suppose that girl . . . Carole? I suppose she thinks she meant something special to him."

Maude shrugged noncommitally.

"Well, let me tell you, each new woman was just another piece of meat to him. And he always had two or three on the side. To feed that over-inflated ego of his. Now the conquering hero is gone . . . for good!"

Andrea turned abruptly away. Her shoulders began to shake but Maude had no idea whether the big woman was sobbing or laughing as she followed the tracks in the general direction of home.

Maude was still feeling sick and rattled when she walked into her own cottage. She met Damien coming along the hall from his room. "Hi, Damien," she said trying to keep her voice even. "How was your day?"

Damien's eyes filled with tears. "You don't care, do you? You don't really care that someone died out there last night, do you? You go for a swim. You go to work. You even take the locals to see the spot where it happened. And you don't give a damn!" He put on a mimicking voice. " 'Hi Damien. How was your day?' How do you think it was – knowing the track is right behind those rocks? Someone murdered Mr. Zadorski – right there."

"How do you know he was murdered?" Maude asked sharply.

A series of emotions crossed the boy's face. In the end, scorn triumphed. "Pretty obvious, isn't it? You don't have to be a brain surgeon to figure it out. I mean, like, the guy was going to lie down on the tracks and let the train run over him – because he was famous and he had a good-looking girlfriend and a Ferrari. Right! What do you think I am – a retard or something?" With that, he turned back to his room and slammed the door.

Maude and Tom were getting the evening meal together when a corporal from the Sûreté knocked on their door. It was routine, she said. Just checking again with everyone in the neighbourhood to see if anyone had remembered anything more about the hour leading up to the "train accident."

Tom shook his head.

"Not really," Maude said. She called up her memory of the scene. "You could hear the train whistle up the river. There were the usual hassles about parking . . . but everything looked normal, in fact, everything looked particularly beautiful last night when I got home. That was half an hour, maybe forty minutes before the train got here."

"Could I speak to your son again?"

Reluctantly Tom went to summon Damien.

Damien faced the corporal sulkily. "No, I told you before. I didn't see *anything*. I was talking on the phone with a *friend*. I didn't have time to do any spying. Anything else?"

The corporal shook her head.

"*Good*," Damien said, and disappeared down the hall.

After the corporal left, Tom went back to dicing vegetables, while Maude got the salmon steaks ready for the grill.

"You know," she said, "when I drove Andrea Zadorski over here this afternoon, I kept thinking about what a jerk Bruno could be. Remember how he turned up at Andrea's birthday party – uninvited – with Carole in tow?"

"Pretty hard to forget," Tom chuckled. "Those were some fireworks!"

Maude didn't think it was funny at all. "When Andrea picked up that poker and started waving it around, I really thought she was going to beat them both to a pulp. And the look of pure hatred on her face!"

"If she were going to kill Bruno, she's had ample opportunity long before now," Tom said.

"I'm just considering every possibility, Tom. A lot of the neighbours use the tracks for a footpath. She could have been walking there last night. What if she saw Bruno?"

Maude thought a moment. "Here's another possibility: Carole. What if Bruno did have another woman or two on the side, the way Andrea says he always did? Do you think that could have made Carole angry enough to kill him?"

"If she wasn't here, she couldn't have done it," Tom said.

"Well, I know Carole says she was at the airport, but we don't know what time her mother's plane arrived. Is all her time accounted for? And what if she and Bruno had quarrelled again?"

Tom pulled a face. "She doesn't seem like much of a killer to me."

"I know she's blonde, rosy-cheeked and wholesome-looking, but . . . " Maude's voice trailed off.

"I thought you said she was pretty devastated by the news."

"You're right. But remember that Carole is an actress. She could have faked the shock and disbelief." Maude looked off at the hills across the river. "I really don't know what to believe."

By the time dinner was over, life in the cottage had settled down. Damien's mood had eased back to sullen and morose. "The men" took on the dishwashing detail, while Maude tidied up the verandah. She took a load of Damien's belongings down the hall to his room.

The moonrise caught her eye and she stopped to look out at the scene. She'd never noticed how much you could see from Damien's room. No wonder he kept a chair turned so he could look out the window.

A couple from a cottage on the other side of the railway tracks came into view, walking up the hill from the river's edge. It was late for them to be coming up from the beach. They turned into Maude and Tom's parking area. In spite of the recent tragedy, they took the short-cut through the parking spot and started down the steps to the railway track, heading for a path on the other side. They were doing a clumsy job of carrying a large picnic hamper between them.

Something stirred in the back of Maude's mind. She blinked. Then she blinked again. "Damien," she called. "Damien. Could you come into your room for a minute?"

Damien was still holding a dish-towel when he appeared in the doorway.

"I think we should sit down because I have something to ask you," Maude said. "I wouldn't pry – except that – well, it's important."

The light from the hall revealed a wary look on his face.

Maude took a small stool, and that left the armchair for Damien. Reluctantly he sat and looked out the window, avoiding her eyes.

"Damien, I need to know what you saw last night, when you came in here to take that call from your friend."

Damien put his head down and scuffed the side of his shoe on the carpet. "I told you. I told that policewoman. I didn't see anything. I was talking on the phone." He continued to stare at his shoe.

"Let's think back to yesterday evening. You come into the room. You flop down in the chair and pick up the phone beside it. You're talking to your friend – "

"To Sheila."

"O.K., you're talking to Sheila here in the dark – and you notice some movement out there in the moonlight. It's two people. You get a glimpse of them struggling with something very heavy – and very awkward – between them. Maybe you recognize one of them at this point. Maybe you don't. How am I doing so far?"

Damien's face had gone white and frozen.

"At the time you don't think much about it. You go on talking. But a few minutes later the train runs over something on the track behind the cottage." Maude waited but Damien did not react. "And then we see Mr. Zadorski's body."

There was a long silence.

Maude took a deep breath. "You believe you might hurt someone – someone you like a lot – if you tell what you saw."

Maude thought she saw him flinch.

"There's something I have to tell you, Damien. Mr. Zadorski was still alive – alive but probably unconscious – when someone laid him across those tracks. That means that the people you saw carrying his body through the parking lot – those people intended him to die."

Still the boy said nothing.

"Listen, Damien. Do you want to go on wondering for the rest of your life – wondering if someone you know did this terrible thing? Isn't that worse than knowing the truth – whatever it is? Tell me what you saw. Please."

Misery and defeat swept over his face. "I don't know what to do! I don't know what to do!" He turned away from her and stared out the window.

Tentatively she reached out and touched his arm. And she waited.

Suddenly Damien sat up straight. Maude realized he was watching two teenage boys and a girl take the short-cut to the railway track. His mouth dropped open. "Those guys are all wearing baseball caps," he said in wonder.

"Yeah? Is this important, Damien?"

"They look just like my New York Yankees cap – the one I gave to Carole."

"In this light I suspect all baseball caps look pretty much the same."

"You think so?" Damien's face seemed lit from the inside. "I just saw them for a minute the other night – and I thought one of them was Carole for sure – because she was wearing my baseball cap. But maybe it wasn't my Yankees cap! Maybe it wasn't Carole! Maybe it was somebody else!" There was elation in his voice. "It couldn't have been Carole, could it? She wouldn't do a thing like that, would she?"

"What did she look like – apart from the cap, Damien?"

"Well she had these long legs . . . " Damien's face fell. "It could still be Carole, couldn't it? Carole and somebody else. I couldn't see much of the guy who was with her." He thought about it for a moment. "But it doesn't have to be."

Once Damien had talked to his father, Maude picked up the phone. She caught her friend the inspector just as he was leaving the office.

"Not much new," he said. "They've pretty well established that the girlfriend has an air-tight alibi. There's an independent witness who puts her at the airport 45 minutes before the police officer met her at the cottage – but apart from that they're – "

"Let me get this straight," Maude interrupted him. "You say the police are satisfied with Carole's alibi." Damien and Maude's eyes met. "She couldn't have been here at the time of the murder. That's great! Thanks. Thanks a lot. You're still a sweetheart!"

Damien sank down in his chair and began to sob. It took a while before he could tell them anything more about the man and woman he'd seen so briefly, carrying a big bundle, wrapped in a blanket.

Maude tried to probe gently. "Do you remember seeing anything else out there that night?"

Damien screwed up his eyes, concentrating.

"I could see your car and Dad's . . . and I think Mr. Zadorski's Ferrari was across the road . . . and there was the other car."

"Another car?"

"Yeah. I couldn't see it very well." He looked back out the window at the path down to the parking area. "I guess it was mostly behind that hedge in front of the house."

Maude considered the information. "Any idea of colour or model?"

"I couldn't see much of it. But I could tell it was light-coloured – there was enough moonlight for that."

Maude pulled on a sweater and walked down towards the river. Cloud was sliding up the sky from the northwest, but it hadn't yet covered the moon. Lightning flickered along the horizon.

When she knocked at the Pelleys' door, the major answered. "Suzanne has gone out for a breath of fresh air. I think she wanted to be alone," he said, giving Maude a meaningful look.

"Well, I'll probably look in on her tomorrow," Maude said. "I just wanted to see how she was doing."

"She's fine – just a little upset – you know, about the accident."

"Right," Maude said. She was going down the steps when she stopped. "Oh, I meant to ask you about the game last night."

"The game?" Winston Pelley looked surprised.

"Weren't you and Suzanne going to watch a Lynx game on the big screen in Chelsea?"

"No. Where did you get that idea?"

"I don't know. It must have been somebody else," Maude said.

"We had a video I wanted to see. In fact, we were watching it when we heard the train."

Maude found Suzanne at the beach, sitting huddled on a log forty yards or so from her cottage. They sat together for a while looking out over the water. The moonlight picked up every detail on a little island just off from the shore.

Maude decided to take a chance. "I was thinking about Bruno," she said, "and how he must have felt watching that train coming at him – knowing he was going to die."

Suzanne shook her head violently. "But he didn't see it coming! He was already dead!"

"What makes you think that?"

"He had to be, didn't he? I mean, he wouldn't just be lying there, would he?"

"Listen to me, Suzanne. He was simply unconscious. Whoever left him on the tracks actually murdered him in cold blood."

"But Winston said he was already dead! He said no one would ever know . . . !" Suddenly she clamped a hand to her mouth and turned a stricken face towards Maude.

"Suzanne, the police have evidence that Bruno was alive when the train hit him."

Suzanne wouldn't look at her.

"How did it happen?" Maude asked. "You and the major probably got into his big Cadillac to go out to watch the Lynx game at the pub. When you got to the top of the hill, there sat Bruno's Ferrari blocking the road."

Suzanne began to tremble.

"There was an argument out on the road – "

"It was an accident," Suzanne said quickly. "Really it was. Winston was already so angry with me. You know. I – I was late and I'd scratched the car. And then Bruno laughed at him, and told him to get a life."

Her voice began to quiver. "Winston didn't mean to hurt him. Really he didn't," she insisted. "Winston just pushed him around a little and Bruno fell backwards against the Cadillac. He hit his head on the bumper. And then he lay there on the ground."

Suzanne's face was full of misery now.

"Exactly what did Winston do?" Maude asked.

Suzanne closed her eyes. "Well, he felt for Bruno's pulse – at the wrist and at the neck. And then he straightened up and he didn't say anything for awhile. I said, 'Is he going to be O.K.?' And Winston said, 'Shut up, will you? I'm thinking!' "

"And then what?"

"He said Bruno was dead. He said if I didn't want his career to go up in smoke, I'd help him move the body to the tracks. I didn't want to touch a dead body, so Winston got an old blanket out of the car and we wrapped him in it."

"If Bruno had regained consciousness," Maude said, "he'd have been sure to press charges for assault. We all knew Bruno. He'd milk every opportunity for all the drama he could find. And that would have meant the end of your husband's chance at a big job with the Minister of Defence."

"Oh, Winston wouldn't think that way, he wouldn't . . . " Suzanne's voice trailed off again. She met Maude's eyes. The moonlight illuminated her thin face and now Maude watched it fill with horror.

"Are you saying he wouldn't be ruthless enough to commit murder?"

Suzanne's body sagged. Tears began to roll down her cheeks. Maude dug into her pocket and found her a kleenex.

They heard the cottage door open behind them. "Suzanne?" Major Pelley called. "Come here."

Suzanne stood up in answer to his command but Maude put out a restraining hand.

"Hi, Major. We're just watching the clouds move in," Maude called.

He ignored Maude. "Suzanne, I want you in the cottage. *Now!*" His voice was angrier.

"Come on, Major." Maude put on a jolly tone. "I promise Suzanne will be under cover before the storm breaks."

She could see him silhouetted against the light in the open doorway as he peered into the darkness.

Thunder rumbled in the distance.

Maude held her breath. Would he come out to get his wife?

The landscape began to darken as the first clouds drifted across the moon.

He stepped forward to the edge of the deck.

"Just a few minutes." Maude kept her voice cheerful. "I promise."

He hesitated. In the silence they could hear the thunder growing closer.

He turned back into the cottage and slammed the door behind him.

Suzanne began to shake violently.

Maude draped her sweater over the woman's shoulders. "Are you O.K.?" she asked.

Suzanne hunched her body under the sweater.

"Let's go up to my cottage," Maude said, taking her by the arm. "We can call the police from there."

IT'S NO MYSTERY TO ME

Black flies in the deep woods,
Mosquitoes in the reeds,
Hawks up in the tree tops,
Rattlers in the weeds,
Badgers in the burrows,
Foxes in a den,
Wasps on every tree branch,
Skunks in every glen.

I'm surrounded by a bevy
Of naturally scary things,
Of toothed and furry killers
And criminals with wings,
So I'll stay within my cottage,
I won't even take a look.
I prefer my "Nature" indoors
And my mayhem in a book.

Joy Hewitt Mann

HEAR NO EVIL

by Linda Wiken

"Have you thought of garrotting him?"

"What? Get real. In a hotel full of conventions? Not a guarantee you'd get away with murder."

"We'd plant clues all over the place. Implicate someone from each convention and watch the cops go crazy."

They couldn't be serious. She couldn't be hearing this! Martha Ingram waited until her hand trembled a little less before cautiously separating the leaves of the Dieffenbachia. Two blondes, one with long hair tied up in a pony tail, the other an obvious perm, facing each other in two straight back green chairs. Two coffee cups on the squat glass table. Empty love seat. No one nearby to overhear the plot.

Except for Martha. Blending in with the plants she tended, every morning, 7 - 10 a.m., at the Lakeshore Hotel. Start with the lobby – loads of Ficus, Dracaena, Calathea and others lapping up the light from all those floor-to-ceiling windows – the most recent attempt to update the seventy-year old lodge since its purchase by a national chain last year. There'd also been a total re-decorating scheme – nouveau rustic they'd called it, new plumbing, renovations to the conference area, and of course, a new name. The Lakeshore Hotel on beautiful Flange Lake. The new windows had begged for plants, which meant an ongoing contract for Martha and a nice balance sheet for the business.

She'd planned to trim some brown tips before moving over to the potted Fatshedera near the bank of elevators. But would they hear the scissors? She took another look. Both attractive young women, probably in their thirties, with badges pinned to their tops. What were they doing talking murder? Maybe she'd skip the trimming for now.

"I tell you, Susan, they were planning to kill some guy," Martha said, a little louder than the first time.

"People don't just sit around a hotel lobby and talk about murder, Mom. But if they do kill someone, you're a witness. Can you identify them? Did they see you? Are you safe?"

Martha eyed her daughter over the rim of her coffee mug. She was enjoying telling this story. Not a dull moment at the Lakeshore. "I guess. Or maybe I should just confront them. Tell them what I heard," she paused to savour the look of incredulity on Susan's face, "and demand to be written into the book."

"What?"

Martha laughed then sobered quickly at the look of annoyance on her daughter's face. "I asked Georgia about them. They're writers, Sisters in Crime they call themselves, and they're holding a writers' retreat at the hotel. You know, back to nature basics and far away from the madding crowd."

"Writers." Susan threw a soggy cloth at Martha. "Not very funny, Mom. I thought this was for real and you'd be in some sort of danger."

"Don't even think it. Owning *The Cottage Garden* is as dangerous as I want it. Bill collectors scratching at the door. Late shipments of soil from suppliers. Humourless daughter as a business partner grousing around about second-rate manure. Whatever made me think this would be fun?"

"What about poisoning him?"
"With what?"

Oh Gawd, here they go again. Martha shook her head as she peeked through the Monstera. They were sitting in the same spot, except these three females were not the same ones who had been plotting yesterday. What a weird bunch of women. You'd think they'd do all this in their workshops. Or at least, in the bar.

"I've got an idea," said the brunette. Obviously the oldest or maybe the swatch of grey bang was out of a bottle. "Get him down to the dock, tonight after the banquet. Give him a good whack on the head and shove him in the water. He'll be so pissed he won't know what hit him. The cops will rule it an accidental death, a drunk who slipped, hit his head, and drowned."

"But, will he die?" asked the petite redhead.

The brunette shrugged. "Hold him under."

"Oh, no, I couldn't do that."

"We'll all do it. Together. Like an Agatha Christie novel."

The smoker spoke up. "I vote for poison. Jill, you cosy up to him during cocktails – he'll go for that, as we all know. And I'll waltz by and slip a slow-acting poison in his drink. Sharon can add an extra diversion to make sure he doesn't catch on. Then, later in the evening, when we're all set up with alibis, he'll take the big one."

"But, could we actually kill him?" The redhead sounded scared. "That would be murder."

"Justifiable homicide, I'd call it. And it would definitely put him out of action. We've got to do something fast, before he chalks up another victim. Ashley's too naive to defend herself when the boss makes his moves."

"Just like we were," the redhead added.

The brunette shuddered. "If he rapes her . . . "

"We'll make sure he doesn't get the chance." The smoker stubbed out her cigarette. "We should have castrated the creep last time."

"What would we use for poison? I can't see waltzing into the local pharmacy. And I doubt anyone's brought samples."

"It doesn't have to be the skull-and-crossbones type. I've read that some of the over-the-counter stuff can be just as lethal depending on what it's mixed with. Nasal spray's like that. Think of it, next time you're working."

"How do you nasal spray a drink without being spotted?" The redhead again.

"Just an example. Any type of 'Mickey Finn' will do. Oh, looks like they're getting started. Give it some thought before coffee break."

I'd hate to get on the wrong side of a mystery writer, Martha thought as she pushed her cart towards the front desk. Poison, drowning. And whose story was it? Maybe a collaboration. She should get their names. It might be a best seller and she could say she knew them when they'd plotted in the lobby of The Lakeshore Hotel on the shores of beautiful Flange Lake, Ontario.

She grabbed a plastic mister from her cart and detoured to the concierge's desk. "Hi, Frank, how's it going?"

"Been pretty busy. How're things with you?"

"Not bad. At least the plants don't complain."

He looked shocked. "Nobody's been complaining about you have they?"

"No need to be concerned," but sweet, she thought. Too bad he was one step away from retirement. "You sure have some weird clients these days. Anything spooky been happening with all these mystery writers here?"

"Nope. Went smooth as punch. Great group of girls. Some of them were kinda crazy but I sort of miss them and their snappy lines."

Martha stopped wiping the Schefflera leaf. "Miss them? Are they gone?"

"Sure, the thing ended yesterday noon."

"Then what . . . ?" She whirled around to look at the now-empty corner. "You sure? What's going on today then?"

"Oh, a sales meeting for some drug sales reps. Like in the prescription type. Two days. The Blue Heron, Mallard, and Osprey rooms are booked from 8 to 5. Banquet tonight in the Gannets Room. They were here last year, too. Not big tippers.

"Too bad," Martha mumbled.

What were the chances that some of the mystery writers were also pharmaceutical sales reps? Three of them, in fact? Pretty slim. She glanced at her watch. If she did the mezzanine now, she could be back down in an hour, hopefully in time for that break. Those three needed to be kept under a watchful eye. And ear.

How many females did this company have on staff? Martha did the rounds of the lower level break tables twice looking for her elusive trio, then by-passed the slow elevators in favour of the stairs to the mezzanine, even though it was a bad day for her knees. Lots of brunettes, some redheads, but not the combination she wanted. Where the hell did they take their break?

She spotted them coming out of the washroom and heading right back into the Mallard Room. Damn. Why hadn't she checked there? Now she'd never know what they were up to. She watched as the doors closed, then went to search out the one person who could and should be doing something about this. The Hound.

Jack 'The Hound' Hounecker came by his nickname in two most appropriate ways. First, the deep shadows under his eyes, testimony to his late night activities; and second, his job as Chief of Hotel Security.

Martha found him in his 'office,' the corner booth in The Shoreline restaurant that flourished amid the flowering Campanula next to the lobby. He sat facing the large picture windows and the circular drive. She often suspected he used the window as a mirror, keeping an eye on his territory. As usual, he spoke before she reached him.

"Wondered what was keeping you, Martha."

"Some of us have work to do around here. Especially if we want to get paid." A cup of steaming coffee arrived as she slid into the booth beside him.

"You will let me know if we're missing any cacti or such, won't you?" He flashed Martha a lopsided smile that reminded her there was a short but determined line of unwed hotel employees with their sights on him. Of course, he was the only single male over the age of 20 on staff. Now, if she were 20 years younger . . .

"Glad you've nothing more important to worry about these days. Did you enjoy the murder and mayhem group?"

"What? Oh, the Sisters in Crime. Yup, a great bunch of gals, uh, sisters. They even had me speak at one of their sessions."

"Does that make you one of the gals?"

"Damn straight." He stuck out a lapel sporting a red and white enamel pin.

"Congratulations. By the way, Susan says 'hi'." A little white lie now and then didn't hurt. Susan would sooner sit on a cactus than send Jack a message, but he didn't need to know that.

Jack's eyebrows perked up. Not half bad looking, Martha thought, plus a good, steady job. Chance of advancement with a big hotel chain like this, even though it was the country cousin. Much better than that abusive bum Susan finally got rid of. Just needed some shaping up, a good, steady guiding influence. A Susan.

"So, how is Susan these days?" he asked.

"She's working too hard. I keep telling her she should take some time off, have some fun. Do her good to go out once in a while." Hint, hint. "Of course, if the new O.P.P. officer has his way, she'll be pretty busy."

"Lathem? He's been coming around?"

Martha brushed his question away with a wave of her hand. Keep him guessing. "A funny thing happened this morning. You know that northeast seating area in the lobby? The one with the huge Dieffenbachia?" Jack nodded even though his eyes had glazed over at the mention of plants. He'd have to get over that if he wanted to make points with Susan.

"As I was tending to them, I overheard three young women plotting a murder."

"You sure it wasn't yesterday morning? Sounds like something the Sisters in Crime group would do."

"I'm not senile yet, Jack. I know they're gone, that's why it's so crazy. But here these three were, trying to decide the best way to do this poor guy in."

Jack was giving her his full attention now. "You've got good ears, Martha. Your tips have paid off in the past. But, like you said, it's crazy. Were they guests?"

"Better than that, they're with the pharmaceutical convention."

"I don't suppose they gave you their names and room numbers?"

"No, but I got a good look at them. I can identify them."

"And then what? I can't stake them out for the next two days. Unless I go undercover, say as a 'plant' . . . man." He chuckled.

She ignored his attempt at humour. "You won't have to wait that long. It's going to happen tonight. At the banquet . . . or after . . . depending on which method they choose to do the deed."

"This is really the dumbest idea you've ever had, Mom."

"Nice of you to say so, Susan dear. I think the green dress would be better. You wouldn't stand out so much." Hard to blend into the surroundings with that flaming red hair, though. The only good thing her Dad gave her.

"You didn't invent this murder plot, did you, Mom?"

Martha stopped brushing her hair. "Now, why would I do that?"

"You've been trying to get me and Jack together for about three months now. And you never have been known to give up."

"The Hound? You think I'd want my only daughter with that overweight, sexist lush?" Sorry, Jack. I know what I'm doing.

"Don't you think you're laying it on a bit thick, Mom? So, he's got a slight pot belly. He could easily get in shape after a few weeks of running. And he does have a cute butt."

Martha was glad her back was turned so Susan couldn't see the smile on her face. "Whatever. You're Jack's date, his cover. We'll mix and mingle."

"Date? Don't think for one minute I'm thinking of Jack as my 'date'."

"Whatever. As soon as I've pointed out the lethal ladies, your non-date and you will make sure they don't victimize this poor sucker while he's enjoying his happy hour. I'll be ready to cover the dock in case they opt for plan two."

"You will be careful, won't you, Mom? It *is* murder we're talking about."

"Don't worry. The Hound will take over if there's any sign of trouble." I hope.

"Who moved those Norfolk Pines? They shouldn't be that close to the air conditioning."

"Give it a rest, Martha. You're not here with your watering can tonight." Jack grinned.

Martha glared.

Susan laughed and asked her mother, "Okay, so where are the bad gals, Master Sleuth?"

Martha scanned the crowd. Too many assorted hair colours and styles. She hoped the two brief looks she'd had of their faces would click in, even with the stylish outfits and after-eight make-up. "Well, let's schmooze our way on through here. They're obviously not going to form a line-up for me."

She led the way at a snail's pace through the sixty-plus bodies. The count came from Jack.

Twice she thought she'd spotted them. Third time lucky. All three were dressed in short chic, standing casually beside a potted palm which thanks to Martha's Tender Loving Care, had green leaves once again.

"That's them," she whispered, grabbing Jack's sleeve. "The blonde, brunette and redhead. Over there in the corner."

"Very nice."

Martha scowled at him. "This is work, remember?"

"Of course," he answered, turning to Susan. "Let's you and I ease our way over towards them. Remember, we're looking for the lone male who's their target. Keep a sharp eye on his glass. Martha, you come around on the other side."

"Right, chief."

Martha shivered as she checked her watch for the third time in ten minutes. Maybe she should have encouraged Jack to stake out the dock. Crouching behind a rack of overturned canoes was hard on arthritic knees. Oh, for a deck chair or at least a pillow.

And after this, she would ignore any strange conversations she heard in the lobby. Gawd, it was getting chilly. She thought longingly of her Hudson's Bay parka, packed away in her old cedar chest for at least another month. She made a slight adjustment to her knee angle, then flapped her arms and tried thinking warm thoughts . . . toasty fire, blazing sun, hot toddy.

She peered around the canoes and surveyed the scene one more time. They'd have to come straight towards her hiding spot at the end of the dock. The rowboats were tied in the water at her left side; the boathouse nestled in the 'U'-shape of the dock to her right. There was no other way for them to approach. She'd have a clear view of all that happened.

Martha tried shifting her weight, then froze at the sound of voices approaching. Male, female, and then some giggles.

She took deep breaths to slow down the noisy beating of her heart. Was Jack on his way, too? The dock shifted slightly then creaked as the first footsteps hit the wooden deck.

"Oh, Petey, you're going to enjoy this. Bet you've never been in a foursome before." A giggle.

"Nothing I can't handle," boasted the male voice.

"Oh, I wouldn't be too sure," a second female tittered.

Martha cautiously peered around the side of her cover. Three females and a male. She'd recognize those short skirts anywhere. This was it, but where was Jack? She couldn't see the end of the dock. He'd better be there.

"What about in that row boat, Petey?" the first woman asked. It was the brunette.

"Better than a water bed," the man agreed as he wobbled a few steps in Martha's direction, then leaned over to take a look at the boat.

The brunette reached down into the next boat, grabbed an oar and raised it above her head.

Now, Jack, Martha urged. Where the hell is Jack? No Jack. Guess it's me.

"That's not such a good idea," Martha yelled out, at the same time scrambling around the rack. Her skirt caught and ripped as she pulled free. She muttered curses as she stumbled over to the group.

The women stared at her. The brunette had at least lowered the oar. A good sign. The man had a hard time straightening up.

"Who'zat? Another party girl?" He leered in Martha's direction, then belched.

"Who the hell are you?" asked the brunette.

"I'm your conscience and just maybe your guardian angel." Martha cleared her throat, trying for an authoritative tone. "I know what you're planning to do and believe me, it's not in your best interests."

"You've got a great imagination, lady. You see pink elephants, too? Now why don't you toddle back up to the bar and finish off with a night cap."

"Great idea. I will 'toddle off' as you put it, and I'll take Petey right along with me."

The brunette's grip changed on the oar. Getting ready to bash me, too, Martha thought. Where are you Jack?

The blonde stepped over to Petey and eased her arm around his waist. "We're just having a fun evening with our friend."

"Right on," Petey agreed, tipping into her, his left hand sliding across her thigh.

The oar inched upward. Martha reached forward. "It's all fun and games to you? You couldn't fix his drink so you'll whack him on the head. Some fun." Let them have it. Show them she was on to them. Then run like hell if that oar moved again.

The blonde looked at the redhead. The quiet one finally spoke. "I think we'd better all go back to the hotel."

"Now you're thinking straight," Martha said.

"You stay out of this," the brunette shot back. She looked at her two buddies. "We don't do it now, you know what he'll do. And to whom."

"Aw, com'on girls." Petey belched. "Let's get this party going."

"Shut up," the blonde screamed, slapping his hand away. She shoved him into a sitting position at the edge of the dock.

"Go to the police," Martha urged. "Surely you can prove what an asshole this guy is. Let them handle it."

"And if they don't? You want to know what this shithead does to sweet, unsuspecting young females under his power? He sexually harasses the lucky ones." She reached behind and grabbed the redhead's hand. "He raped Sharon, last year at this very convention."

Martha could see the tears on Sharon's cheeks. She glanced at Petey, momentarily wanting to grab the oar herself. He sat hunched over, smirking. Probably in anticipation.

The brunette continued. "Shithead here gets his kicks that way. And now he's at it again. A sweet, young naive clerk. Her first job, finally away from an equally disgusting home life. She's already got problems and then jerk-head here starts coming on to her. Well, this time we've got to do something. We've got to protect her. And get even."

Martha had her eye on the oar. The brunette's grip tightened. Her stance shifted slightly towards Petey.

"I know you're hurting," Martha spoke directly to the redhead. "But like I said, tell it to the police. Tell it to his bosses. Not too many corporate types like scandals under their noses."

"Yeah, and let everyone gawk at Sharon."

"No, we can't do that," Sharon cried. "I'd die if everyone knew."

"Is it better if they know you as a murderer?"

"Shut up." The brunette was back in control. "You don't know what you're doing. You're ruining everything."

"You're not a murderer. None of you are. And he's certainly not worth what it'll do to your lives." Martha prayed he'd keep silent. She glanced at his body, swaying back and forward. Maybe he'd rocked himself to sleep. "Come on, let's go back to the hotel. Tell the cops. Let them deal with him."

The three looked at each other. Each nodded slightly. The brunette put the oar down. Sharon looked down at Petey then reached out and pushed him over into the water.

It took Martha a few seconds to realize what had happened. The water wasn't deep, but he wasn't in control. "Just hang on Petey, I'll help you. Pass me that oar," she said to the brunette who picked up the oar and threw it out past Petey's head.

"Damn, damn." She kneeled down near the edge. "Here, grab my hand. Try to reach out. Petey, get my hand." She tried grabbing him but couldn't connect. After a few minutes she struggled up to a standing position. "I'll get a ladder. There's one in the boathouse. Someone go for help."

She ran around to the end of the dock and tried the door. It was locked. "Damn. I need a key. No, I need an oar. There's got to be an oar in one of the other boats. This stupid long skirt," she muttered, grabbing at the hem and running back to where she'd left the others.

She hadn't heard them leave the dock. But they were gone.

Petey floated face down, his head bumping the bow of the rowboat, his body at an angle to it.

"So, where the hell were you, Jack?" Martha took another long drink from the mug of hot tea then continued to glare at him.

"The women didn't all leave at the same time, Mom." Susan answered for him. "By the time we realized they'd gone, we came running, and well, here you are."

Martha looked at her daughter, then back at Jack. Interesting. Susan defending Jack. Maybe once she got over feeling so goddam empty she'd think about that.

"Anyway, I'm sorry you had to be the one, Martha." Jack touched her hand. "You did your best to save him, you know. You can't blame yourself."

"I know that. I just don't feel it. Yet."

"Did you tell the police about the plot?" Susan asked.

"I'm the only one who heard them." She looked at Jack. "And, it ended up an accident."

Jack sat silent a moment before talking. "Justice, it would seem, has been served."

"My thoughts exactly."

They were seated at the corner booth in the darkened Shoreline restaurant. She'd just finished giving a statement to the OPP.

Two hours she'd waited in an empty office while the three women had taken turns at being questioned. Once she'd left to go to the washroom. The blonde was in there, too. She'd be the next to talk to the police. She'd told Martha not to feel too badly. It was an accident. They'd left the dock. Martha had searched for the ladder. And drunken Petey had drowned.

The blonde had even patted Martha's shoulder. The dampness from the thick satin cuff of her sleeve penetrated Martha's thin blouse.

Martha stared at the cuff. "You'd better dry your sleeve before seeing the police."

ACCIDENTS CAN HAPPEN

by Joan Boswell

"Kenny MacDougall needs help."

My husband, who lay stretched out on the top bench of our steamy sauna opened his eyes, rolled over and stared down at me.

"I know." He sighed, "But we can't do anything. I keep telling you we can't ignore the basic fact about life in Tremblayville. Kenny's dad is my boss and the boss of the town. Even though you and I suspect Marlene hurts Kenny, there's nothing we can do about it."

"My head says you're right, my heart says you're wrong." Without giving myself time to think I said, "Right now I'm finding living in this town pretty tough. I thought I knew what I was getting into when I married you . . . " I shook my head. "I realized logging engineers spent a lot of time away from home building roads into the woods. And I was prepared to live in company towns in remote areas and make a life for myself when you were away." Running my fingers through my moisture-laden hair I willed myself to keep my voice from rising. "But I had absolutely no idea how difficult, how bizarre, life in a company town would be."

Jorma swung his feet over the edge of the bench and sat up. "Give it a chance. We've only been here a year."

"It isn't how long we've been in Tremblayville. It's what it's done to my illusions. Before we moved here I believed if something was wrong in a community somebody would take action. The police, the Childrens' Aid Society, the church, some organization would fix whatever was wrong." Wrapping my arms around myself I rocked back and forth. "But, it could be 1361 instead of 1961. When there's trouble there's nowhere to turn and nobody to intervene." I stopped swaying and looked at Jorma. "Here we are, two hundred souls isolated in northern Quebec. No road in. No medical facilities. No nothing."

I stood up, winding my extra large yellow towel sarong style around me. "Dave should do something about Kenny. How can a seven-year-old's father not see how often he has something wrong with him?"

"Maybe he accepts whatever fairy stories Marlene tells him. And he can't monitor what happens at home when he's away 90 percent of the time."

"He could divorce her and hire a housekeeper ."

"If the courts granted him a divorce they'd give Kenny to Marlene. Maybe he loves her. Marlene does have her virtues. She's a terrific housekeeper."

"And a lousy mother. If only she didn't mistreat Kenny. Poor Kenny. Poor baby."

For a second I allowed myself to remember our Patrick, the premature baby Jorma and I had treasured for three weeks before his frail lungs failed. I could almost feel his tiny fingers wrapped around mine. Thinking of Patrick always made me replay the accident that had precipitated his birth. For the millionth time I wondered if I would have stayed on the road if I'd been driving more slowly. Drawing a ragged breath I changed the subject.

"Wait until your parents see what we've done to fix up this old trapper's cabin. And the sauna." I clutched my slipping towel with one hand and ran my other hand along the warm, smoothly sanded bench. "They'll be pretty impressed."

Jorma examined the tiny, cedar-lined room. "Well, I have to vent it so it won't smell, and if I put a hook on the inside like the one on the outside, the door won't swing open unexpectedly."

"Then it'll be perfect."

"Maybe not perfect but okay." Jorma checked his watch. "We should call the dog and head back."

I stepped over to the shower.

Standing with his back to me, Jorma said, "Gloria, don't get upset again, but I have to tell you something you're not going to like hearing."

He turned. "On Wednesday afternoon Dave and I are doing a road location walk near here."

I ran a terminology check. After a year I didn't have all the logging terms worked out but I remembered. Jorma had done a location walk in the spring. He'd fought his way through alder swamps, fallen timber and fast-moving streams searching for the cheapest and safest location for a road to let the huge pulp trucks drive in and remove cords of pulp wood from a cut.

"Dave said Marlene wants to drive up with him to see our cabin." Jorma shifted uncomfortably. "Since Dave and I will be gone for a couple of hours, I invited them to stay for dinner."

"Wednesday afternoon. Are you crazy? The cabin's a mess and there's no time to clean it now. And we have to hurry back or we'll be late for dinner at the Poiriers. Why didn't you tell me earlier?"

"Relax. On Wednesday morning you can drive up early in our truck and clean before we arrive. I'll come up with Dave and Marlene."

Monday afternoon as I stood at the sink doing the dishes Prince pulled his leash from the hook beside the back door, dragged it across the kitchen floor and dropped it at my feet. Three o'clock. Time to mosey across town to the two-storey red asphalt-brick house the company had converted into a combined residence for the teacher and classroom for the eight English-speaking Protestant children in Tremblayville. Prince and I had started this routine shortly after we arrived the previous year.

It began one day when I stood in our yard tossing the ball for Prince. Kenny MacDougall came past on his way home from school. When the ball bounced out on the road, Prince retrieved it and dropped it at Kenny's feet. Kenny looked anxiously at me.

"It's okay. Prince wants you to throw it."

Kenny tossed and Prince brought it back to him two or three times before Kenny stopped and glanced up the road where his own house was visible but separated from the other employees' houses by a long stretch of unoccupied land. He caught his lower lip with his two new oversize front teeth. "I have to go. I'm not supposed to talk to anyone or stop anywhere on my way home."

I wondered if there was a special reason for Marlene's insistence, if Tremblayville was dangerous for children.

The next time I met the wife of one of the other forestry engineers, I asked about Kenny.

"Marlene keeps him on a short line. He's the same age as my son but she doesn't allow them to play together." She seemed to want to say more but her husband gave her the kind of look husbands give when they want you to drop a subject.

Soon after our first encounter with Kenny, Prince and I happened to wander past the school at three-thirty. The door banged open. Eight children erupted into the warm afternoon.

"Hi Mrs. Suomi. Hello Prince," Kenny called as he hip-hopped out to the street.

Prince greeted him with a slathering kiss of welcome. I said hello and dug the ball out of my pocket. Kenny and the other kids took turns throwing it. But Kenny didn't stay long. After he'd tossed it two or three times he hugged Prince, produced a sigh far too big for his small body and set off down the road.

And that's how Prince and I developed the habit of walking past the school and escorting Kenny from the side street up to the main street where he headed for home and we crossed the railroad tracks to the main part of town where the church gloried over a huddle of houses, five hotels, the general store and the station.

On Monday we followed our usual routine. We started from our own bungalow, one of a line of brown company houses strung along the dirt road. We reached the school as the bell released the children for the day.

The children streamed out. Kenny was not among them.

Tuesday afternoon Prince toted his leash to me in the living room where I was listening to the Northern Messenger on a CBC punctuated by static. Because I lingered to catch the last exotic messages to trappers and storekeepers living on the shores and hinterland of James Bay, we left on our daily trip a little later than usual.

The bell had given the all-clear to freedom before we arrived. As we turned the corner, Kenny trudged toward us with eyes down and feet scuffing up clouds of dust. He had a cast on his left arm.

"Kenny, what happened?"

"I broke it," Kenny whispered and patted Prince with his good hand.

"How?"

Kenny stared at the ground, dug into the dirt with the toe of his sneaker. "I fell."

"Where?"

We stood silently while he concentrated on tracing a circle with his toe. Finally he spoke in a voice so low I almost didn't hear.

"Down the cellar stairs." After a long pause he added, "On Sunday."

"You had to wait until yesterday to go to the doctor," I said and thought how awful it was to live in a town inaccessible by road. Kenny had endured more than a day of pain because the train didn't run on Sunday and the nearest doctor lived an hour and a half up the railway line.

"We'll walk you up to the corner. It's a good thing you can still throw the ball for Prince," I said. At the corner we separated. With tears in my eyes I watched him set off for home.

At dinner Jorma and I sat at our red painted kitchen table and tested one of my newest recipes, a liver and onion casserole.

"It's really bad," I said.

"No. It's good. I'll have more."

"Not the casserole. The Marlene situation."

Jorma dug into his casserole and shoved a forkful in his mouth.

"I've told you how I keep track of Kenny's comings and goings?"

With a mouthful of casserole, Jorma nodded.

"He has a broken arm."

Jorma continued to eat.

"Did you hear me, Jorma? A BROKEN ARM. She's done it again. She pushed him down the cellar stairs. What are we going to do?"

Jorma put his fork on his plate and leaned toward me. "Gloria. He's not our kid." Jorma stopped. By the remoteness of his gaze I knew he was remembering Patrick. As if he was clearing his mind of the painful thought, Jorma shook his head. "Did Kenny say it was his mother's fault?"

"No. He's scared of her. He wouldn't tell."

"Despite your suspicions, we can't be sure she pushed him. Kids do have accidents that are just that – accidents."

"Come on Jorma. We've catalogued the things that have happened to Kenny in the last six months: a sprained ankle, a bad burn, a dislocated shoulder, a concussion and now, a fall and a broken arm. Let's face facts. Marlene hurts him and the injuries are getting more serious."

"Gloria, forget it." Jorma used the index finger on his right hand to tick off the fingers of his left hand. "Dave's the boss. I'm not ready to interfere and neither of the other two foresters is likely to be either."

He moved to his second finger. "Dave hires and fires the teacher. The teacher needs his job. He won't say anything."

Third finger. "We can't go to the priest because the MacDougalls are English-speaking Protestants. The Anglican minister visits once a month and he's totally useless."

Little finger. "The nearest police detachment is in LaTuque. There's one law for the French and one for the English." Jorma shook his head. "No one's going to prosecute an English manager's wife for how she treats her kid. There's nobody we can turn to."

"Well, someone has to act. Marlene scares me, but the idea of Kenny dying and our not having tried to change his situation . . . I couldn't live with myself."

"Dying? Isn't that a little excessive?"

"No. It isn't. I know how you feel about a child's funeral . . . " My voice quavered to a stop.

Jorma started to speak, stopped and cleared his throat. After exhaling noisily he breathed deeply and tried again. "Gloria, you're thinking of Patrick."

I opened my mouth but Jorma didn't give me a chance to speak.

"You're seeing Kenny and thinking of Patrick. You have to get hold of yourself and stop. It's not the same." He scrubbed at his eyes. "Don't use Patrick to involve me. And don't tell me how I feel." He swallowed hard and his voice shook. "You have no idea how I feel."

I clamped my lips together to keep them from trembling. When I regained control, I said, "I'm sorry. Truly, I am. You're right. I do keep thinking of Patrick."

Jorma picked up his fork and mashed a chunk of potato into the onion gravy before he said, "If YOU feel something has to be done, YOU'RE going to have to do it yourself. Why don't you talk to Marlene next week at the cabin? Offer to take Kenny on a picnic or for a walk. Tell her how much you like him. Say what a great kid he is. Maybe if she realizes you care about Kenny and are watching her she'll back off and leave him alone."

"I will talk to Marlene." My voice quivered but I forced myself to smile. "Decision made. What else can we talk about?"

Jorma reached over and held my hand. "I can tell you something to make you smile. When I came back to the office this afternoon I told Dave to be prepared because every first-time visitor to a Finnish home has a sauna. He asked me what happened if you didn't. I shrugged and said the question had never come up because new guests always took saunas."

I visualized Marlene in the sauna and, as Jorma had predicted, I smiled. "Marlene may not come when she hears that story. She won't like not meeting the challenge, but, being a cleanliness freak, she probably won't risk contamination. I bet she'll make up an excuse. What do you think?"

"She'll take one. She won't risk losing face, risk being the only guest who doesn't."

"You sure?"

"Absolutely."

"In that case I'll clean the sauna tomorrow morning. I wonder if drain cleaner would get rid of the smell?"

On Wednesday morning, at the cabin I unloaded the groceries and lugged my town vacuum cleaner inside. Once I'd put away the food in the propane refrigerator, I started the portable generator and attacked the cobwebs, dust balls and dog hairs in the main room. Then, armed with drain cleaner, cleanser and bleach I waged war on the smelly sauna.

Back in the cabin I lit the wood stove to dissipate the chill before I went outside and collected an armload of goldenrod and Michaelmas daisies from the roadside to arrange in mason jars. After a quick sandwich lunch I perked a pot of coffee and parked it on the back of the wood stove before I returned to the sauna.

Inside, I switched on the artificial coals and poured buckets of tap water on the coals until steam enveloped the five by six foot building.

I sniffed.

It didn't require the nose of a bloodhound to tell me the room still smelled of stale water. Hoping to block the odour, I saturated two sponges with drain cleaner, lifted the grates, and shoved them deep into the pipes in the floor of the sauna and the shower. A few scatterings of black mould in the corners of the shower had resisted my earlier attempts to eradicate them. Preparing to try again, I poured bleach into the pail.

Prince barked frantically.

I set the pail down and rushed outside. Jorma and the MacDougalls had pulled into the yard to the accompaniment of Prince's hysterical yapping. When Marlene climbed out of the cab my heart flip-flopped and my mouth got that dry feeling it gets when you have to speak to a crowd or do something you've been dreading. I felt sure no words would come out but I managed to shout 'hi' and ask if the men had time for coffee in a perfectly normal voice.

Inside the cabin Dave and Jorma drank quickly before they drove off and left me to cope with a long afternoon with Marlene. Having promised myself to talk to her about Kenny I waded in before I lost my nerve.

"Kenny is the greatest kid . . . "

"How do you know?" she snapped.

First mistake. Since Kenny wasn't supposed to talk to anyone, how would I know? "I see him now and again when I'm out with Prince. I'd love to bring him with us on our walks if it would be okay with you."

"It wouldn't. I want him at home where I can keep an eye on him."

"I can understand that you're worried about him. He does have a lot of accidents."

"Accidents can happen," Marlene said.

"People are saying . . . they may not be accidents."

Marlene's eyes narrowed as her head snapped up and her body swayed back and forth. Like an enraged viper she caught me with her hypnotic gaze.

"What – do – you – mean?"

"They claim he broke his arm because you pushed him down the cellar stairs."

Malevolence flashed from her slitted eyes. Her voice dropped and she enunciated each word. "Who said that?"

"Two men. I overheard them talking when I was shopping." I couldn't stand to look at Marlene. Instead I moved my coffee cup aimlessly on the table.

Silence.

I risked a sidelong glance and saw Marlene's mask of pseudo civility drop back into place.

"People always talk, but accidents can happen and Kenny is accident-prone," Marlene said in a neutral voice. "Of course you'd know all about that. If you'd been more careful you'd have your own son to worry about."

I felt as if she'd shoved a two-by-four in my stomach. For a minute I couldn't breathe, I couldn't speak.

Marlene pushed her cup away, stood up and focussed on the log walls of the one room that served as living room, dining room and kitchen.

"A lot of creepy, crawly things must be in here," she said.

I wanted to scream, 'only today' but I didn't. "Not so far," I said in my best imitation of a normal voice. "Would you like to go for a stroll? We've cut trails along the lake."

"No." Marlene stepped to one of the two easy chairs, bent and brushed the seat cushion. "Dog hairs everywhere. Cleanliness is clearly not next to godliness as far as you're concerned." She lowered herself into the chair, lifted her quilted tote bag to the coffee table and removed a half-done piece of needlepoint. "I always carry sewing with me wherever I go."

After she unloaded everything she needed, she took a needle already threaded with lime green and began to stitch. Once she finished the strand, she picked up her folder of wool to find a matching piece. With the greens laid out on the tapestry, she examined them carefully before she put them back with the other wool.

"I don't have the exact shade I need. I always work right down a piece. I can't go any farther."

She returned everything to her bag.

"Now what do you suggest we do," she said, folding her hands in her lap.

Sitting opposite her I leaned forward, "Perhaps you'd like a sauna? It's traditional for first-time visitors."

"Dave told me," Marlene said. "He's going to have one but it seems to me like a wonderful way to spread germs."

I sat back. "If you'd rather not . . . "

With her jaw lifted and a determined glare in her eye Marlene said, "And have you tell everyone in town. No sir. No one says Marlene MacDougall isn't a good sport." She peered around as if challenging an invisible audience to contradict her. "What do I do?"

"The sauna and the shower are in the little shed behind the house. Change in our room. There's a terrycloth dressing gown on the back of the door."

"You mean I'll be naked."

"That's how it's usually done, but keep your underwear on if you want. It'll be damp but it's up to you. Wear your shoes until you're in the sauna." I stood up and moved toward the bathroom. "I'll fetch clean towels for you."

Moments later, Marlene, wrapped in the robe, emerged and followed me out to the converted shed. I unhooked the door, pulled it open and released a warm wave of steam. We stepped inside and pulled the door shut. "Put a towel on the bench to sit on. When you're ready, empty the bucket onto the coals to make more steam. The idea is to make as much steam as possible."

"I won't like it."

"You know how good it feels to soak your hands in the dishwater on a cold day, how relaxing it is when the steam rises in your face? A sauna is a hundred times better."

Marlene made a moue of distaste. "I'll end up hot and sweaty?"

"No. The steam is the first part. In Finland they beat themselves with birch boughs before they dash out and jump in the lake or roll in the snow, but we don't do that. Usually, we swim after a sauna. Or shower." I pointed to the supplies beside the shower stall. "That's a loofah hanging on the wall. It's like a huge sponge and your skin feels great if you scrub yourself with it. Or, if you'd rather, use the long-handled scrubbing brush. Shampoo and skin lotion are on the shelf. In the shower there's wonderful Finnish herbal soap Jorma's mother sends to us."

Marlene stood like a monument. Finally she said, "All right. A sauna and a shower. " She wrinkled her nose. "It smells of bleach."

"Yes. I've been cleaning. If you have everything you want, I'll clear out and give you some privacy. Prince and I will go for a walk."

Marlene nodded dismissively and plunked herself down to remove her shoes.

"Enjoy yourself," I said as I let myself out, fastened the door and whistled for Prince.

When we trotted back from our uneventful foray into the woods I left Prince investigating a hole under the cabin and walked to the sauna.

"Marlene, how was it?" I called as I unhooked the door.

Silence.

"Marlene?"

More silence.

I pulled the door open.

A cloud of stinking, choking steam swirled out. I jumped back. When I felt sure the air was clear I took a deep breath and went in.

Marlene lay motionless on the floor in front of the door.

I bent to feel her pulse.

But of course she had no pulse. She was dead.

I returned to the cabin, poured myself a cup of coffee, found the number of the radio dispatcher at the company office in Tremblayville and lifted the phone. "C'est Gloria Suomi ici a Lac des Rapides . . . " I sobbed and gulped for air. "Il y avait . . . "

The dispatcher interrupted me. "I speak English. Where are you?"

"At our cabin on Lac des Rapides. Mrs. MacDougall has had an accident." My voice climbed the panic scale. "I think she's . . . dead."

When they arrived in town the Quebec Provincial Police accepted my explanation.

Leaving the bleach in the bucket had been accidental. I would reproach myself forever because I hadn't finished cleaning the sauna, but I'd been distracted.

Distracted. What had taken me away from the job?

Prince had barked because Jorma and the MacDougalls had arrived. I'd gone out to greet them and completely forgotten to dump the bucket of bleach.

And why had I stuffed sponges saturated with drain cleaner into the drain?

The smell. To get rid of the smell. How was I to know bleach and drain cleaner combined to make chlorine gas?

Had I never read the warnings on the bleach bottle?

Who reads labels? I knew now I should have been more careful and I'd never forgive myself, but, as Marlene said, accidents can happen.

IT MUST HAVE BEEN THE SHERRY

by Brenda Missen

"Have another glass of sherry, Winona."

It was the last thing I wanted on a scorching July day, sitting on Mr. Ashman's deck, but I didn't want to hurt his feelings. I was here on my mother's orders, more or less. She'd phoned to see how my holiday was going, and how the pump was holding up.

"Oh, and go see Mr. Ashman, Winnie. He just lost his wife last summer. You remember. He'll be lonely up there on his own. You can keep each other company."

This last remark was the closest my mother was going to come to sympathy for the fact that I'd recently lost my own companion. Not to cancer, like Mrs. Ashman, but to another woman. The reason her sympathy was lukewarm was that I was, in her opinion, at age thirty making far too much of a habit of losing companions.

The sherry was cloying and sticky, and giving me a headache, but I sipped it dutifully and listened to Mr. Ashman talk about his wife.

"Lucy was the most wonderful cook. The dinners she put on!"

I nodded, though I'd never been to an Ashman dinner. It was, after all, my parents' cottage. For the past ten years or so I'd been coming up when they weren't using it, with whichever man I happened to be attached to at the time. I had only heard my mother's descriptions of Mrs. Ashman's elaborate spreads. Courses carefully chosen to stimulate the palate, not fill up the stomach, on a hot summer night.

"It seems the neighbours are going to have to forego the pleasure of my dinners this summer." Mr. Ashman spread his hands in a gesture of resignation that was somehow contradicted by his smile.

He was a trim and tall man, with tanned leathery skin from years of summers on Lake Rosseau. I knew for a fact that he was almost sixty, but except for the silver in his otherwise dark tight curls, he looked at least ten years younger. (Lucy had been just fifty-eight, my alarmed fifty-seven-year-old mother had informed me.)

"I could help you put together a dinner if you wanted to have a few of the neighbours over." The words were out of my mouth before I was even aware of what I was saying. Was I crazy? I *never* cooked. It had been one of the sore points between Joel and me.

"Do you think you're up to taking on the neighbourhood?" There was a challenge, as well as amusement in Mr. Ashman's eyes.

I laughed. "No, not the neighbourhood. But maybe a select few." Why not? The idea of entertaining with Mr. Ashman was beginning to appeal. As was the idea of how annoyed Joel would be if he ever found out I was *volunteering* to be domestic.

Before I'd finished my second drink, we'd drawn up a list of guests – one couple and two widows. Before I left, Mr. Ashman had talked me into braving barbecued shrimp and scallops on skewers, with baba-au-rhum (whatever that was) for dessert.

"It must have been the sherry," I muttered to myself, hiking home over the hill of lichen-covered rocks that separated our two properties. How in the world was I going to duplicate Mrs. Ashman's famous dinners? What had possessed me to volunteer? I banged the screen door behind me and changed into my swimsuit. "It must have been the sherry," I grumbled again and dove into the lake to get rid of my headache.

"Winona," came Mr. Ashman's deep voice over the party-line the next morning before it was a decent hour to be awake. "I've found Lucy's recipe box for you. Get up and enjoy the day. I'll see you around four for drinks."

Emerging from sleep sometime later, I groped for my watch and swore when I saw what time it was. The day was already half over. I would have time only for a quick sail before I was expected at Mr. Ashman's. I almost wished I'd got up when he'd told me to, much as his attempt to dictate my day had irritated me.

He's a grieving man, I told myself for the tenth time, rushing to get the rudder for the Laser. Besides, I had to admit I was looking forward to the visit; it wasn't as enjoyable as I'd expected being up here by myself. (How can you miss someone who was never there? a mocking voice asked in my head.)

Putting up the sail of the Laser that Joel and I had bought, but rarely sailed, together, I thought back to our three-and-a-half year relationship; and to my year and a half with Mark before that; and to my two years give or take a few months with Jeremy before that. I couldn't imagine living with someone for thirty or forty years and then – bam – they're not there. And harder for the man to be the one left, my mother always said. My mother had already decided my father was going to be the first to go. It was a family joke: "How are you going to bump him off, Mom?" "I won't have to," she would reply in a grim voice, watching my father eat his roast beef. "*That's* going to do it for me."

But it wasn't beef that had killed Lucy Ashman before she'd hit her golden years. The rumours had been rife around Lake Rosseau last Labour Day weekend when the news of her death had spread. Rumours that Mr. Ashman's claims of cancer were unfounded; that she'd actually died of alcoholism. She'd been a bottle-of-sherry-a-day woman.

But they were whispered rumours, accompanying the other whispers that Mr. Ashman refused to acknowledge his wife's drinking problem. And no one was about to confront him.

I dismissed the rumours. If anyone indulged in the sherry, it was Mr. Ashman. And how could you deny your wife drank that much? The signs would be obvious. He'd have noticed the dwindling contents of the bottle, or the smell on her breath. The only way he could have avoided acknowledging *that* was if he never got close to her. And you couldn't live with someone and not get close to them. (No? said the mocking voice in my head.)

Promptly at four, I showed up on Mr. Ashman's vast cedar deck, surprised he wasn't sitting in one of the Adirondack chairs looking out over the lake. I had even put on a sundress for the occasion. Would wonders never cease.

A shadow appeared at the French doors. Mr. Ashman opened them and greeted me with obvious pleasure in his eyes. "You look lovely, Winona," he said. "It's nice to see a young woman in a dress."

His comment irked, but I let it pass.

"Come inside. It looks like it might rain."

The sky was overcast, but certainly not threatening. I hated being indoors when I could be outside. Summers were too short as it was.

I shrugged. *He's a grieving man, Winnie. Humour him.*

Mr. Ashman led me into the cottage. Although "cottage" wasn't quite the image the Ashman summer dwelling conjured up. It was large and spacious, with cathedral ceilings and large plate-glass windows spanning the entire lake-side of the house. The furnishings were not, like at our cottage, the usual mishmash of cast-offs, but exotic Asian antiques from Mr. Ashman's lucrative import business. The kitchen was more luxurious than my parents' in Toronto.

Of course, Lucy couldn't have put together her marvellous dinners without a *kitchen*. I could only hope it would help *me*. It had been awhile since I'd put my culinary skills to use. It wasn't that I wasn't capable. Just unwilling. Stubbornly so, my mother liked to tell me.

A dozen index cards had been laid out on the kitchen table. "Salade de moules," "brochettes de fruits de mer," "asperge Andoulouse," "baba-au-rhum," I read in Lucy's meticulous hand. (Not the shaky hand of a bottle-a-day drinker, I thought irrelevantly.)

The recipe for baba-au-rhum covered the front and back of three cards. I began reading, then looked at Mr. Ashman in dismay. "Oh, Mr. Ashman. I can't possibly do this – I've never worked with yeast . . . "

For a moment I thought he looked annoyed. No, it was merely disappointment. "Oh, well, if you can't do the baba-au-rhum, we'll find something else. There's the dessert box – but where are my manners?"

He steered me into the living room towards one of two richly upholstered armchairs that faced the lake. "Please. Sit down . . . this was Lucy's chair. Will you have your sherry now?" Without waiting for my response, he crossed over to the dining area and opened a beautiful black lacquered cabinet with two golden dragons locked in a circular chase of perfect symmetry on the doors.

Moments later, a crystal glass was put into my hands – it was rather nice to be waited on like this – and Mr. Ashman settled himself in the matching chair. He raised his own glass, and his eyebrows. I had never noticed how his eyes glinted – like he was sharing a secret with me. My own sparkled back. I couldn't help it.

"You know," he said, crossing his legs and leaning slightly in my direction, "Lucy never touched a drop. I could never get her to join me. It's good to have someone to have a drink with."

The sherry went down better in the cool interior, out of the sun. I even welcomed the second one. It was relaxing . . .

Absently I stroked the gleaming wood of the arm of my chair. "Your furniture is all so beautiful, Mr. Ashman – "

"Please, call me Michael."

"Michael. How often do you go on buying trips?"

"Oh, two or three times a year to China and Japan, sometimes India."

I sighed. "It sounds fabulous, all that travel. I've never been off the continent."

"Well, we must remedy that. You'll have to come with me next winter."

"Yeah, sure," I laughed.

"You'd see an Asia you'd never see as a tourist," he continued. "My clients would see to that."

He couldn't be serious. Mr. Ashman and I travelling together! The idea was absurd.

"I guess you're wined and dined in style when you go abroad," I said to deflect the topic from us.

Mr. Ashman nodded. "Speaking of entertaining, Winona, have you phoned the neighbours yet?"

I stared at him. "Mr. Ashman, I – "

"Michael."

"Michael, I really think you should be the one to do the inviting – after all, it's your party."

"*Our* party. It would be so much more effective if you did the inviting, don't you think? Playing the true hostess. Lucy was always the one – " He sighed and looked away.

"Oh, Michael. Of course I'll do the calling. We want them for next Thursday evening, right? What time shall I tell them?"

"Thursday?" Mr. Ashman looked puzzled. "But, Winona, we agreed on Saturday. Lucy and I always did our entertaining on the weekends." A sudden smile drove a crease down his cheek. "Unlike *some* people, I'm an early riser. I'm always in bed by ten o'clock on weeknights."

I suppressed a prick of annoyance. I'd begun spending Saturday evenings at Trapper's Bar in Rosseau, sharing a beer with some of the other cottagers around the lake. We had definitely agreed on Thursday. I'd explained to Mr. Ashman about my new Saturday night ritual. Ah well, I guessed I could give it up this once.

I felt Michael's eyes on me. To my horror, I found I was blushing. I suddenly had the impression he was looking at me as . . . a woman. That was crazy. He was almost double my age. I must have imagined it. He was merely smiling at me expectantly.

I smiled back, and he nodded. "Saturdays are the night to do a dinner party." He cocked an appraising eye at me. "I can see you now. You'll wear your most elegant evening dress. Mm . . . yes . . . and you'll put up your hair. You'll look lovely. You'll see. We'll do it in style."

His hands weren't anywhere near me, but I swear I could feel them on the back of my neck, sweeping my hair up onto my head. My neck tingled – the hairs were actually rising . . .

It must have been the sherry, I repeated (it was becoming my mantra) as I made my way home over the rocks with a pillowcase full of Michael's whites the next day. He'd confessed his attempt at washing had broken the machine, and I had a load of my own to go to the laundromat anyway. I could just hear Joel: "You never did *my* laundry." But Michael was another generation. He couldn't be expected to do these things. Lucy had obviously taken good care of him. That's what that generation of women did – even my mother. Besides, I was enjoying myself; what harm a mild domestic romance with an older man? It wasn't as if I was going to make a habit of doing his *laundry*.

Julia Baker was the first to arrive. "So Mike has seduced you into hosting dinners for him" was her greeting as she stepped briskly up onto the deck. "I hope, for your sake, the seduction hasn't moved on into the bedroom. I've heard he's older than he looks. But, then, age has nothing to do with capability – so I've heard." She halted and looked at me appraisingly. "Well, Winona, you're looking more like your mother every day."

I gritted my teeth behind my smile. It had been awhile since I'd heard what my mother called "Julia-isms" – Julia's blunt (and amusing if they weren't directed at you) remarks.

But in one respect she was right. It was my mother I saw in the mirror once I had put my hair up and raided her closet in a panic for a dress – the one she kept at the cottage for just these occasions. I had never dressed for anyone in my life. It was kind of fun.

The whole day had been kind of fun, though exhausting. We'd spent most of it in Michael's kitchen, while I prepared sauces and marinades *et al.* and tried to figure out how I was going to time the cooking of everything. Michael had hovered, giving ineffectual instructions. We'd laughed a lot, flirted mildly. He'd filled my head with visions of escorted travel in China.

Julia perched herself on the broad deck railing and looked around. She was a thin woman in her mid sixties, yet there wasn't one grey hair on her head. And that wasn't thanks to the tricks of a bottle, according to my mother. "All the grey hair landed on her husband's head and then fell out" was how my mother put it. She could sound remarkably like Julia when she wanted to. "It was either eat or be eaten, with Julia," she would add. "That's why *he* went first."

"Well, Lucy must be glad she no longer has to look after this place," commented Julia. "Some holiday, taking care of this mansion every summer. As if one big house weren't enough."

I looked anxiously through the open French doors.

"*Now* you're looking like *Lucy*," she observed. Then: "Don't worry about Mike. He's used to me. Besides, he knows the truth when he hears it – at least when he *chooses* to hear it."

"Would you like a – "

"So I gather the boyfriend's gone," she continued, as if I hadn't spoken. "No great loss there, I suppose. He spent more time on his sailboard last summer than with you from what I could see."

"Oh, Julia, leave Winnie alone." Myrna Martin had arrived at the bottom of the steps, followed by the last of the guests, Norbert and Noreen Billings. Just in time to save me from a rude reply.

Puffing slightly, Myrna came up onto the deck and held out her plump warm hand to me. I returned her smile. It was rumoured around Rosseau she'd also sent her husband to an early grave. If she had, she'd done it in the most cajoling way. I liked Myrna Martin; she'd always seemed a sympathetic presence in the cottage community.

The Billings were a short, squat, white-haired couple who'd grown to look almost identical over the years. Neither of them looked like they wanted to bump off the other. Had this couple managed to achieve the elusive domestic harmony? If they had, they weren't saying. Norbert wanted to talk about sailing.

"How's the Laser?" he asked.

"Lonely," I replied before I could stop myself.

Norbert smiled as if I'd said "lovely" and launched into a description of his latest sailing expedition.

Finally Michael emerged, in a jacket and pants that managed to look both casual and elegantly expensive. It struck me what an attractive man he was. And by the look he sent my way, I knew he was pleased with my own efforts.

The look was not lost on Julia. "Watch out, Winona," she warned in a not-so-low voice, "You'll be the next Mrs. Ashman."

I ignored her and offered Noreen a napkin to go with the hors d'oeuvres. They were looking a little soggy; I'd put the tapinade on the toasts too early. I watched nervously as Michael bit into one. He caught my eye and crooked a finger at me.

When I trotted over, he gestured for me to bend down close. His breath was warm in my ear. "Take these away, Winona. We'll make do with the humus and pita."

Shit. I could be sailing out there on that sparkling blue water. What was I doing here humouring this demanding man?

"Pour yourself a sherry while you're inside," he added, still speaking softly in my ear. There was a warm pressure on my hand, and an electric shock ran through me.

My grumblings evaporated.

When I finally stopped running from the barbecue to the kitchen and back, I was almost too tired to eat.

"Very well done, Winnie," said Myrna. The other guests politely echoed her compliments. And everything considered, I had to admit it hadn't turned out badly. The scallops were maybe a little rubbery, and the asparagus had been left too long in the steamer, but on the whole, not bad.

Once or twice, Michael had had to give me gentle reminders about something I'd forgotten. But now, his eyes above his glass across the table made everything worth it.

I was clearing the dinner plates when Michael suddenly folded up his napkin and rose to his feet. "You must excuse the host for abandoning his guests – it's long past my bedtime. Thank you for the dinner, Winona. Goodnight all."

I stared after him in disbelief as he disappeared down the hall. And then, suddenly, in my head I could hear my mother: "*Every* time . . . I don't know *how* Lucy puts up with it . . . I could have thrown that trifle after him myself . . . " How could I have forgotten?

"You'd better get used to it, my dear." Julia's tone was sardonic. "I can tell you from fifteen years of experience: Mike always toddles off to bed before dessert. Of course Lucy would have slaved all day over some creation or other. You'd think after thirty-five years she'd have caught on. Especially since none of the rest of us – well," – she glanced over at Norbert, who was gamely finishing everything on his plate – "*most* of the rest of us just aren't dessert eaters. Did you make something special? I hope you didn't spend all day on it. Maybe you should bring it out, so we can at least *look* at it."

"Stop teasing the poor woman, Julia," said Myrna. "*I'll* have some of it, whatever it is. As long as it's not trifle. Lucy's trifle was always a bit too . . . s*trong*."

"*Soused* is the word, Myrna. Why don't you just come right out and say it: she soused it. Or *doused* it. With sherry."

I blushed, but no one noticed.

"I thought we weren't going to talk about that tonight. The poor woman hasn't even been in her grave for a year – "

"I'm talking about dessert, Myrna. I never said we couldn't talk about dessert. Anyway, it wasn't *I* who said we couldn't talk about the sherry – "

"I'll – just go and get the – dessert," I said.

"Poor Michael," Noreen was saying when I came back. "The cancer claimed her so quickly."

"Cancer," snorted Julia. "My eye. That's Michael's story. When did you ever see any signs of cancer – or hear Lucy speak of it? That man controlled her right up to her very death – even dictating what disease she died of. It wouldn't do for Michael Ashman to have an alcoholic wife. But as sure as I'm Julia Baker, it was alcohol that did that poor woman in. For that matter, it wasn't the alcohol, it was the *husband*."

"Julia!" Myrna cast a glance towards the hallway down which the very husband had disappeared. It seemed to me she didn't look so much shocked at *what* Julia was saying as *where* she was saying it: in his house, perhaps within his hearing.

"Oh, Myrna, you know it as well as I do. Even here at the cottage, she never had a break from that man's tyranny: 'cook for me, entertain the neighbours, dress this way, wear your hair that way.' "

I blushed again.

"You carted off your share of Lucy's bottles to the garbage dump," Julia added, nodding at Myrna.

Myrna sighed. " 'Thank God for the sherry,' " she murmured. "That's what she always said."

My mouth was open to say something, anything, when Norbert cleared his throat. "It was cancer of the liver," he said in a surprisingly authoritative voice. As if that were the end of the discussion.

"Liver, yes," snorted Julia. "It was as soused as Winona's trifle likely is." She nodded at my end of the table, and three surprised sets of eyes landed on my dessert.

I ignored them all and spooned myself a generous helping, hoping to souse my own liver a little.

The dishes were piled high on all the counters. Michael had emphatically told me not to touch them; he'd do them in the morning. There was a dishwasher, of course, but he didn't have the foggiest idea how to use it; he was an old fashioned man. He'd laughed ruefully. "I like my men old fashioned," I'd teased back.

Now I looked around the kitchen in dismay. He'd be doing dishes all day. Not that *I* wanted to do them, but . . . I'd just load the dishwasher. Do one load anyway.

I picked up a plate. It was caked with leftovers. I'd have to scrape and rinse everything first. I fought back my rising irritation. Why was I even *looking* at someone else's kitchen mess on a Saturday night? It was only 11:30. Still time to drive over to Trappers for a well deserved drink . .

Drink. Sherry . . . sherry would get me through this.

Looking for a clean glass in the liquor cabinet, I thought back to Julia's comments at dinner. Even my mother had her doubts about the cancer. Though she'd never outright accused Michael. It was a terrible thing to say about anyone. But there hadn't seemed to be any doubt in Julia's or Myrna's minds . . .

On my way back to the kitchen, I blew out the dripping candles on the dining room table. There was no moon, and in the sudden darkness I tripped over the carpet and almost lost my drink.

One glass got me only through the plates. I felt my way back through the living room to the liquor cabinet. The two golden dragons on the doors gleamed in the dark. Their luminescence somehow made them look as though they were actually moving, chasing each other. Was it my imagination or was one overtaking the other?

I squeezed my eyes shut for a moment to get rid of the illusion, then opened the doors, fumbling for the dark bottle. I weighed it in my hand, trying to gauge how much liquor was left. Oh well . . . if Michael noticed, I'd just tell him I'd given the guests more after dinner.

I poured half a glass, hesitated, then shrugged and topped it up. There, that would get me through the pots and pans, too. Just leave them for Mr. Ashman, an angry voice said inside my head. Drive over to the bar and forget about this mess.

I took a generous swallow. Oh hell, I could handle the pots and pans. It was only this once anyway. I pulled off the stopper to top up the glass again.

Behind me, there was a sound. I whipped around. The sherry spilled onto my hand.

I managed to put my glass down on the cabinet and brought my hand up unconsciously to my mouth to lick the sherry off.

A shadowy robed figure was standing not three feet from me.

"Oh! Michael!"

The figure remained motionless, and silent.

I put the back of my hand in my mouth and bit down hard to keep myself from screaming.

The figure came suddenly to life. Instantly, he was by my side. "Did I startle you? Look, you've spilled your drink. Here's a napkin." He picked one up from the table, took my hand away from my mouth and wiped at it with the dry cloth as one might try to wipe away sticky drying blood.

"You're shaking," he exclaimed, and I was suddenly enveloped in his arms . . . Surprisingly strong arms . . . A surprisingly hard body. His fingers on the back of my neck were not, this time, my imagination. I relaxed against him.

Abruptly Michael let me go. "There, I didn't mean to startle you, my love. I thought you were a prowler." A mocking – no, a *teasing* – look came into his eyes. "I see I shall have to put the liquor cabinet under lock and key. Goodnight, Lucy."

It must have been the sherry, I thought. I wiped the towel over the last pot and felt my face grow hot thinking how much I'd enjoyed being in Michael's arms. So what if he was double my age. He was a handsome man. An attentive man. A nice change.

I thought of Joel, and it was like a sudden revelation: we'd been fighting so hard *not* to take care of each other, each so determined not to be taken advantage of, we'd given nothing to each other. In fact, that seemed to have been the pattern with all my men. No wonder they'd never lasted. *This* was how it should be . . . And the way he'd looked at me . . . as if I were someone he *knew* – someone he knew *intimately*. It was almost scary.

He'd even called me Lucy . . . a natural slip for a grieving man.

No, Mrs. Ashman had been *lucky*, not a lush. Julia and Myrna were just a couple of vicious gossips. Probably jealous because he didn't lavish his attention on *them*. It was all just ugly rumours . . .

It was one a.m. before I stumbled over the dark rocks back to my cottage. I felt a little sick. Mrs. Ashman may not have needed alcohol, but then, I wasn't Mrs. Ashman. Thank *God* for the sherry – all this domesticity was going to kill me.

UNNATURALLY INCLINED

I cast into a tree branch,
I cast into the weeds,
I've caught nothing but minnows
And lily pads and reeds.
I guess I'm not a fisherman,
I guess you'd say I'm hexed,
But if you don't stop taunting me
I'll take up hunting next.

Joy Hewitt Mann

THE LANGUAGE OF FLOWERS

by Maureen Jennings

The flowers arrived by special delivery ten minutes before I was about to fly out the door for the office. At first I thought Charles was trying for a reconciliation but then I saw the address label. They were from Aunt Ally.

I hurried back to the kitchen and opened the box. No fancy florist for my aunt. She'd picked the flowers herself. A large bunch of Michaelmas daisies. My heart jumped. That was bad enough but in their midst was a single stem of purple meadow saffron. I thrust the flowers back, phoned work to say I wouldn't be in and raced upstairs to pack my overnight bag.

Aunt Ally is my mother's older sister and has been my guardian since I was eight when my mother was killed in a stupid unnecessary car accident. I never knew my father as I was conceived during a brief encounter on the Trans-Canada train. It was my aunt who told me later, that although he was virtually a stranger, Mathilda had assured her he had very good vibrations.

In my early desperation to be exactly like everybody else I found that small consolation. After Mom died I continued in an exclusive boarding school in Toronto, thanks to her insurance policy, and spent all vacations with Uncle Jack and Aunt Ally at their cottage in Muskoka.

She was eighty-four now, a widow, and a woman with very decided opinions about life. Not for the first time, as I hurtled along the 401, I was annoyed by her refusal to move into the modern world. She wouldn't get a phone or electricity, claiming the hydro lines drained energy from the body.

By the time I got to the Bracebridge turnoff, my head was aching and I could feel a knot of irritability forming between my eyebrows. I took the old road to the lake, opening the windows to let the warm grass-scented breeze blow in my face. The shorn fields were dotted with giant rolls of shredded wheat and Three-Mile Lake glittered in the sun, sailboats scattered around the islands like wounded moths.

Ten minutes more and at the crest of a hill appeared the familiar driveway and the sign, TREE TOPS. The blue paint was almost faded away and tall grasses were climbing up the weathered post. I parked in the weed-grown lay-by above the cottage and as soon as I shut off the engine, I heard my aunt's voice calling a greeting. I jumped out of the car and like a child, ran down the steps. She was standing at the kitchen door beaming in delight. I caught her up in my arms and twirled her around. She was as fragile as a bird, and smelled of cinnamon. I held her longer than necessary because I didn't want her to see that I was close to weeping.

"Was the traffic bad? I expected you half an hour ago."

I laughed. "Oh Auntie."

I'd long since stopped questioning Aunt Ally's knowledge of my whereabouts. Like Sherlock Holmes she always had some logical mundane explanation but we both knew it was something else. She had the Gift.

"Come in," she said.

"Hold on a minute. What's up? Why are you sending me daisies? Where are you going? And meadow saffron? Don't pull that one, Auntie. Your best days are far from past. You're going to live to a hundred."

She smiled impishly, her face cracking like parchment.

"I'm glad to see you remember your lessons."

"Of course I do. But if I knew I was going to be tested I'd have studied."

"Dora, please. You know how I hate sarcasm."

"Well? Is that what you're doing?"

"Not now, dear. You need a swim, look at you. I could mangle a sheet in that jaw it's so tight. Go on, shoo."

I obeyed because I knew it was useless to do anything else and taking off all of my clothes there and then, I ran naked down the stone steps to the lake. Aunt Ally believes passionately in the healing properties of fresh air and sun and she'd have been upset if I'd waited to put on a swim suit.

Fortunately for my urban sensibilities, the cottage is nestled near the bottom of the hill amidst a thick grove of pines and hemlocks which afford complete privacy.

The cool water caressed my bare buttocks and breasts and I dived down to touch my Wishing Rock which was dappled with the sunlight filtering through the clear water. Fat grey minnows watched me, reproaching me for staying away so long. Aunt Ally and I wrote letters, hers long and chatty, mine brief and hurried but I hadn't actually seen her since Christmas and I felt bad about that. I'd been too caught up in my own stormy life.

I splashed about and swam until my headache disappeared and the tightness left my neck and shoulders. When I finally got out, Auntie had cold mint tea and warm bread set out on the deck and my old blue terry cloth robe at the ready.

She nodded approvingly. "That's better. You look like somebody I know again. You were quite orange when you arrived."

She meant my aura. She reads auras as nonchalantly as other people read newspapers. She went back to her rocker and as I sipped on the tea, I watched her with increasing dismay. Since I saw her last, she seemed to have shrunk and in spite of the patina of health given by the outdoors, she looked drawn and tired. Uncharacteristically she wasn't chattering at me, asking a dozen questions about my life, the office gossip, the latest with Charles my fickle lover. I put down the cup.

"All right, enough already . . . tell me! How are you?"

"Check me out."

"Auntie I can't do that. I don't know how anymore."

"Nonsense! The Gift isn't something you forget like a school lesson. Come on."

She leaned forward in her chair. Reluctantly I got up and placed my hands on her shoulders.

"Ready?" I asked.

She nodded. I closed my eyes and concentrated on co-ordinating my breathing to hers. One and two and three. I stopped.

"Auntie I can't get anything."

"Theodora, concentrate."

When Aunt Ally calls me Theodora, she means business. I tried again, breathing deeply, letting go of all the distractions that wanted to crowd into my mind. It's difficult to describe this kind of reading if you've never done it. It's not seeing and it's not exactly touching but another sense altogether. I began to feel the movement of Aunt Ally's energy as if there was a river flowing from my hands down into her body. I was also that river and I could feel as we hit the heart area how the flow speeded up. Not surprising, I knew she'd been born with a leaky valve and her heart had to pump harder than most people's to get the blood circulating. We moved on, a tiny bit of sluggish in the liver but the stomach was terrific. It was when the energy reached her abdomen that I felt the trouble. There was a blockage at the bottom of the large intestine like a damn across the river bed. I removed my hands.

"Well?" she asked.

"What is it?"

"Probably cancer."

I didn't ask her if she'd seen a doctor because I knew she hadn't.

"You can treat it, Auntie," I burst out. "You know how. You've done the same for dozens of people."

"I don't want to."

"What do you mean?"

"Dora, I'm eighty-four. I've had a long and mostly wonderful life. I think it's my time to go."

"No, that's not—"

"Try to listen, dear. I'm tired, the dratted thing hurts. No, hear me out. My old friends have all gone except for Ethel and she's in Florida all the time now. I miss your Uncle Jack and I'd like to join him and all the others who have gone ahead. Like your mother for instance."

Uncle Jack had died from an aneurysm two summers ago. It had happened suddenly while he was working in his pottery shed up by the road.

She stood up and went into the cottage, returning with a spiral notebook that had a picture of a foal on the cover.

"Here's the deed to the cottage inside this envelope. It's in your name of course. And I've written down everybody's name and telephone number that you will need to contact when I'm gone."

"Aunt Ally, what are you talking about?"

She sighed. "Dora I don't know what's become of you. I'm trying to tell you I am going to pass on tonight."

"What!"

"I rushed you up here because I need your help . . . stop gaping, you'll get a fly in your mouth."

"Aunt Ally, back up will you! What do you mean you're going to pass on tonight?"

But I knew full well and had since receiving the daisies with their message of farewell and the saffron saying, 'my best days are past.' I just didn't want to face it.

"I thought if I went tonight, you'd have the weekend before you went back to work. I've told all the neighbours I'm off to visit you in the city so nobody will question anything. When you're ready all you have to do is call them up and say I've passed—"

"No! You can't do this to me."

She frowned. "Dora, I'm not doing this *to* you. You know very well how I feel about these things. I refuse to end my days in some horrible hospital drugged into unconsciousness. Jack passed away while he was doing something he loved right here in his home and I don't see why it should be any different for me. I want to leave this earth in my own good mind." She paused. "And most of all I want to be buried here, by the lake."

"But . . . I - I don't think that's allowed."

"Exactly. That's why I have to die unofficially as it were . . . I've dug the hole but obviously I can't fill it in myself if I'm dead so I need your help for that."

"What!"

"Dora if you don't stop saying 'what' after every sentence I will have serious misgivings about the value of your supposedly first-class education."

She studied me for a moment. "You're not worried because it's illegal are you?"

"No. Well, maybe . . . somewhat."

She gave a little snort of disapproval. "I've always thought it a pity that legal and moral don't always coincide."

"I agree with you but there's nothing I can do about that."

"May I continue?" she asked frostily.

"Be my guest."

"I do wish you wouldn't sulk, Theodora. Anyway, what I'll do is lie down beside the grave so it will be easy for you. I'll wrap myself in the quilt."

"Auntie, you said I could have that quilt," I moaned childishly.

"I know I did but I decided to be selfish about this. But don't mind. In the bedroom closet there's a Simpson's box and in it are all the pieces of cloth I've saved for you over the years."

I could feel sobs stuck in my throat, lumpy and hard.

"What about a death certificate? You need one."

She smiled. "Listen to how ridiculous you sound. Why should I? As far as the government is concerned I don't exist. I never took a pension. How could anybody know I've gone if I'm not a number on a list somewhere?"

She was probably right about that but I couldn't sort out my thoughts. I concentrated on watching a tiny, iridescent green hummingbird zoom in to the lip of the red feeder and hover there, its wings a fan-shaped blur. Across the bay children were laughing and splashing as they jumped into the lake. Ally reached over and took my hand in both of hers.

"I was wondering if you'd sit with me for the passage. It won't take long."

I pulled away and jumped to my feet turning my back to her.

"I can't! Don't ask me, Auntie, I couldn't possibly do it."

"You did it for Molly. That wasn't so bad."

"She was a dog."

"But you loved her too."

"No, I can't."

She got up and went back into the cottage. I heard the side-door open and close with an emphatic slam. After a few minutes I heard her return.

I went inside. She was putting a fresh-picked bunch of buttercups in a vase.

"Auntie, that's not fair," I wailed pointing at the flowers. "I am not ungrateful. You've been my anchor as long as I can remember. I love and appreciate you more than I can say."

It was my turn to leave and slam the door.

I went straight to my favourite spot on the hill where there was a thick stand of silver birch. I pushed through to the centre braving scratches and mosquitoes. A flat rock heaved out of the ground making a natural seat, with a patch of soft green moss a perfect cushion. I knelt down and put my arms around the closest tree, pressing my cheek against the smooth white bark. I held on tight until my knees ached and my face began to hurt. Years ago Aunt Ally had taught me how to hear the bloodflow of the trees and now, as the branches swayed and creaked above, I began to listen again.

After a long time, I got up stiffly and went back to the cottage.

Ally was in the tiny kitchen stirring something herb-like in a jar. She turned towards me and I could see she had been weeping.

"I'm sorry, dear. I obviously underestimated how much of a shock this would be to you. Come."

She held out her arms and I fled into them, towering over her but comforted nonetheless as the hot cries tore out of my throat. She waited until I was cried out then she handed me a handkerchief.

"Blow your nose. I'm thinking it is selfish of me to ask you to stay. Perhaps it's better if you just give me a few moments then come and cover up the grave."

"No, it's me who's being selfish. And childish. It's just that I want you to live forever. Of course I'll be with you."

She touched my cheek. "Thank you dearest. Death is still an undiscovered country after all and there is some place in me that cannot help but be fearful."

"When do you want to . . . ?"

"As soon as it's dark enough. We're secluded here but you know how cottagers are with binoculars. I don't want anyone getting alarmed. In the meantime we've got a gallon of mint tea to get through and we can talk."

And we did. Not the tea part but we talked. About my childhood, "I knew early on you had the Gift." About my mother, "She wasn't named Mathilda, one deserving of honour for nothing, Dora." The family was big on names that had meaning. Ally was short for Althea, one who heals. My name means 'gift of God.' I'd always longed to be called Debbie or Linda or Sharon like all the girls I'd gone to school with.

As the sunset flamed over the lake, the mosquitoes chased us inside and we sat in the soft yellow light of the oil lamps. My aunt talked about herself, then, in a way I'd not heard before. Of her life with Jack who for years after his discharge from the army was troubled with terrible black moods which he vented on her. It was a long time until his soul healed, as she put it.

I laughed when she said that. "When he'd been particularly bad-tempered you used to say that his soul was hurting and for years I thought you meant his foot."

Finally only a single strip of light lingered over the lake, caught in the dark clouds like a golden scarf. Aunt Ally yawned.

"I think it's time. Give me the flashlight, I'll empty my bladder before . . ."

She didn't finish and in spite of everything my stomach squeezed with dread. While she went up to the outhouse, I fetched the quilt from her bed. So many stories of love and heartache and joy were sewn into that quilt and I knew every one of them. I caressed the squares: there a piece of pearl-grey satin from her wedding dress, here the soft red plaid of Jack's flannel shirt, a corner of my mother's blue taffeta blouse. When she came back I was ready. She slipped off her dress and old-fashioned white cotton bra and knickers. She stood naked in front of me. I put the quilt around her shoulders and we went outside.

"Gaiea's cut her fingernails, Auntie," I said pointing at the sickle moon.

She smiled. This was a story I'd believed when I was a child.

"Indeed she has," she said. She was holding onto the quilt with one hand and in the other she had a thermos. The homeyness of it brought a burst of tears into my eyes which I hoped she didn't notice. Together we walked carefully down to the water and she led me into the grove of evergreens. For the first time I noticed the mound of earth beneath the hemlocks.

"How did you manage to dig that?" I asked.

"It took me a whole week. It had to be quite deep, I don't want a raccoon digging me up."

At the edge of the grave she paused. "I'll just lie down close here so it won't be hard to get me in. Even a bag of bones like me is heavy to move."

She sat down and leaned back against the trunk of the hemlock tree.

"Do you remember how you used to talk to the trees, Dora? You'd rattle on about what they'd told you. You were quite a big girl before you realized not everybody could do that."

I nodded, not trusting myself to speak too much.

"If you want to put in electricity you can," she continued. "I know how much you hate the outhouse. But no television, promise?"

"I promise."

She raised her head towards the sky. Through the branches, the stars glittered above us, thick and brilliant in the dark night. Her white hair was a pale halo like milkweed fluff. She sat like that for a moment then she said.

"I'm ready now. Give me a kiss dear child of my heart. And don't grieve too much. It's much better this way."

I kissed her soft, papery cheek.

"You smell like lemons."

"I put on some citronella oil. The mosquitoes are bad tonight."

She undid the lid of the thermos, poured some dark, viscous liquid into the cup and quickly swallowed it down. She grimaced.

"Ugh, it's bitter."

She lay back and took my hand. I sensed her fear.

"I'm here, Auntie."

She closed her eyes and very soon her breathing grew shallow and more rapid. Then her entire body shuddered, once, and then again. Her breath stopped. A trickle of saliva came from the corner of her mouth.

She had gone.

I stayed beside her until her skin was quite cold. Then I wrapped her tightly in the quilt, rolled her into the grave and pushed in the soft earth until she was covered.

Eventually I climbed back up to the cottage where I sat until the dawn crept over the bay to blot up the darkness.

I went out onto the deck. The lake was still as glass and tendrils of mist were drifting up from the surface, silent and slow as departing spirits. A loon called his lonely liquid cry. The leaves of the birches rustled softly.

After a few minutes, I went out to the garden beside the cottage and scanned the flower bed. I selected some of the carnations and gillyflowers and went back down the hill.

There were dozens of dainty blue forget-me-nots growing wild in the grass and I gathered a large bunch and added them to the gillyflowers. I put them in the lop-sided jug I'd made with my uncle when I was ten years old and placed it at the head of Aunt Ally's grave.

The bonds of affection are everlasting.

I broke off a sprig from the hemlock tree that had sheltered her last night and placed it on the mound of earth.

Farewell to thee.

Finally, even though she'd think I was moping too much, I laid the bouquet of deep red carnations at her feet.

Alas for my poor heart.

FULL MOON, BLUE LAKE

by Mary Jane Maffini

Those two old gals were drunk as lords the night they rammed the speed boat into Judge Greely's fancy new dock and roared off laughing across Blue Lake, backlit by the full moon. At least, that's the gist of what Clem was blathering around my general store the next morning, collaring everyone who came through the door.

I always say you can tell a lot by a person's eyes. Clem's were lit up like a top-of-the-line torch from over in Practical Hardware. And you could bet your fancy new dock the whole of Blue Lake would have all the details of this Judge Greely thing plus a few extras before noon. As if the return of the Beaton girls after nearly fifty-six years hadn't been enough to get the tongues flapping.

I knew something had happened as soon as I spotted the Judge on the other side of the counter just after I opened. His eyes were hard and grey as any pack of rock-solid cod fresh out of the freezer. He checked out the new arrivals in hand-tied flies and picked out a nice little purple number with just a hint of glitter. He never lost that don't-mess-with-me look for a minute.

We don't often see the Judge in the store, which is fine by me. Usually he sends his housekeeper, Annabelle, to flit around, nibbling her nails, sniffing and blinking her little pink eyes, trying to pick out stuff that would be fine with the Judge. Annabelle always makes me think of a rabbit used to test cosmetics. Of course, Annabelle couldn't be trusted to pick out a new fly.

The Judge wasn't big on small talk. No one would have had the nerve to ask him about the dock. He loomed in and out before eight o'clock when the youngest Phillips boy sashayed through the door.

Clem, on the other hand, hung around practically every minute (although you'd think there'd be something for him to do over at his funeral home). As the morning went on, Clem's eyes flickered faster with excitement, like his battery might be running low. The rumours and tales came fast and thick. The Summer People had their versions and the Residents had theirs. Except when it was over, there was no doubt at all about what happened to Judge Dawson Greely. Don't you listen to Clem on this. Listen to me. Anyone will tell you I'm the most honest man in Blue Lake.

"I don't deal in speculation, you know that, Clem," I said.

"Since when?"

"Since you don't know what you're talking about. Since then." My heart thumped like a pickup with a flat tire. It did whenever I thought about those Beaton sisters.

But Clem wasn't done. "Of course, I know what I'm talking about. People saw them, heard them. Respectable people. What's the matter with you, Earle Maddore? And when did you start wearing that ridiculous tie?"

I fingered my new bow tie but I wasn't about to get side-tracked by my wardrobe. "Who told you about the Beaton girls, Clem? Eye witnesses who'll come forward and give their names?" You can't be too subtle around Clem. "You know wild talk goes round Blue Lake every summer. Since we were kids, for Pete's sake."

Clem's eyes gave off little red sparks. He knew I had him there.

"Too bad there's no money in talk. If there was, I'd have a Tall Tales section and make a bundle," I said.

"Not a tall tale." Clem's spark level went up.

"No? What about the sea serpent? What about the ghost of the Scottish piper? What about the fleet of holiday-making aliens?"

Clem started to sizzle. "This is different. These two old gals were alive and real. And everyone knows who they are. Plus speaking of different, who ever heard of wearing a bright red bow tie in the morning just to work around your old general store? You think it's Christmas in July?"

"And speaking of general stores," I said, "it would help business quite a bit if you didn't park that goddam hearse of yours in front of this particular store every morning. It scares off the customers."

"Don't change the subject," he said. "It's those Beaton gals, isn't it? You always had a flaming crush on that Janet. That's why you won't listen to reason."

I didn't give him the satisfaction of a reply.

It was Ellen really.

"If I remember I wasn't the only one with a crush. You forget how things were, Clem. That's because you're an old crock. In fact, it's time you gave the town a break and retired."

"Can't retire," Clem said, "business is booming."

Well, maybe Clem's funeral business is booming, but he always seems to have plenty of time to hang around my store chewing the fat and making my customers jumpy. A lot of people don't care to have the undertaker following them around asking how they're feeling.

"And anyway," Clem said, "even if it was more than fifty years ago, I think you still got a crush on Janet Beaton and it's getting worse because you're a withered up old fool."

Ellen. It's Ellen. And deep in my guts, I figured Clem was right. But I'd be a fricassee in hell before I'd give him the satisfaction of admitting it.

He leaned over the counter. His whole head was damn near as red as my tie.

"Speaking of business booming, Clem, you better watch that blood pressure," I said. "You don't want to go making work for yourself."

I laughed, but only on the outside. On the inside, I was a real mess. Clem was right. After fifty-six years, I still had that damn crush and it was getting worse.

The bell over the front door jangled just as I was about to tell him to take his hands off the fresh seven-grain rolls in the bakery display. Did he think I was having those rolls baked on the premises to have him squeeze the shape right out of them? Clem jerked himself upright, ran a big liver-spotted hand over his scalp and hightailed it over to the newcomer to spread his latest bit of news.

My knuckles were whiter than the stone-ground flour over in Bulk Products. The flat tire in my heart still hadn't been fixed. If I didn't start getting over these reactions every time the Beaton sisters were mentioned, then I was going to end up on a slab in Clem's place with a formaldehyde cocktail and those girls would have no one to defend them.

At ten in the morning, Clem was in front of the Cheeses of the World counter, still telling his story with a lot of arm-waving and a wild screeching laugh to capture the sound of two crazy old women howling across the water after a bit of midnight vandalism. He even threw back his head and shook his imaginary hair.

Didn't the next jangle at the door turn out to be Gwennie. Nicely turned out in her Ontario Provincial Police uniform. Golden curls just so. Knife-edge crease in the pants. Still looking cool as one of those new mint sorbets everyone's buying, even after she'd been sitting in that cruiser all the way from the OPP detachment in Langston. Even though that bullet-proof vest must have been hotter than our super salsa.

Down in Novelties, the youngest Phillips boy slipped something out of his pocket and slid it onto the shelf.

Clem stopped laughing when he spotted Gwennie. I noticed he tucked his shirt in and stood up straighter. As if a good-looking gal not even thirty years old would give a hoot about old Mr. Liver Spot.

"Mr. Maddore," Gwennie said, "Mr. Wampole."

"Good Morning, Officer Honeywell." We always call her Officer Honeywell to her face. The fact is we feel kind of flattered Gwennie would choose to be posted back to our neck of the woods and that she'd give either one of us the time of day. Personally, I like the fact she picks up all her provisions right here. Plus she's a lot easier on the eyes than the rest of the OPP officers and she doesn't mind a bit of polite chat. Except when she's serious, like she was at that particular moment.

"What brings you all the way over from Langston this early in the day?" I asked. "Nice weather," I added, giving Clem an extra moment to collect his wits.

Gwennie had her cap in her hand and a little crease between her eyebrows. "Well," she said, "we got a call from the Judge about some vandalism at his new dock. You two always know everything that's going on in Blue Lake. Thought you might tell me if you heard anything."

Boy, you think Gwennie, growing up in Blue Lake, would have figured out by now the taboo about telling the police anything about anything.

"Vandalism?" I said.

"Dock?" Clem said, like he'd never heard of one and would have had to have the idea explained to him with an illustration.

Gwennie's eyes might be pretty and the exact colour of cornflowers but they have a dangerous way of boring right into you like the better quality drill bit I keep over in Tiptop Tools.

"Sure you haven't heard anything?"

I opened my mouth.

"He doesn't deal in speculation," Clem said.

"That a fact?" Gwennie said.

"But if I find out anything for certain, I'll let you know," I added. "Officer Honeywell."

"That's right," Clem said. "After all, someone's bound to have seen that speedboat." Honest to God, sometimes I think he's inhaled too much embalming fluid.

Gwennie's eyes sparkled like the sun hitting a carving knife. "What speedboat would that be, Mr. Wampole?"

Clem goggled. There's no politer way to put it.

"Hmmm?"

"No speedboat in particular," he said, "just assumed vandals must have used one. No way to sneak past the Judge's house without being seen by the Judge or Annabelle."

Nice save, you old fool, I thought.

"We'll keep our ears open, Officer Honeywell," I said.

Gwennie's lips twitched. "You do that, gentlemen."

I couldn't look at her when I loaded up the cruiser trunk with a bag of provisions. I didn't want her boring into my brain and seeing the image Clem had planted there of the Beaton girls ramming that dock while their silver hair blew wild in the moonlight.

They nearly took my breath away stepping into my General Store on the Tuesday morning before the dock incident. After all those years, the Beaton sisters were damn fine-looking women, just this side of seventy-five and proud of it.

They still had the same bright tempting dark eyes and the same elegant bearing as when they were girls, visiting with their racy Aunties in that sprawling log camp on the lake where every night you hear the clink of glasses and the laughter. You can imagine those Aunties were the talk of Blue Lake. The sisters too.

Janet and Ellen had been blonde. Their hair was silver now. They sure made me stand up and straighten my old brown bow tie. Even the youngest Phillips boy gave them a look bordering on respect.

"Well, if it isn't Earle Maddore," one of them said. I think it was Ellen but it might have been Janet.

My jaw dropped. I hadn't laid eyes on those Beaton girls since I was twelve years old peeking at them through the trees and they were the most glamorous creatures ever to light on the shore of Blue Lake.

To tell you the truth they still looked mighty good in their khaki Bermuda shorts and sandals. Something about those bottomless dark eyes, though, when they looked straight into yours, could give you the shivers. I would have known the two of them anywhere. And why not? There was a time when I had memorized every line of their long lovely bodies.

I wasn't sure I liked them knowing me right off, at sixty-eight, with my hair nearly white and the bum knee and the cane. I would have preferred to run into those girls when I was in my prime, with my shoulders broad and my arms strong and my hair brown and wavy. Not when I was starting to see some old stranger in my mirror.

Now on the two of them, that silver hair didn't look old. It looked right, like they selected that exact shade from among all the colours that hair is available in. It looked kind of wild too.

Brought to mind a pair of lynxes.

By the afternoon after the dock incident, Clem was claiming he saw the whole thing and the two of them were silhouetted against the full moon. He swears he personally heard them howling with laughter. I think he was starting to believe it himself, the old blowhard.

"Odd there was no damage to their boat," I said.

"You're peevish enough, Earle," Clem said, leaning across the counter, practically crushing the display of M and M's. "Are you sure it's not time for you to think about taking your retirement? Do your disposition a world of good."

"I don't see any sign of you retiring, Clem Wampole, so don't be badgering me." Not a very witty comeback, I'll be the first to admit, but my brain had not been at its best since the shock of coming nose to nose with those Beaton girls. And now this dock business.

"Me? Retire? Why would I want to do that?" Clem said, leaning even further into the M and M's. "I'm making a fortune. I'd have to be crazy to quit now. Say, how you feeling? You look a bit pale."

"I'll outlive you by a good ten years, you old goat." I must have shouted it because a couple of Summer People dropped a Sara Lee cake. The youngest Phillips boy's head popped up over the counter in Children's Toys. "You better be prepared to spring for those M and M's if you smush 'em any more."

Clem only wheezed with laughter. "I hear they're still swimming naked in the lake."

He would have gotten a pretty chilly reception from me but he hadn't said it to me, he'd said it to Summer People clucking up and down the aisles hunting for decaf espresso and tofu and low-fat, sugar-free mango yoghurt.

The couple looked more fascinated than shocked. The younger people around Blue Lake are just as captivated as us old fellas by those Beaton sisters.

In fact, Blue Lake still whispers about what happened that summer fifty-six years ago. Of course, being a small town, folks were inclined to blame the girl not the fella. And no one was ever too certain that anything took place at all. Just a bunch of hissing rumours. Some said yes it had happened and some said no it hadn't.

And there was me.

I knew for sure.

I'd been so overcome with twelve-year-old love for Ellen Beaton, I got a pain in my chest whenever I thought about it. And sure enough those girls were gone overnight and no one ever heard anything about them for years until Clem's second cousin, Francis, said he saw one of them, Janet he thought, at the Eaton store in Toronto looking like a million dollars, for what anything Francis Wampole says is worth.

But with what we knew about Dawson Greely, every kid in Blue Lake believed that story could have been true. It was only the grown-ups who shook their heads and clucked their tongues and said what a disgrace it was for anyone to even suggest that Old Judge Hamilton Greely's fine young lad, Dawson, could do something like that and those city girls were no better than they ought to be and good riddance to them both.

When I opened my mouth to protest this horrible injustice and dirty lie, my own mother flicked her dusting cloth and said poor Ethel Greely, imagine how she must feel having people say something like that about her son, just wickedness to repeat it. There'd be no bad talk about young Dawson Greely in her house. And sure enough there wasn't. It would have got me the belt.

Over the summers we heard many sly rumours about things Dawson Greely had done to other young girls but no stories ever made the papers. No charges were ever laid. Just girls leaving town. Or staying, trapped in Blue Lake, with dark secrets tucked away behind their eyes.

Even poor Annabelle who'd been pretty enough in her time, there was talk about her.

As for me, I told no one. To tell would have been to admit I'd been sitting high in the big oak tree, watching those Beaton girls swimming by the light of the moon, staring at their beautiful bare backsides slicing though the silver water while their Aunties were inside drinking bathtub gin with other people's husbands. A wicked thing for those girls to do, people would have said, and probably even wickeder to watch.

Even though I would have got the belt for sure if I'd been caught, I went every night, until Dawson Greely showed up and did what he did. That night I ran off choking and shaking and throwing up, not able to help my beautiful Ellen. A dirty little coward who deserved fifty-six years of guilty nights. People may say I'm the most honest man in Blue Lake but I know better.

"Strange, isn't it," Clem whispered to me, although there was not another person in the store at the time, "Strange, them showing up right after he retires and moves back to the old place."

"What's so strange about it?" I thought it was strange too. And worrisome. But I'd have been filleted and fried before I'd admit it to Clem.

"Just strange, that's all."

"How come you got so much time to hang around here gossiping if business is booming?" I asked. "As you claim it is."

"Just a quiet patch," Clem said. "Things will pick up soon, they always do. Say, you don't have a bit of indigestion and a numb-kind of feeling in your arm, do you?"

"Pay up for those M and M's," I said.

Clem was hopping up and down in front of the door when I drove up the next morning at seven. The hearse was parked under the Fresh Meat sign. The youngest Phillips boy waited, patiently blowing pink bubbles.

"Would you mind," I said, "moving your hearse."

"Not now. Have you heard the news?"

"Now," I said.

The man sure can fuss. He was pretty hot and bothered by the time he moved the hearse and thumped through the front door.

"You look a bit flushed," I said, "You don't have a numb-kind of feeling in your arm, do you? Bit of indigestion?"

"Very funny. Get any funnier and I won't hang around to tell you the news."

I was tempted.

Clem must have figured that because he started yapping. Before I even got the lights on.

"They did it again!"

"Did what?" I didn't have to ask who.

"You'll never guess."

"I don't want to guess. Either tell me, Clem, or head back to your slabs and let me get on with making a living."

"No need to be so damn cranky. You ever think you might have a brain tumour or something?"

"I do not have a brain tumour," I said, banging in the computer code to set up the cash register.

"Really? Then how do you explain the wearing of that particular bow tie if not a brain tumour?"

"There's nothing wrong with my tie. Now stop handling those baguettes."

"Nothing wrong with it? You think that colour green is found in nature? Looks like you found it in a vat of radioactive waste."

"Clem. Maybe you have nothing to do since people are too inconsiderate to die, but I have. So share the load or hit the road."

Clem's eyes glittered like the sparkle ropes over in Children's Toys.

"Boy, you aren't going to believe this, but . . . "

I considered beaning him with my float except he'd probably have found a way to keep the cash.

The front door jingled.

Gwennie stalked toward the counter with a snap in her step and big dark circles under her cornflower eyes and a pinched look around her mouth. "Mr. Maddore. Mr. Wampole. You gentlemen know anything about a ring of fire burning around Judge Greely's place last night?"

The youngest Phillips boy scrambled to safety over in Pet Food.

Quarters clattered as I dropped the float. Ring of fire. In the night. Just when those Beaton girls got active. Now I knew what Clem had been so anxious to blab.

He goggled at Gwennie. "Ring of fire?" he said. "First I've heard about it."

"I doubt that."

"What do you mean?"

"I mean people tell me you were first with the news about the dock."

Clem blushed to the top of his liver-spotted head. He didn't want Gwennie to think badly of him. As if a real looker like Gwennie would give a thought about an old windbag like that.

She turned to me.

I said, "I don't deal in . . . "

Gwennie interrupted. ". . . speculation. So you say. You telling me that ring of fire doesn't mean anything to either of you?"

"It doesn't," I said, truthfully.

"No, Ma'am," Clem said, lying through his dentures.

"Any idea who's got something against Judge Greely?"

Clem actually snorted. "Everybody in Blue Lake's got some grudge or another against Dawson Greely."

Gwennie would know that, of course, growing up here.

My heart was tripping like one of those new compressors over in Automotive Necessities. Couldn't be anybody in Blue Lake with a bigger grudge than Janet and Ellen Beaton. I sure hoped Gwennie never heard the rumours about why.

Gwennie's shiny pink lips twitched as she looked us over. "Everybody?"

Business was booming.

That ring of fire really got the imaginations cranked up, Summer People and Residents both. Of course, everyone kind of liked the idea of Judge Dawson Greely getting a touch of the stuff he'd handed out all those years.

People did a lot more shopping than usual. I even sold those plastic lawn penguins I'd been carrying as Dead Inventory for two years.

As far as I could tell Dawson Greely didn't have a friend in the world. Everyone in Blue Lake figured the Beaton sisters were behind the doings and everyone figured the old bastard had it coming.

I didn't like any of it. If they were behind it, I figured they were playing with fire in more ways than one.

If I'd had a cap, I would have held it in my hand the night I went to see them. I had to content myself with fingering my tie and hoping it wasn't hanging at some foolish angle.

Just a casual drop in, as suggested by Janet, I believe, on her second visit to the store. By the time I reached the edge of the Beaton property, anybody standing next to me could have heard my heart. But it was a twelve-year-old heart, full of romantic excitement, finally getting to encounter the mysterious and glamorous Beaton sisters.

I stopped near the oak tree to catch my breath.

A bevy of rusty pick-up trucks blocked the view. The entire Phillips clan, parents, grown-up children and a bunch of wild-looking babies, plus the family dogs, were camped on lawn chairs around the foot of the tree, catching the cool breeze from the lake. I was willing to bet every one of those lawn chairs had been pinched from Summer Residents over the years. You never saw so many bare, hairy bellies in your life. Clem probably would have said, "And that's just the women."

Even Mrs. Phillips was there. These days you didn't see her around all that often, except on the way to court with one of her boys. But I remembered when she'd been beautiful, back in the Sixties, before getting herself in a family way at fifteen, marrying Wilt Phillips and producing a bumper crop of layabouts and poachers. Her formerly long blonde hair was cropped and frizzy with grey. It had been years since I'd seen her smile. Her teeth had gone the way of the waist-length hair and the slender body. Her eyes were still the same though, like the finishing nails I stock in Building Supplies, tiny, sharp and dangerous.

She sure was in a good mood that evening.

"Hey, there, Earle Maddore," she said, raising her beer bottle and showing her gums.

Her oldest boy belched in greeting. With the exception of the youngest boy, the babies, and the dogs, everyone was drinking beer straight from the bottle. They kind of ruined the scenery around the oak tree but the Phillipses are something you just have to accept but watch out for, like leeches or black ice.

Gwennie must have had them under surveillance. I saw the cruiser slide by but she didn't return my wave. Gwennie had plenty on her mind that night, what with the Judge Greely thing and the Phillipses all out in a pack.

I could see it in her eyes.

I forgot about Gwennie and the Phillipses the instant I walked through the door of the Beaton girls' log camp.

I imagine I was grinning like a real old fool even before they served me that rich dry sherry with the same wicked sparkle as their eyes. I never stopped grinning the whole night when we talked and laughed, remembering the old days and sipping that fine sherry. If you asked me to repeat what any of us said, I couldn't, although I do remember them admiring the tiny embroidered ducks on my tie. Mostly, it was as though my brain just stopped working. Time turned around and everything seemed to be just wonderful.

When I warned them about the danger of playing games on a man like Dawson Greely, they laughed even more. They let their eyes sparkle. They refilled my sherry glass and told me not to worry. But of course I worried. What chance would two old women have against a man like him? And while we were on the subject, what chance did an old man like me have against them?

At two in the morning, I found myself outside their lodge, headed home with my tie at an angle and stars swirling around my head. As I got further from the Beaton girls, that twelve-year-old feeling faded.

You are a dolt and a failure, I told myself. Never had the guts to open your mouth and say the right words when your were twelve, when it would have made a difference.

They hadn't paid a speck of notice to my warnings. So now I'd probably failed them again.

I passed the oak tree, feeling pretty sorry for myself and not paying any attention to where I was walking, when Dawson Greely socked me in the eye.

I never saw him coming.

The combination of the sherry and the surprise knocked me right on my keister. The full moon illuminated the Judge, hanging by one foot from that old oak tree. His dead-fish eyes staring.

Snared.

The hand still swung where it had connected with my face.

It took a minute for me to make sense of it all. When I did, I sank back onto the grass a second time. I felt a bit short of breath. My arm tingled. If I wasn't careful old Clem was going to have himself a double-header.

It took a long time before I could steady myself enough to stumble back to the Beaton sisters' place to phone for Gwennie.

Clem said Dawson Greely's face had been the colour of a red cabbage. Clem said it showed up something terrible in contrast to the bright, yellow rope he was dangling from.

It was true enough but I would have been battered and baked before I would have agreed with Clem, since he enjoyed the telling so much. Dawson Greely had been hideous in death. Even though he got what was coming to him, hanging by one foot, like a Deli sausage, that hadn't made it any easier when Gwennie arrived with her roof lights flashing and the siren blaring and blue fire in her eyes.

Of course, word was all over town before Gwennie even slid her cruiser into PARK. Lucky the telephone lines didn't ignite. Half of Blue Lake had hopped into its pickups and raced on over to see the sight. Clem led the pack in the hearse. Gwennie had a helluva time keeping them all from obliterating any evidence.

"Dead a couple of hours if you ask me," Clem said.

"Nobody did," Gwennie snapped. "Mr. Maddore," she said, turning and boring into my head. "You want to tell me what this is about?"

"You tell me, Officer Honeywell. I spent the evening visiting the Beaton sisters, got there at eight. Left just before I found the Judge. No idea how he got there."

I could feel Gwennie's cornflower eyes exploring my brain. I wasn't worried about what she'd see there this time. The Beaton sisters had the perfect alibi. Me, the most honest man in Blue Lake. This time I didn't have to let them down.

"There wasn't any snare there at eight o'clock when I went past that oak tree," I told Gwennie. "The entire Phillips clan was there with all their kids and dogs. Running all over the place."

Gwennie nodded. "Don't I know it. They were there until nearly midnight when I followed them home to make sure they didn't cause any trouble."

"Everyone knows the Phillipses are the world's biggest poachers. Maybe one of them set the snare when they left," I suggested.

"Well now that would be convenient for sure but no such luck. I watched them get into their trucks. I walked around and checked to see if I could get them on littering. For the first time in their lives, the Phillipses left a place spotless. There wasn't any yellow rope then."

All around us people were clucking their tongues and saying what a terrible thing. Those who didn't express disappointment in the solid alibi for the Beaton girls expressed it over the Phillipses. But underneath all the fuss was a mood more fitting for a church picnic than the finding of a body. The feeling that Dawson Greely finally got what was coming to him. I wouldn't have been surprised to see fried chicken. Or fireworks.

But who had done the deed?

The next morning, half the town was in the store, busy buzzing about the news. Although, every single person stopped talking the minute Gwennie walked in. Clem stopped in the middle of a word and clamped his lips shut like there were still a couple of syllables trying to bust out through his teeth.

Everyone in Blue Lake already knew the Judge was alive and snarling when Annabelle whimpered good-night at eleven o'clock and gave him a message that some fella had called about meeting him that night. The coroner was saying (according to Clem) the Judge was dead by twelve at the latest, going by the onset of rigor and body temperature. And Clem was saying didn't I tell you so. The coroner figured Dawson Greely most likely died of a stroke brought on by rage at being snared and hanging upside down. But it would take an autopsy to tell for sure.

I figured somebody had set that snare especially for Judge Dawson Greely sometime after the Phillipses had finished their picnic and sometime before midnight.

"That's right," Clem told the world, "When old Earle here called me it was two o'clock and the Judge was already starting to ice over. Not Earle though, he was hot to trot, just reeking of Chanel No. 5 and gin. Shaking like a leaf though."

Chanel No. 5 and gin. Sometimes I think the old loon is ready for the bin, although to tell you the truth, I was grateful he'd shown up the night before and driven me home after the excitement died down. Even if, at that very moment he was leaning against a pile of crinkle chips I'd probably never be able to sell afterwards.

I couldn't concentrate on anything at the store, not that I had two minutes of peace and quiet what with all the chattering and squawking and citizens pretending to be outraged. I noticed nobody was grief-stricken over the late Dawson Greely. Some of the ladies even seemed to have a glint of celebration in their eyes. Eyes that made me think of music boxes: lift the lid and the whirling and dancing begins; close it and all of that's hidden again.

Dawson Greely had left his miserable mark in a lot of eyes around Blue Lake. A lot of ladies probably figured those Beaton girls had done the world a favour. However they'd managed it.

And another thing, I had to admit, despite all the fuss, it was good for business. Since everybody who came in bought something to justify their visit and a lot of people came back more than once for news updates from Clem. I had to change the tape in the receipt machine twice, that'll give you an idea. I had to subtract the cost of the baked goods that Clem squashed, but even so.

It was only when I was tidying up in Bait and Tackle that I spotted it. That yellow rope. And I remembered where else I'd seen it.

Clem was badgering a couple of tourists with talk of our local mystery and the youngest Phillips boy was busy trying to remove the batteries from a flashlight when Gwennie came in to pick up ice cream and vegetarian lasagne and a few other things.

"You got everything you need now?" I said, as I punched in her purchases.

"I do." Gwennie's eyes twinkled. She was looking a lot more relaxed than usual. Sort of uncoiled.

"Help you load up your cruiser?"

"Sure."

I hoped when she drilled into my head with her next look, she couldn't read my thoughts.

"By the way," I said, trying a little normal conversation, "How's the investigation going?"

"Looking more and more like a freak accident. We'll most likely never find the poacher who set that snare," Gwennie said. "I imagine the Coroner's Inquest will find it's Death by Misadventure. Don't you?"

"Wouldn't be surprised." My guess was the Coroner's Inquest would never hear Gwennie no longer had that length of yellow rope she'd been carrying in the trunk of her cruiser the last time I loaded it. Wouldn't hear it from me, anyway.

It wasn't the place of the Coroner's Inquest to wonder why a pretty blue-eyed blonde like Gwennie suddenly left Blue Lake at sixteen. Or yet again, why she asked to get posted back here years later, when she probably could have had her pick of postings.

It probably wouldn't occur to anyone to wonder why an OPP officer sat watching the Phillipses swig right out of their beer bottles in full view in a public place on that very same night the Judge died. Sneering at the law. The Phillipses always came to mind for anything remotely connected with poaching. But Gwennie herself provided a solid alibi for the whole clan.

Of course, you could look at it another way: they provided one for her.

And as for the most honest man in Blue Lake, I made an excellent alibi for the other two most popular suspects in the entire area, those

Beaton sisters. Wasn't it lucky for them they chose that particular night to invite me over?

I figured the Coroner's Inquest would never raise the right questions, like whether rabbity little Annabelle really took a late night phone call from some fella asking the Judge to meet him or why so many Blue Lake ladies seemed to have a bit more music in their eyes lately.

I wondered what started it all. What words got things rolling? Who all else was involved? Was it Gwennie coming back? Was it the Beaton sisters? Was it just the full moon? But it didn't matter. I'd never know. Not even much point thinking about it. Nothing but speculation. Pure speculation.

And like I told you before, I don't deal in speculation.

I have more important things on my mind such as dinner with the Beaton girls this very night and such as whether to wear the new tie with the ladybugs and such as whether we might go swimming in the moonlight.

ZEBRA MUSSELS

by Vicki Cameron

Lake Hashaga used to be a quiet lake. A slow-moving, long deep lake emptying into a slow-moving winding river.

A man could spend time at his cottage here and not see another living human for days. Sit on the end of his dock with a beer and his private thoughts, watching the water wander past. Hardly any cottages, as the shore is rocky and often steep. Few swimmers, just the young men who hitch-hike to the diving cliff at the far end of the lake and jump the hundred feet into the deep water. Hardly any boats. Certainly no divers.

But all that's changed now, because of those damn zebra mussels.

A couple of years ago, somebody must have chugged into Lake Hashaga with a zebra mussel or two clinging to the bottom of his motorboat. That's all it takes. One or two.

Pretty soon you've got a colony of zebra mussels, lurking on the posts of your dock. And then another colony sets up shop on a submerged log somewhere. And they all get to work filtering the water. That's what they do. Suck all the water through their tiny striped shells, filter out all the plankton, and spit out pure clear water.

Clear water. Doesn't take too many years of that until the whole lake gets clear. Take Lake Erie. The zebra mussels cleared that up in about three years. Didn't take them that long here on Lake Hashaga. Person can see right to the bottom in the shallower places.

So then the divers started coming, in their fancy boats, with their floating warning buoys. Swimming around on the bottom of the lake, looking at stuff. Looking for stuff.

There's a bunch of them out there now. Environmentalist divers. They dive in groups and collect garbage from the bottom of the lake. Then they create a big fuss about fishermen dropping empty beer cans overboard.

Looks like they've found something bigger than a beer can. A pair of them have popped up to the surface, spit out their mouthpieces, and yelled at the others lolling around on the boat. Now the others are scrambling into their gear, leaving one loser to look after the boat. He isn't doing a good job of it. He's hanging over the side staring down into the water, and trying to raise somebody on his cell phone.

They've probably found a body. That's the only thing that would get them so pumped up. People really love gruesome stuff. Like driving slowly past a car accident, trying to see the blood.

They've probably found a hitch-hiker. A handsome young guy with a big chip on his shoulder, running away to the city because he can't have his own way at home. Still a boy, thinking he's invincible, and too naive to spot a pass until it's too late. Too naive to watch his back.

The divers are popping back up to the surface now. They've all had a good look. One of them hasn't taken it too well, and is vomiting into the water. Somebody is giving him a comforting pat on the back. The police will be here soon. More divers and more boats, and the coroner to pronounce the kid dead. As if that isn't obvious. He's been under the water for over a year.

Those zebra mussels are to blame, clearing the water like that. Might as well have hung out a neon sign.

There'll be no stopping them now. Every diver for a thousand miles will be visiting this lake this summer. The macabre draws a crowd. They'll all be out looking for bodies.

They'll find them, too. Hitch-hikers from the crossroads. Heading for the city or for the cliff.

They'll find the cute university kid with the curly blond hair and the slow dimples. He'd heard about the diving cliff and wanted to prove himself a man.

They'll find the ex-con with the silky skin and muscular thighs who thought he knew the score. He'd learned lots in prison. But not enough about staying alive.

They'll find the native lad with the long shiny hair. A real pretty boy. Knew how to use what he had. I thought of keeping him, but that never works out.

Lake Hashaga is ruined now.

They'll start calling it Lake Hitch-hiker.

Damn zebra mussels.

AN ACCIDENT WAITING TO HAPPEN

I'm not one of your model-types
Who walks with style and grace;
I'm tall, but if I don't wear flats
I fall right on my face
I don't use things with pointy ends,
I fear a knife that cuts
And dull it well before its use:
I'm just your average klutz.
But after I had married Joe
I got more clumsy still.
At twenty-seven I felt sure
That I would need my will.
It seemed I often fell down stairs
When carpets went awry,
Although I'd always straighten them –
Or goodness knows, I'd try.
My darling Joe was always there.
He never would chastise.
He'd smile at me and chuck my chin,
"You win the graceless prize."
Once Joe got me to wash some clothes
He said were stained with soil.
The fireman said, while Joe held me,
"The stains were probably oil."
Who would have thought washing machines
Could burst into a flame?
"There, there," said Joe, and kissed my burns,
"I don't hold you to blame."
He didn't blame me for the time
The brakes failed on the Ford
Or for the time while hanging drapes
I strangled in the cord.
I really was a lucky one;
Each time I struggled free.
If it wasn't for my inheritance
Could Joe stand clumsy me?

So I never did deny my Joe
His chance to be alone,
To monthly get away from one
So badly accident prone.
Joe had a little hideaway,
A cottage on a lake,
But two days on our honeymoon
Was all that I could take.
"My lovely little klutzy-poo,
I'll miss you at the shack.
Don't make a move without me, love.
Just wait till I get back."
This last time that he went away
He looked so sad that I
Decided to be brave for once
And give the lake a try.
I told myself to "get a life" –
I knew I once had guts.
I wasn't born with aptitude
For burns and falls and cuts.
I first put on my flattest flats,
Then drove with extra care,
Staying well below speed limits,
Making sure that I'd get there.
I steered with infinite caution,
I parked beside the lake,
Walked carefully down the long trail –
Discovered my mistake!
Joe was giving wet farewells to
A girl 'bout half my size.
It wasn't his first such farewell
I came to realize.
I ducked in behind the dogwoods
Waiting for her to go,
I watched till she was out of sight
Then went to confront Joe.
Then it hit me like the low beams
That used to mar my life,

An Accident Waiting To Happen

I wasn't half as clumsy 'til
Joe took me as his wife.
He'd cultivated all my faults
And it was plain to see
That if I were to die a klutz
It was *me* killing me.
I pulled an ax out of a log
And walked around the back.
I caught Joe at his barbecue
And gave his head a whack.
My hands held tight, my shoulders tensed,
I had such acumen;
If I were being judged for it,
It was a perfect ten.
I dug a hole without a fault,
I didn't stumble once.
Without Joe there to comfort me
I didn't feel a dunce.
I wiped the ax most carefully
And put it back in place,
Then swept the ground with a pine branch,
Erasing every trace.
Cottagers' cars would cover up
My tracks eventually.
There would be nothing to connect
Poor Joe's demise to me.
I'll play the grieving widow if
His body's ever found.
I'll be so weak and helpless (with
My two feet on the ground).
My broken heart's an accident
That only romance seals.
I'll have more luck with husband two
'Cause now I walk on heels.

Joy Hewitt Mann

To order more copies of

COTTAGE COUNTRY KILLERS

send $18.95 plus $4.50 to cover GST,
shipping and handling to:

GENERAL STORE PUBLISHING HOUSE
Box 28, 1694 Burnstown Rd., Burnstown, Ontario
K0J 1G0
(613) 432-7697 or **1-800-465-6072**
or Fax 613-432-7184
Email: orders@gsph.com